HIGH PRAISE FOR GORDON COTLER'S
"HIP," "WITTY"
SHOOTING SCRIPT

"Cotler keeps the pot boiling merrily while dishing dirt on TV series development. And yes, there's a zinger kept for the end, too."
—*Kirkus Reviews*

"Wry, witty, sardonic."
—*Buffalo News*

"Rich in bi-coastal atmosphere and characters who live and breathe, *Shooting Script* is slick, well-done and never disappoints."
—*Mystery News*

"A slick . . . appealing production in the coast-to-coast mode, filled with denizens of studio offices and back streets alike."
—*Library Journal*

"[A] nifty bicoastal mystery. Cotler's brisk, intricate plot, his TV biz setting and his cast . . . all satisfy, as does the story's neat surprise ending."
—*Publishers Weekly*

By the same author

The Bottletop Affair
The Cipher (as Alex Gordon)
Mission in Black

SHOOTING SCRIPT

GORDON COTLER

A DELL BOOK

Published by
Dell Publishing
a division of
Bantam Doubleday Dell Publishing Group, Inc.
1540 Broadway
New York, New York 10036

ISBN: 0-440-21682-6

Reprinted by arrangement with William Morrow and Company, Inc.

Printed in the United States of America

Published simultaneously in Canada

April 1995

10   9   8   7   6   5   4   3   2   1

OPM

To the Memory of
Jerry Davis

sui generis

SHOOTING
SCRIPT

PART ONE
N.Y. TO L.A.

CHAPTER ONE

I thought I caught a glimpse of Stavros as I was getting out of my car in the network parking lot but I
couldn't be sure; the southern California morning
sun had bleached the scene almost to white on
white. And whoever I saw had climbed into a car in
the section marked "Reserved for Talent." Not even
the most indulgent definition of Talent would have
given the nod to Stavros. Still, real or imagined, this
was a portent. I just wasn't willing to accept that
anything having to do with Nicholas Stavros could
be portentous. He was an annoyance, a minor one I
expected to fade like a bad sunburn.

In any case, his name wasn't in the sign-in book in
the lobby. Neither was Wolf's, but that didn't surprise me. The last date Wolf Waxroth had been
punctual for was his bris. Show me an agent who is
punctual, went his unspoken excuse, and I will show
you an agent who cares more about time than about
working for his clients.

The sign-in book told me that the Blaus, at least,

had arrived; they had signed in at 10:02. It was now 10:09. Our meeting was for 10:15. Ordinarily the Blaus were not much more likely to be on time for a meeting than Wolf, but this wasn't a meeting, this was a *network* meeting. Producers get in line for a network meeting and they stay in line. Networks are the Source: all monies flow from them and all other meetings depend on that flow; the system is like a series of stepped-down fountains. And the Blaus had probably showed up early to prowl the corridors, producer style, in search of a loose deal.

I signed in and made my way to the inner door past the wannabes hanging out in the lobby. The guard buzzed me through to the elevator corridor and I took the car to the fourth floor, where the reception room for the network's creative departments was located. A knot in my stomach the size of my fist wasn't there because of normal premeeting tension; I had been in too many network meetings for that. But this meeting I particularly needed to go well, this job to go well. I had let myself get into a position I had once never imagined possible for me. I no longer had my "Fuck you" money.

This warehouse-sized reception room had been built to humble supplicants with the majesty of the corporation but its design succeeded mostly in reminding us of the network's creative failings. Glass and chrome and wood and leather and marble— there were too many elements, it was too busy, there was no point of view, it didn't work. Like so many of the network's pilots these last few years. In strategic huddles under the vaulting skylights were the usual edgy assemblages of producers, agents, and writers on missions ranging from pitching ideas to fine-tuning scripts. As I had suspected, the Blaus were nowhere in sight.

The receptionist was wearing the smile she set when she came in this morning and prayerfully opened one more button on her blouse. Her verdict on my not quite L.A. attire—the slightly too heavy gray herringbone sport jacket—registered only in her eyes. "You're the first in your group, Mr. Saldinger. Let me know when you're all here. Anyway, Mr. Kornbluth is running a little late. Did you have a nice flight?"

They could smell when you had just come in from the East. I said, "Except for losing an engine over St. Louis. The Blaus are somewhere on the floor. We won't wait for my agent. Call me when Oscar is ready." I would find the Blaus. Punctuality counted for more on this floor than in this month's hot restaurant. Any hint that our party wasn't assembled and the table would go to someone else; Oscar Kornbluth would start taking his phone calls.

I didn't have to find the Blaus. They knew the drill. They materialized at 10:15, Werner from the north corridor, Seth from the south. They didn't bother to ask about my flight and they didn't care whether my agent showed up. The Blaus hadn't gotten where they were by servicing the amenities. Their focus was entirely on product—finding it, developing it, selling it, exploiting it. Their first sale had been their own idea, a syndicated series built around a boy with a flying bicycle, a shameless steal from *E.T.* That had exhausted their creative juices; and ever since they had vaguely resented having to depend on writers like me to fuel their operation.

Werner nodded curt recognition of my presence and asked, "Is Oscar ready?" Werner, the hot-eyed, wiry one, spoke for the brothers. Thin lips that forewarned of miserly negotiating stances were the only clue that the two had genes in common. Seth, younger, softer, better-looking, a good-time guy not ambitious enough to have made it on his own, would have shaken my hand limply and tried to make small talk if he was alone, but he followed his brother's lead and merely nodded.

We were going to have to wait and we didn't have a damn thing to say to each other. We had bled each other dry on the one subject we had in common in endless cross-country communication—conference calls, faxes, FedExes, even a brief visit east from Seth. So we flopped down on deep leather couches in a corner and by unspoken mutual consent retreated into separate worlds. I caught up on the trades I found on the slate coffee table, and the Blaus fell on the phones and made scattershot calls. Anything to appear busy. Waiting was something of an embarrassment to Werner; it gave the impression there were minutes in his day he could afford to throw away.

Kornbluth made us wait so long that we were still planted on the couches when Wolf finally showed. He tried to mask his chagrin at Kornbluth's running even later than he was by asking, as if he really cared, about my flight and my hotel and my kids. On a roll now, he started to ask about my wife before he remembered the divorce and checked himself. I felt a twinge of pain I didn't need right now. I had been separated for over a year and every so often I found out that wasn't long enough.

The waiting was more than Wolf could bear. A phone might have pacified him but they were all in use. He was about to take off on a prowl of nearby offices when Oscar Kornbluth himself showed up from down the hall, no jacket, sleeves rolled up, all smiles and shambling cordiality. He hadn't sent his secretary to fetch us. Was that behavior white smoke or black? We weighed the question separately as we followed him back to his office. Even when he smiled—maybe especially when he smiled—Kornbluth was hard to read.

Kornbluth's people were already in place in his cluttered office. Sheila Bannister, his Director of Development, who, at our previous meetings, took a lot of notes and in between stroked the spirals on her notebook like a harpist. And Matt Clay, Manager of Development—everybody gets a title—black and young. They were all young, but Clay was practically fetal. Anyway, that's how it looked from the disadvantage of my forty-four years. Neither the Director nor the Manager was likely to say more than hello and good-bye during the meeting, but that didn't mean they could be ignored. One or the other could be Kornbluth the next time I came west.

We made the obligatory small talk to reestablish the pecking order. At least, the others did. I kept my mouth shut, dug a toe in the figurative sand, and looked agreeable; it was the safest posture in my financial condition. Wolf opened with some gossip about an impending disaster on a pilot in production for another network; apparently the chemistry between the male and female leads was producing a toxic substance. Bad news somewhere else served to put the group at ease. Werner Blau followed with some questions about the network schedule that were meant to show how much wiser than he Kornbluth was. My guess was that in actuality he could have taken Kornbluth in a single gulp, spitting out only bone fragments.

Not that Kornbluth was stupid. I didn't know him well but he seemed to do the job. Then again he'd have done the job of managing major appliances at Sears. He was no minor-league Louis B. Mayer or

Harry Cohn, with show business instincts that proclaimed the whole world was wired to his ass. He was a generic middle-management executive who had come to the creative arena from a network-owned-and-operated station where he sold the most time two years running. Only a slight tic at one corner of his mouth made me wonder if something was ticking elsewhere in the awkward body that looked as if it had been designed by whoever did Richard Nixon's.

While Kornbluth and Werner played out their ritual dance I fixated on the tchotchkes on Kornbluth's desk. They included a plastic alligator, a pyramid of marble cubes, a clutch of quill pens, a windup clown, a sepia photo of . . . his grandmother? More likely, his great-grandmother. Development executives who run story conferences keep stuff like that on their desks to distract writers from their rising gorge.

Kornbluth's voice was changing color, signifying there had been enough small talk, he was ready for substantive matters. A stillness fell over the group while he opened his copy of the script. He turned toward me as he started to flip pages. I spotted very few pencil marks; that was good. The rattling of paper was the only sound in the room. Finally he said, "Well, Mike, you've got the franchise focused nicely, and I like the way you've turned up the gas on the jeopardy. We needed the added running and jumping. And now the human side of our hero is finally emerging—where he's coming from, his flaws and so forth. This rewrite just about does it for me."

It damn well should; it was the third, although we were calling it, for purposes of the payment schedule, Second Draft. A grudging but unavoidable gift from me to the network and the Blaus. But I felt a flood of relief as Kornbluth closed his script. And so, I could tell, did the Blaus. "What I have is mostly line notes," Kornbluth said. "Window cuts, clarifications. No point discussing them at this point in time."

Or this point in space, Oscar. Already I was beginning to feel uneasy again, as if someone were nudging me out into oncoming traffic. If everything was so damn peachy, why had Kornbluth sprung to bring me out here on one day's notice, first-class airfare—a Writers Guild requirement—with a two-hundred-and-fifty-dollar per diem that included hotel, but not car rental, for which I would send him a separate bill? When network profits were down and they were firing half the people who weren't covered by a contract, and squeezing the production companies for every penny on licensing fees?

Kornbluth had turned to Sheila. "Sheila, why don't we do Al's stuff first?" I didn't have a clue what he was talking about. Sheila did; she nodded and went out to the corridor. Waxroth was getting restless; he had been sitting in one seat for nearly fifteen minutes, the script had been approved except for a pro forma meeting with the star, and he didn't see any profit in hanging around here.

He said, "Listen, Oscar, if you need me, I'll be down the hall—"

I said, "No, Wolf, wait." I didn't know why. Who was Al? And what did Kornbluth mean by doing him "first"? Two unknowns, two too many.

Wolf stayed, his bony ass edged to the front of the couch, perched for takeoff. But he had caught my concern. "Who's Al?" he asked.

Kornbluth said, "Al Vecchi. We've put him under a short-term contract."

Who the hell was Al Vecchi? At moments like this I

regretted having given up the trades. But three hundred-plus dollars a year for a daily paper that arrived in New York a week late was an extravagance I could ill afford at the moment. Then I saw the blank looks on the faces of my people. If Werner Blau and Wolf Waxroth didn't know an Al Vecchi, forget it, he didn't exist. Anyway, not in the business, which was the same thing. And yet the name niggled somewhere at the back of my memory.

Werner had never in his life admitted ignorance on any subject. He knew how to cover. "To do what?" he asked.

"Never heard of him, eh, Werner?" Score one for Kornbluth. He turned to me. "Why don't I let New York fill you in."

"New York" often tasted sour out of the mouths of L.A. executives. If you work in the business, went the accepted wisdom, live in the town. Don't run up first-class airfares from that sinkhole where you and your elitist friends make Tinseltown jokes behind doors you have to triple lock. But "New York" tripped my memory. Al Vecchi. Now I remembered the name. At the time the story broke I had pitched it without much conviction as a Movie of the Week and understandably got a pass from every network. The tearsheets were yellowing in my files. I said, "That's the cop, isn't it?"

Kornbluth allowed himself a grudging nod and I turned to the others. "The cop who broke the Raymond sisters' killing."

I had their attention. They might not know Vecchi but everyone remembered the Raymond sisters, two girls, eight and ten, who disappeared from their Queens Boulevard apartment one afternoon and turned up five days later, after a massive search and screaming headlines, in Poe Park, near the landmarked cottage in the Bronx, brutally murdered. The "Edgar Allan Poe Murders," the media called the case, a bum rap for the poet. The killer didn't know "The Raven" from the park pigeons.

"I remember the story," Wolf said, suddenly interested. "How come that was never in development?"

"How did this Vecchi solve the case?" Werner wanted to know, more to the point. Maybe the Edgar Allan Poe Murders had TV potential and maybe they didn't.

I said, "This Al Vecchi—I'm sure it's the same cop —figured the killer as someone who worked a day shift somewhere in Queens, got off work at maybe three or four in the afternoon, and lived in the North Bronx."

"Kind of a reach, wasn't it?" murmured Seth Blau. "Would an audience buy that?"

"Vecchi didn't do an audience survey," I said. "He had this hunch and he followed it."

"Followed it how?" Werner asked. He was totally sucked in. He turned on his brother. "Why didn't I see coverage on this?"

Waxroth and Blau had both picked up the scent of a property: a true-crime story told through the eyes of a hero cop. Totally foolproof. They had stopped wondering what the hell Vecchi or his exploits had to do with this meeting. Wolf's nostrils quivered at the prospect of a kill. He turned back to me for the rest of the story.

I worked the moment, gave it a couple of beats. "What Vecchi did," I finally went on, "was spend six weeks in Queens combing the personnel files of companies with shifts that ended at three or four in the afternoon. When he'd find a worker who lived in the Bronx—men only; it had to have been a man

—he'd do a little snooping. He checked on maybe two dozen office and factory workers. Eventually he followed a loading-dock worker at a soft drink bottling plant to a two-family house in, I don't know, some place like Gun Hill Road. When the guy left his Chevy parked out front Vecchi looked it over. He spotted a drop of caked blood on the trunk lid. That did it. As soon as he confronted the nut he broke down and poured out the whole story. Shortwave signals from Jupiter or maybe Mercury had made him do it."

"That's it?" said Waxroth.

"A real nail biter," Werner said sourly. "I'm wringing wet."

While the air went out of their balloon I turned to Kornbluth. I could take a pretty good guess but I asked, "What's Vecchi got to do with our project?"

"What else? A little expertise most production companies won't pay for. Not necessarily you, Mike, but too many writers today won't get off their fat asses to find out how police procedures actually work. Al Vecchi had twenty years on the NYPD, commendations up the kazoo. I put him on for a few weeks to eyeball our crime shows and give the network a renewed air of authority. I want to weed out some of the crap that gets generated by word processors instead of by life."

Waxroth jumped in. "Wait a minute, Oscar. Does this mean you're giving us another set of changes? No way. You've had three bites of the apple, three chances to fold your police maven's notes into your own. Mike's met you more than halfway. You have something else, I don't care what, hold it for the polish." Whether his passion was felt or he was showboating for me, his point was well taken.

Kornbluth's voice went silky. "Contractually,

Wolf, you may be right, although I'd have to have our lawyers take another glance at the applicable paragraph. But look, what are we doing talking business in front of Talent . . . ?''

My heart thumped and I broke in fast. Talent or no, I could no longer afford the luxury of playing hardball with the Kornbluths of the business. This deal was my salvation. And it was potentially so sweet I'd have taken script notes from Kornbluth's great-grandmother in the sepia photo. I said, ''Why not hear what Mr. Vecchi has to say? It wouldn't hurt to get another point of view.''

I was saved from further mealymouthing. The door had swung open and Vecchi himself stood there. It had to be Vecchi—five seven, barrel chest, open shirt collar around a seventeen and a half neck, mock-alligator belt, lightweight zippered wind-breaker. A subway door had opened and let out a little rush of Times Square air. I half-expected to see a rolled-up *Daily News* sticking out of his back pocket. I couldn't say whether he was Bensonhurst, Arthur Avenue, or where, but it didn't much matter. He ate at Puglia's, on Hester Street. Him or his twin.

He acknowledged Kornbluth's pro forma introductions with pro forma nods and sat down. Werner quickly went to the point. ''So, Al . . . you read Mike's script?''

''Mike?''

''Byron Saldinger. Mike.''

''Yeah, I read it.'' It wasn't cordial, it wasn't hostile. It was a statement.

Werner was waiting for more—hopefully something at the level, at least, of ''it wasn't half bad.'' When it didn't come he asked, ''Any problems?''

Vecchi cleared his throat. What was I in for? His Adam's apple bobbed while a hand like a catcher's mitt searched for his first turned-down page. I decided he wore neckties only at weddings, and not all weddings. He was handling the script as if he were holding it for the bomb squad. When he found his place he said, "You don't 'frisk' a suspect, you 'toss' him."

"I know," I said quickly. "But 'toss' would confuse the viewers."

"I just call them," he said. "What you do with them is your business." He found another page. "A body in the water six hours wouldn't be floating."

"We need it to be on the surface," I said. I couldn't believe that eight more or less grown people were grappling with this problem. "You tell me how long the body would float and I'll shorten it to that."

"Right." Vecchi turned pages. "Your man is on a major investigation. Four cops? One of them a woman? There'd be a hundred detectives on this case."

"If I put a hundred cops on the case the viewers would start rooting for the killer."

"Like I said," he said, "I just call them."

"How many cops were there," Werner asked testily, "on the Raymond sisters' murder?"

"A hundred and sixty in the task force."

"I mean how many with you, thumbing through Rolodexes in Queens. You have pretty good backup?"

"None. I did that on my own time."

So much for Blau. He retreated and my agent took over. "Oscar, is this the proper forum for a technical adviser? Why not let Mike meet somewhere with Al over Al's notes, whatever those may happen to be, and if we think they're do-able without renegotiating the contract—"

"They're do-able, Wolf," I cut in. "Based on what I'm hearing I don't see having to take the piece apart."

"So, end of meeting?" Wolf proposed. And this time he got to his feet.

"Hold it, Wolf," Kornbluth said. "There's one other thing."

I had been waiting for this, whatever it was that went with Kornbluth's foreshadowing "first." He hadn't brought this group together to watch him introduce the technical adviser to the writer. Wolf sat down and now Vecchi got up. "I guess you guys won't be needing me." He pointed a thick finger at me. "Catch you later?"

"That's all right, Al, you can stay," Kornbluth said. By which he meant, Stay. Vecchi sat down and now I understood the purpose of the meeting to this point—it had been to make sure Vecchi was on hand for what was up next. Werner looked at his watch. Like the rest of our group, he could foresee nothing in what was to come that could do him any good.

"Oscar, will this take long?" he asked. "Seth and I are expected on the other side." By which he meant at Galactic, their deficit financiers on this deal, who had offices at a studio in the Valley.

"I don't think so," Oscar said in a reassuring voice from which I drew no reassurance. "It's about this Nicholas Stavros."

I had a mildly sinking feeling. So it *was* Stavros I had glimpsed in the parking lot. Kornbluth turned to me. "Did you know he was in town?"

"No, I didn't. What of it?"

"He knew you were here. *Variety* had it. He came in to see me this morning."

There was a minor explosion from Wolf and the

Blaus. "What is this?" Wolf demanded. "Why don't you let your lawyers deal with this kind of crap?"

"Stavros came without a lawyer. He says he hasn't hired one yet. I decided to see him. Informally, just the two of us."

"Nice going, Oscar," I couldn't help saying. "What next, you underwrite a roast for him at the Friars?"

Now Oscar's voice took on an edge. "Let's keep it civilized, okay, Mike? We're locked in, all of us, in maybe the biggest deal you've ever had." Or was likely to have, we both knew. A two-hour pilot, twenty-two guaranteed hours—not scripts, *film*—plus a major movie star who had never had TV exposure. "There are big bucks going out of here," Oscar reminded me, "even with participation from our foreign partners."

"Big bucks will come back in," said Wolf.

"Bucks we damn well don't want to share—to say nothing of triple damages—with some half-assed civilian who claims Byron Saldinger stole his property," Oscar shot back.

"This is a used-up subject," I said. "I have nothing more to add to it."

Werner came in. "For Chrissake, Oscar, why don't your people give the Greek a few bucks and close the books on this? There are nuisance suits every season from nuts like him."

"Exactly why the network has a firm no settlement policy," Kornbluth said. "Anyway, there is no suit. Not yet. I'd like to keep it that way."

"For Chrissake, Oscar." Werner's voice was heavy with weariness, boredom, contempt—it was hard to tell.

"Right. I know. This is a drag. To tell the truth, there's so much at stake here we might have made an exception, grabbed a settlement. But this nut won't deal. He won't even hire a lawyer. I don't know where he's coming from. Yes I do. What was that place the ancient Greeks dug in their heels, wouldn't quit?"

"Thermopylae," said Matt Clay. Another county heard from.

"Thermopylae. Exactly," said Kornbluth. "Talk about pig-headed stubborn. Frankly, you know what the cleanest out is for the network? The least headache? Close out the books on this deal and find another property for Trig Bascomb."

My heart dropped to my arches. A deep rumble of alarm came from the others in my group.

"Just a minute, my friend," Wolf said.

"Yeah, I know, we can't do that," Oscar said, "we're under time pressure, and anyway, Bascomb is welded to your concept." Thank God for our movie star and his clout.

"So what are you getting at, Oscar?" Werner wanted to know.

"We're boxed in with your group," Kornbluth said. "We have to go to the mat with this Stavros. And if it comes down to a trial, you know when the case will make the calendar? When we've got a good three seasons in the can and the real money is starting to come in from overseas and syndication. And I don't have to tell you what's been happening in the courts lately—the judges trying to murder us with a redefinition of profits that could deliver every dime we make on this series to somebody like a Stavros. So Mike, here's what I absolutely have to know: that you're totally clean in this situation. You know what I mean?"

"I know what you mean," I said as slowly and evenly as I could manage and knowing that I was making a major mistake. "You mean is the concept mine, or did I steal it, you son of a bitch."

"Mike, I understand why you might get upset, but I thought we agreed to keep this discussion on a high plane. Look, I'm a person totally on your side in this situation. And yet this Stavros managed to make a case, a reasonably convincing case. So what worries me, if he can do that with me, a professional, how would he play to a jury, to people who don't know how the business works and don't know you the way I do?"

"I don't know, Oscar. I told you the facts, I told the Blaus, I told Galactic, I told you again, and I told your lawyers twice. What do you want me to do? Hire a blimp and trail a banner, '*Corrigan's Way* is entirely and solely the creation of Byron Saldinger'?"

"Mike, take it easy, huh? I want you to tell me again. How you don't know Stavros, never met him—"

"I didn't say I never met him. I said that until he started yelling that I stole his property I can't recall ever exchanging more than hello and good-bye with him."

"Christine's. You said you eat there practically once a week."

"Sometimes twice. Sometimes more. Since the divorce I mostly eat out."

"It's his sister's restaurant, for Chrissake. And you don't know the man?"

"He doesn't work there. I hardly know the people who do. I go in with a book or the paper after the crowd leaves that's going to the theater. Correction. I know the bartender. I know the waitress I usually get. My surrogate mother."

"So you go there when the place is nearly empty.

But you never talk to this putz, Stavros, who also comes in when the crowd clears out?"

"Sure. How's the veal, how's the scrod, how's the weather. Why would I talk television concepts with Nicholas Stavros, who owns a health food store? Why?"

"So it's more than hello and good-bye, it's how's the veal. And you know Stavros owns a health food store."

"We got real close one night. Intimacies poured out."

"This isn't funny, Mike."

"Damn right, it isn't funny. So tell me what it is?" My team was watching from the sidelines, pretty much reduced to spectators; I couldn't tell anymore how much they were with me. I said, "We've gone over this before. Ad nauseam on the phone, Oscar. What is it you're looking for this time?"

"Reinforcement. Conviction. I want to hear you crush Stavros's story like it was a matchbox."

"Nah. I don't think so, Oscar. I don't think that's it." I was coming to a boil. Considering my record of temper control, I should have shut up at this point. But I was too far gone. I said, "You know what I think? You brought me in here with this rent-a-cop so you could grill me again while he sized me up. Then later he'd tell you whether he had pegged me as a liar. Based on what he used to watch for behind the one-way mirror at the precinct house while his buddies grilled suspected flashers and pickpockets. What are the telltale signs, Al? White knuckles? Shallow breathing? Enlarged pupils?"

Vecchi nodded. "Those will do for starters."

Kornbluth said, "Mike, you've got this all wrong—"

I said, "Fuck you. As far as I'm concerned, this

meeting is adjourned. You want me for a script meeting—a *script* meeting—Wolf knows where to find me.''

I stormed out of the room. Sheila Bannister's slack jaw and unbelieving eyes were the last things I saw. Even before I slammed the door some part of me already knew I wasn't necessarily behaving in a wise and responsible manner.

CHAPTER TWO

The traffic was light to Sunset and I made the turn easily and headed, for no particular reason, west. In New York I would have run off my anger—a couple of five- or six-minute miles, depending on the season, around the lower rim of Central Park and across the transverse. Since moving to the Upper West Side, where I rented an apartment after Helene and I split, I had not played tennis, my major outlet for stored angers in Westchester. In L.A. if I was staying at a hotel with a pool, I tried to swim off my mad. Otherwise I went for a drive. This was a good hour to drive, halfway between breakfast and lunch, when I might not have to wait more than a light or two to make a left turn. What I wasn't going to do was drive back to my room at the Desert Palm in Hollywood, where there was no working pool, and wait for the phone to ring. Let the messages pile up and let the pack of them wait for me to return the calls. It would be a small edge, but an edge, and I needed whatever I could get. The shakier your career and the more thoroughly some business manager had screwed you, the more firmly you had to stand on pride.

Standing on pride was one thing; getting the messages I was temporarily disdaining but had to have was entirely another. I wasn't sure how well I could count on the Desert Palm for that service or any other. When I checked in the night before I had to shout and play distress signals on the desk bell before the night clerk sleepwalked out of the office, his T-shirt caked with pizza sauce, and fumbled through the registration procedure as if for the first time. I was counting on the day man being relatively wide-awake, and probably more careful about messages. The Desert Palm's clientele relied on getting their messages: they were mostly in film or television. You got a ten percent discount if you showed a card from one of the industry unions—WGA, SAG, DGA, whatever. This was the principal attraction of what was, not to put too fine a point on it, a dump. The old Hollywood charm in the whimsical, Casbah-inspired architecture was more than offset by the ten-dollar cash deposit you had to lay out for the key to the lobby, locked after eleven P.M. It took two more keys to open the two locks to your room. The neighborhood had seen better days. Better decades. But the Desert Palm was a prudent choice for me, considering where I stood in the business and in my personal finances. It allowed me to put a few bucks from the per diem in my pocket. I would save a few more, depending on how many Chinese take-out meals I ate in my room while they kept me here doing revisions.

That prospect triggered an unhappy memory. Some time before the long employment drought that ended with the *Corrigan* deal, I had argued long and hard with a producer who asked me to write a scene for two people who are "just beginning to realize they are in love" while they face each other on twin beds in a cheap hotel room eating Chinese food with chopsticks out of take-out containers. My position was that I had sat through that scene so many times it gave me an MSG headache. I eventually won the argument and lost the match. The producer nursed his grudge, determined to take the next story point.

That turned out to be a demand that A kill B by running him down with his car. No matter how heatedly I tried to convince him there is no more unreliable and inefficient way to blow someone away than with the hood of a Buick Le Sabre, I got the same reply I had always gotten. "Fuck that," the producer explained. "It's visual." I wrote it. Slow, late, and lousy. Word gets around: "Saldinger is a hardnose." It had been getting around more and more during that time of increasing personal and financial problems. And finally the calls from production companies stopped coming.

I slowed for a light. The almost unchanging commercial face of Sunset along the Strip was as comforting in its stability as upper Broadway at home. I even failed to be put off by what I might otherwise have taken as an omen, a gas station to my right where the T had apparently fallen off the beginning of a string of tinseled letters hung between the pumps. IRE SALE, it read. Here too they were vending their wrath.

Where the Strip doglegs into the perfectly manicured estates of Beverly Hills, a parking place suddenly opened up. That seemed reason enough to stop for the breakfast I had never got around to before the network meeting. There would be nothing between here and the beach but the Beverly Hills Hotel and I wasn't nearly self-destructive enough to spring for a thirty-dollar breakfast. So I sat at the counter at Rascals' Retreat—almost empty at this hour—read the paper, and shoveled down bacon and eggs. Feed an ego, starve a fever.

Back in the car, I continued west. When I couldn't find any music on the radio to match my mood, I settled for a talk show that dispensed cooking advice to people who called in. I followed an in-depth discussion on bay leaf. Better in the morning than mariachis. Out both side windows the American dream repeated over and over through Beverly Hills, Bel Air, Westwood, Brentwood, all the way to the beach. I ended up somehow in Venice, maybe because Venice's grittiness was a match for the Desert Palm, forty minutes to the east. I parked, and strolled aimlessly on the beach.

I was calm enough now to weigh the damage. On reflection, there didn't seem to be that much. Kornbluth could have me fired from the project but what would be the point? Stavros was going to make trouble whether I was in or out. And a new writer now, with the pilot about ready to go, would cost more money without bringing new benefits. Our movie star seemed to be comfortable with what he'd seen, and the last thing anybody wanted to do was shake Trig Bascomb's confidence. Anyway, I had a safety net. It would take more mucking with the script than Kornbluth would be willing to do at this point for him to endanger my back end position on the deal. If I was eased off the series and found no other work, I wouldn't be able to pay off my debts but I could support Helene and the kids on my royalties from *Corrigan*.

Once I had a fix on where I stood I began to feel

better. The sand was firm underfoot, and getting warmer, the air was clean, the ocean pacific. A few sunbathers were beginning to set themselves up with chairs or blankets and were cautiously peeling off a layer of clothing, unwilling to make a major commitment this early on an April day but prepared to go further when the sun did its part. I threaded my way among them along the beach for a few blocks, and then doubled back, asking myself the same question I asked in Central Park: who are these people and why aren't they at work? Eventually I walked back from the beach to the cement beach path and sat on a low concrete wall and took in the passing parade—joggers in bizarre one-of-a-kind outfits, Day-Glo roller skaters, muscle-bound exhibitionists, octogenarian health fiends. The regular Venice scene. It had the same calming effect as a tank of tropical fish.

After a while a female skater in a head-to-toe outfit that may very well have been sprayed on spun to a stop in front of me. "Hi! Is there a rip in the back of this thing?" she asked, and turned around. The back was undamaged, and every bit as pleasurable to look at as the front.

"Looks good to me," I said.

"Some clown nearly whacked me with a box cutter as he went by," she said, and sat down next to me, chestnut hair framing glowing skin, Lycra straining across her chest. "Honestly! You notice how many oddballs hang out down here? Every one of them screaming for attention."

"I notice."

"The way some of these wackos dress . . ." She stopped to regroup, her eye on my arm. "Isn't that jacket a little heavy?"

"I came in from New York last night. I never get it exactly right."

"New York! You live there?"

I nodded.

"In it? Right *in* New York? Itself?"

"The Upper West Side."

"I wouldn't know where that is." She laughed. "Pretty dumb. I guess it's on the upper west side, huh? Would you tell me something? I always wondered. Where do you keep your car?"

"I don't use a car in the city."

"No car." She shook her head slowly, trying to picture it. Then, "I've never gotten back east. I keep meaning to, I nearly went in October. Last minute I took a package deal to Hawaii. I'd have given them back the welcome lei and the complimentary mai tai for a room facing the ocean. What do you do?"

"I'm a television writer."

"Wow. Anything I've seen?"

"You may have. What do you do?"

"Not gonna tell me, are you? I'm not doing anything at this particular moment. I don't think it's an especially good time for Cancers." She must have read my face. "No, that's my sign. Anyway, it was nothing personal. The whole department went. 'Laid off.' Is there any difference between that and 'fired,' except it sounds less brutal? I can't get anyone to give me a straight answer on that."

"You may be right, there's usually none. Tough luck. Tough times. I'm sorry."

"Don't be. I'm sleeping in for a change and I'm finally using my health club the way it's supposed to be used. I'd love to get these thighs under control." She extended a long, perfectly formed leg.

"You've got a major problem there."

"You think so?" she asked anxiously. She gave me

an intense look, then broke into a smile. "You're teasing. But it is a minor problem and I can get to it now because I have a ton of unemployment coming. Which reminds me. I have a job interview." She stood up. "Even if you don't want the job, you have to go through the motions."

I said, "How come being out of work in L.A. scares people less than it does in the East?" A feeble swipe at a new topic. I was trying to keep her from leaving.

"I suppose if you have a lemon tree in your yard you've got your vitamin C," she said, disposing of the new topic. "Tell me your name so I can look for it on the tube."

"Byron Saldinger. What's yours?"

"Believe me, you're not going to see it anywhere. Jenny. Nice talking to you."

She was preparing to push off and I didn't have time to be clever. "Jenny, wait a minute. Will you have dinner with me tonight?"

She looked at me. "How old are you?"

"Forty-four."

She gave it a long beat. "Does it have to be tonight?"

"I may go back home tomorrow night."

She thought it over again. "Okay."

"Good. I'm staying in Hollywood. You know Musso's?"

"Musso and Frank, on Hollywood Boulevard. I've never actually been."

"Seven-thirty?"

"Sure. See you. Byron." She laughed. And she was gone.

Why had I done that? I would blow much of what I was saving by staying at the Desert Palm and there wasn't one single thing that girl and I would have to say to each other. I knew why I had done it. Because she was so damn great-looking.

An hour or so later I was driving up Benedict Canyon and the overhead sun was finding those deep-shadowed places it touches only a few minutes a day. Tidy new suburban houses alternated with older, weathered country places on the steep, heavily wooded slopes. Neither kind looked completely at home. Rudd Cole's sprawling ranch-style house was set well back on a huge plot up a short cul-de-sac known principally for the house where Jean Harlow's husband killed himself. Not only do the streets in L.A. come with credits, the credits clue you to who counts the most. Rutherford Cole's name has probably appeared on the television screen as often as anyone's in the business. The creator of nine successful series, two or three of them not half bad, the author or producer of countless *MOW*s and mini-series, he had cranked out floods of pop entertainment for thirty-five years. Not infrequently one of his shows had been seen by as many as forty percent of those Americans who had their TV sets on. But on the street where he lived he was lucky to get a mention as an afterthought to Mr. Jean Harlow: "Oh, and up the street there's somebody used to be in TV. Must have been big. That's some house."

Rudd's landscaping had grown leggy and scraggly since I was here last, at least two years before. A couple of years more of inattention and the neighborhood kids would start swapping ghost stories about the place. I had phoned ahead, of course, and was expected, so the door was opened at once by a bowing Japanese servant of advanced years. Nobody has Japanese servants anymore—the Japanese would have Caucasian servants if we were any good at it—

but Jasmine, Rudd's wife, was Japanese. After long study I had come to believe that the cluster of three or four servants I always found in the Coles' kitchen —more than they needed—were poor relatives to whom Jasmine was giving a boost.

She was standing right behind the servant and she greeted me with a hug, uncharacteristically physical for a Japanese, and pulled me along through a warren of rooms to her husband's office. The house looked a little tired, a little bereft—their children were grown and out—but Jasmine looked wonderful, a good twenty years younger than her age. There is a theory that the Japanese look young because they are not burdened by Judeo-Christian guilts. Whatever the reason, Jasmine, who gave up being a Japanese movie actress the day she married Rudd, could have shot additional scenes on this day for any one of her pictures.

"How long will you be in town, Myron?" She never failed to use my real name; it was the only thing about her that had ever bothered me. "Can we get you to come for dinner?"

Dinner at the Coles' was an odd ritual. I had never eaten in the solid, woody dining room, but I had been served many interesting meals in other places —the office, the porch, the yard, the master bedroom. Nor had I ever actually seen Jasmine eat. She ran back and forth between the kitchen and wherever, carrying exotic little dishes and hovering long enough to see if the diners approved. All those servants—you could sometimes hear the excited interchange in Japanese when she entered the kitchen— but none of them, apparently, to be trusted with delivering the master's food. An odd ritual, and not at all relaxing.

"Thanks, Jasmine, I doubt I can make dinner," I

said firmly. "I won't be here more than a day or two. I was able to squeeze you guys in because I'm hiding out from my employers. I want them to ring my phone off the hook. How are the kids?"

"Good, very good. The boys are both away in graduate school. Rudd will tell you about Sarah." Sarah, beautiful Sarah. I sometimes wondered what she was up to. Jasmine knocked on the office door and opened it.

Rudd's office hadn't changed in years; I wasn't sure it had been cleaned in years. His awards—the Emmys, Edgars, and so on—were still piled in a corner, still caught between his desire to put them in a closet and Jasmine's to make a big thing of them. On the walls were the same movie posters that had always been there, now a little yellower and curling at the edges. All they had in common was that Rudd admired these movies and had played no part in writing them.

The years allotted to this couple were unfolding in a lopsided fashion. If Jasmine looked twenty years younger than her years, Rudd had aged a good ten since I saw him last. His tired eyes showed that he was glad to see me, but he rose only an inch or two from the worn leather chair at his computer, and there was no other hint of welcome in his body language. It was hard to tell whether this behavior had to do with age. Rudd was formidably nondemonstrative. "That works" was the highest praise I had ever heard him give a piece of writing. A slightly raised eyebrow was his equivalent of handstands. His low-key demeanor had not sat well with American women—his first two marriages had lasted a total of five years—but it was within the expectations of a Japanese woman, even one as outgoing as Jasmine.

Of such unlikely lash-ups the best marriages are often made, and this seemed to be one of them.

After the usual amenities Jasmine withdrew and Rudd said, "I hear you're a shameless plagiarist." He never eased into a subject.

"Rudd, the guy is relentless."

"A Greek, isn't he? They invented the Furies."

"The Furies were female."

"Consider yourself lucky."

"The Furies. What was the Greek name for them again?"

"The Eumenides," he said. I didn't know why, but I knew Rudd would know that.

"How did you remember that?"

"Because of the joke. Greek tailor examines torn trousers: 'Euripides?' Customer: 'Yes. Eumenides?' There's more, but I forget. Can your Greek make a case?"

"No more than any of the paranoids who came after you all those years claiming they had invented your fat cop and thin one, or your man and dog who live in a house with a pitched roof and solve mysteries together. How many suits were brought against you in all?"

"I never kept score. Close to a dozen. My favorite was the shmock"—all those years in the business and he still pronounced Yiddish as if he'd picked it up in an Iowa cornfield—"who claimed he created *Dan and Ann*. So what if his couple wasn't interracial? They came from different states, didn't they? Anyway, it was good to see your name in the trades for a change, even with bad news."

"When did you start reading the trades again?"

"When I decided to come back in the business."

"Rudd! You?" I was truly astonished. "After you

swore you would never again write a sentence that was going to be read aloud?''

He nodded. "I said read aloud by someone who'd had elective surgery, spoke through capped teeth, or wore store-bought hair. But you caught my drift.''

"You lured me into this lousy business, abandoned me in it, and now you're crawling back?''

"I have no guilt about tempting you from higher pursuits. That sensitive little coming-of-age novel was pathetic. But it did tell me you might be able to write television, if you'll allow me to juxtapose those two words. I don't know how else you would have supported a family.''

"Rudd, you made your pile. If I had made mine— or had even kept what I did make—I'd be out. What are you doing? And why?''

"Why first. Sarah has decided she'd like to write television. There I go again. I think maybe she can, and I called a few people. Nothing. I'm out of the business four years? I might as well be dead. So I signed for a development package for which Wolf Waxroth will get the Deal of the Year Award from the National Association for the Cunning. But Sarah is getting her shot. She's writing a couple of sitcom episodes.''

Sarah again. I realized I missed her. I said, "Good for her. So you're in series development again. How's it going?''

"Terribly. It's hard enough trying to sell to eight-year-old network executives who think they've *heard* of Jean Arthur, but when they call you 'sir,' you might as well give up. They can hardly wait to get me out of the office so they can buy a concept from a writer whose creativity impressed them that morning in the sandbox.''

"Tell me.''

"Mike, not you. I've got twenty-three years on you."

"Not enough. I'm on the cusp of oblivion."

"You've got a lock on a series deal."

"Thank God, out of the blue, and probably my swan song. Werner Blau took a proposal of mine to Trig Bascomb—what made Blau guess Bascomb was ripe for recycling on TV?—and network doors opened. The last idea in my sample case, not that innovative, and so soft I almost didn't show it to Blau. Can you figure the luck?"

Rudd said, "There are no new ideas. Only new Vice Presidents for Development." He picked up his ringing phone. "Hello?" He listened for a moment and the color drained from his face. I've never seen anyone go ashen faster. He turned to me, hand over the mouthpiece. "Mike, would you excuse me for a minute?" I got up and he mimed for me to close the door behind me.

There were voices in the kitchen, so I wandered back there. Jasmine was seated at the kitchen table with a clutch of her retainers, regaling them with a story in Japanese. My appearance interrupted a lot of joyful cackling.

"Myron, you're not leaving so soon?"

"No, Rudd's on the phone. I didn't mean to break up the party."

"Don't be silly." At a few words from her the staff shuffled hastily from the room. "Can I make you some lunch?" she asked once there was no one but her to do it. "I'm being a dreadful hostess."

"Thanks, I had a late breakfast. I didn't have the nerve to ask him. How's the novel coming?"

"Who knows? He has hundreds of pages in the computer. Single-spaced. But he never presses Print."

"Single-spaced. That bastard." I couldn't help but grin. "He hooked me into television by telling me how few words you had to put on a page, how few pages it took to make a script. He said, 'The white space will give you snow blindness.' Now look at him."

She said, "He didn't lie to you."

There was no point in asking how he was feeling, why he looked so old. She wouldn't tell me if she knew, and she might not know. I hadn't the faintest idea what went on between them except that they had been together more than thirty years, a salient fact in this town, in this business.

We made small talk for a couple of minutes. I was afraid she would ask about the divorce—she had always liked Helene—but she was too discreet for that. She told me that Sarah seemed to be following in her father's footsteps as a writer but she seemed to discourage further questions about Sarah, and we moved on to other subjects. And then Rudd beckoned me over the intercom and I went back to the office.

He didn't apologize for throwing me out, that wouldn't have been his style. But he made up for his behavior by asking a lot of concerned questions about my network deal. Not the financial side of it, Heaven forbid; no matter how well you know another writer, he is more likely to reveal the most intimate nuance of his sex life than the dollars and cents of his deal. Anyway, Rudd wouldn't embarrass me about money; he could still command at least twice what I did. He asked about the premise of the series and suggested a couple of adjustments in the running characters. He even generously threw in a story notion. Then he gave me a cautious blessing. "With Bascomb tied up and a full year under the deal to find your audience, this one might make it," he said. "Unless I'm totally out of touch, which is also possible."

After that we swapped anecdotes, Rudd's way of fending off intimacy. We had both been on the outside of the business looking in since we last saw each other, so we had no new gossip. There wasn't a story of his I hadn't heard more than once, and he must have known all of mine. When all the color had returned to his face—it must have taken close to an hour—I made my excuses. Rudd weighed his options only briefly and then actually walked me to the front door. I said if I was around long enough I would come to dinner. He and Jasmine waved me out the driveway. His arm was around her shoulder. When I passed Paul Bern's house—Jean Harlow's husband—I wondered, not for the first time, what had gone on in there.

I drove up Benedict Canyon to Mulholland and turned east. By now the fog had burned off and the views were sharp toward both the city and the Valley. I figured on heading down Laurel Canyon Road to the freeway and back to Hollywood. But when I reached Laurel I didn't make the turn. I suddenly realized I had no desire to return to Hollywood just yet. I wasn't ready to pick up my messages at the Desert Palm. Worse, I didn't want to learn there weren't any. At this remove I was again feeling foolish about my operatic departure from Kornbluth's office.

It was after three. I had spent half a day sulking in my tent. If this was the right course, if I was succeeding in making Kornbluth uneasy, continuing to keep out of reach until the close of business was likely to reinforce the message. I drove slowly along

Mulholland until I came to an overlook. I pulled up, shut off the motor, found some treacly Mexican music on the radio, and stared out sleepily across a gulch to some hillside houses on stilts. They were no more committed to this place than I was. When the big shake came they would bolt for Ventura Boulevard. I drifted off.

The words "Nicholas Stavros" startled me awake. I thought I had dreamed them and probably I had, but they seemed to reach me in the voice of a Mexican radio announcer talking a mile a minute—delivering, I now realized, although I couldn't understand a word of it, the news. Jesus, talk about being pursued by the Furies. Was it important for every bracero and housemaid from here to the border to know someone had accused me of plagiarism? Did any of them care? It had to have been a dream. Stavros was weighing on me more than I was ready to admit.

I looked at my watch. It was nearly ten after four. As usual, jet lag had thrown my sleep pattern off and I had taken a really heavy nap. Perfect, just about the right time to start back to the Palm. I gave myself a couple of minutes to come fully awake, then I continued along Mulholland for a bit, fiddling continually with the radio for an English language local news station. The drive controls on rentals are pretty much uniform, but every radio in them seems to present a different challenge to the mechanically disadvantaged. The only news I could find was the tail end of a CBS network feed out of Washington.

On a whim, I made my way down to the Valley on that steep, breathtakingly twisting road that always makes me think I'm on the Riviera until it meets ugly reality at Ventura, near the entrance to the Universal lot. The rush-hour traffic was already building but I didn't care, I was in no particular hurry. Avoiding the freeway, I made my way to Hollywood on the flat. It was nearly five when I keyed the card to the gate of the Desert Palm's dank garage.

The hotel formed a semicircle around what should have been a camel market but happened to be a swimming pool. In keeping with the desert motif, which included walls of peeling stucco and faded paint, the pool was bone dry. UNDER REPAIR said a weathered sign I remembered from my one previous visit. My room was on the second level of the dopey pileup of rooms that simulated the Casbah. I figured on taking a shower before bracing myself to check my messages, so I carefully avoided the office. I was working my way up the network of exterior ramps, platforms, and stairs that led to the upper rooms when I noticed two men sitting at the pool. From my earlier stay here I knew that guests sat at the pool even though it was no longer a pool, but these two didn't strike me as guests. They were two guys who didn't belong here but were nevertheless sitting at the pool. And they were looking at me. When they saw me looking back, one of them stood up and called, "Mr. Saldinger?"

I had written the scene a dozen times; they were cops. I nodded and said, "Yes."

"Like to talk to you for a few minutes?"

I resisted asking, What for? I said, "Sure," and started back down.

"Okay if we do this up in your room?" He didn't want to say "Police" out loud—the word might send half a dozen guests diving out their back windows—so he held up a leather folder with a shield, which at this distance could have been from a Cracker Jack box but which I was willing to concede wasn't.

Again I said, "Sure," and turned and climbed up

to the room. By the time I had sorted out which of the two keys was for which lock, and remembered which got turned once to the left and which twice to the right, the cops had caught up and I let them in. The cop who had done the talking—good-looking, massive shoulders, just the right mix of gray in his carefully combed-back hair—said, "I'm Sergeant Dunleavy, LAPD. This is my partner, Detective Ossian." Ossian was younger, shaggy, more the cowboy type that works in film crews.

I said, "Right, please sit down, guys. I need a minute while I check my messages."

The red light on the phone was blinking and I called the office. Seth Blau had called twice and Wolf Waxroth three times. Same message from both: "Please call." Nothing from Kornbluth, but I decided not to read anything into that. He would have communicated by way of Wolf or the Blaus.

There was a sprung easy chair in the room and the queen-sized bed with the spread that matched the wallpaper, but the cops were still standing. I wondered if cops on duty aren't allowed to sit when they go to someone's hotel room. I had written plenty of scenes in which they did but they weren't based on research, only on what I needed for the scene. Vecchi could tell me. For some reason it now popped into my head that some playwright—Molière?—had written that in comedy people sit but in tragedy they stand.

I said, "What can I do for you, Sergeant?"

"We're hoping you might be able to help us with a criminal investigation," Dunleavy said.

"Yes . . . ?"

"Am I correct, Mr. Saldinger, that you've had some connection with a man named Nicholas Stavros?"

"More a disconnection. We're on opposite sides in what may turn into civil litigation. Why, what's he done?"

The two cops looked at each other. "You don't know—"

I shook my head.

"—that he was murdered earlier today?"

If there ever was one, this was an act break, and among the emotions I was trying to sort out was irritation that I hadn't seen it coming.

CHAPTER THREE

"I'm sorry," Dunleavy said after a decent interval in which he let me process his news, "we figured you knew. It's been on the radio all afternoon."

"I missed it."

"If I'd known I'd have broken it easier," he said. "Even though, if I'm guessing right, you and the deceased weren't exactly friends."

What was going on here? "We weren't exactly enemies either. Just two men on opposite ends of an argument."

"So you did know him. Good, because—"

"*Of* him, mostly."

"—because we can't find anyone else in town who does."

Either they were holding back or they hadn't done much legwork; didn't they know Stavros had a one-on-one with Oscar Kornbluth this morning? If they didn't, I saw no reason to volunteer it.

"How did you get my name?" I asked.

"Off a TV script we found in the victim's hotel

room. Your name, hard to read, was on it as author. Someone had x-ed it out with a marking pencil. Real heavy. Your agent's name was also on the cover. He told us where you were staying."

Perfect. Send me everyone, Wolf; you never know where the job offers will come from.

"You stay here a lot at the Desert Palm?" Dunleavy continued. Meaning he examined very carefully the bona fides of anyone who did.

"Second time," I said. "Can you tell me how Stavros died?"

"Mr. Saldinger, why don't you let me ask the questions? Filling you in on what you'll hear on the six o'clock news won't move our investigation forward."

"Okay. Ask."

"Stavros arrived from New York couple of days ago. Any idea what he was doing here in town?"

"I can't say for sure. But he may have come in connection with the complaint he has against me, Thor Productions—that's the Blau Brothers—Galactic, their deficit financiers, and the network for which we're making a television pilot called *Corrigan's Way*."

"I don't read the trade papers much—"

"Neither do I."

"What is this complaint in regard to?"

"Plagiarism."

Ossian suddenly spoke up; pleasant western twang. "Oh, sure, *that*. *The Hollywood Reporter* had something. In a story on Trig Bascomb." Dunleavy threw him a look and Ossian mumbled, "Sorry, Ed, I didn't put the two together."

Dunleavy turned back to me. "So Stavros was a television writer who claimed you stole this *Corrigan's Way* from him?"

"No." I tried to keep my voice neutral. *"I'm* a television writer. Stavros was a shopkeeper. He owned a store on Amsterdam Avenue in New York, Nature's Buddy, that sells, for instance, unsulfured raisins. Did you ever eat raisins without sulfur? They make a good case for poison."

Dunleavy was not going to be sidetracked by wiseass observations. "But I'm not wrong if I put it that Stavros *claimed* to be a writer. The author of this *Corrigan's Way."*

"It's not that simple."

He took a moment. "How much money is a writer likely to get for a TV pilot?"

"A two-hour pilot?" None of his fucking business. "Generally speaking, in the neighborhood of well under a hundred thousand dollars."

"And that's it? That's all that's involved here monetarily?"

I didn't like what I sensed to be the thrust of the dialogue, but it would be better if I gave him the facts than if he picked them up elsewhere, which he could easily do. I gave it to him straight. I said, "The pilot is step one. If the series goes, it's the tip of the iceberg. Royalties will follow, and residual payments on reruns." He might as well hear it all. "Plus, usually, a producing role on the series for the author, ancillary rights, fees for supplemental markets—that's foreign and cable sales—and a substantial bonus in lieu of profits."

Ossian piped up. "If there was a lawsuit, wouldn't there also be penalties to the complainant? Don't juries award triple damages in this kind of case?"

"If Stavros went to court and won his suit he might end up with a bundle, yes." I was tired of our dancing around each other.

So was Dunleavy. He said, "Mr. Saldinger, would you mind telling me what you did today?"

"Would you mind reading me my rights?"

His eyes widened. "I guess maybe I should do that."

I forced a grin and said, "Let me do it for you." I rattled them off, substituting "I" for "you." He looked mildly impressed. I said, "I type those words a lot. What I did today from when to when?"

"I'll make it easy. From the time you woke up till now."

"Sure, okay. Let's see. I slept lousy. I always do the first few nights away from New York. I woke up at about four A.M. That's seven in New York. I fell asleep again at six and woke up just in time to make a network meeting in West Hollywood with my agent and the Blaus. You'll find me signed in at reception there at ten oh nine. The meeting ran, I don't know, half an hour. When it broke I went for a drive."

"Just a drive?"

"I needed to cool out, I sometimes do after a network meeting. I drove out to the beach. Venice."

"What time would you have gotten there?"

"Oh, let's see, I stopped for breakfast, so I must have gotten to the beach shortly after noon. Something like that."

"Breakfast. Where'd you have that?"

"Rascals' Retreat. The one near Doheny."

"Will anybody there remember you?"

"Remember me for what? I sat at the counter, I read the paper, I ate bacon and eggs, I left an average tip. But who knows? Maybe the waitress wrote me up in her diary because I was her first Gregory Peck look-alike of the day, only younger."

He said, "This will go a lot faster if you let me do my job. How long did you stay at the beach?"

"I took some sun. Maybe an hour? I don't know. I was looking to stay out of touch with my people for strategic reasons. Then I called a friend and went up and visited him at his home in Benedict Canyon. Rutherford Cole." I could see the name meant nothing to him. "The TV producer/writer?"

Ossian was Johnny-on-the-spot. "Didn't he create *Calling Smith and Wesson?*" The man was practically a show business encyclopedia.

"That too. I worked for him years ago when he had his own production company."

Dunleavy wasn't interested. "How long did you stay at the house in Benedict?"

"Till three, something like that. Then I drove up to Mulholland—you can believe this or not—and found a place to park. I was still jet lagged and I sacked out."

His face showed maybe he didn't believe it, but he said, "It doesn't matter whether I believe it or not. The time I'm interested in is between sometime after you left your network meeting and when you say you got to that house in Benedict. Roughly eleven and one."

"That's when Stavros was killed?"

"In there, yeah."

"The M.E.'s established that already? Pretty fancy. He couldn't narrow it down any more?"

"Actually, it was twelve twenty-seven P.M."

I took a beat. "So there was a witness . . ."

"You can say that."

"But the assailant is unknown."

"Right. Listen, if you'd like to talk to a lawyer—"

"I don't need a lawyer. This is goddam ludicrous. I'm sitting still for it because I'm a good citizen. You think I'd actually go out and kill someone because he might possibly sue me?"

"I never said you killed anyone. But if you did, the reason you cite could be motive enough. People kill each other for a parking space."

"True, but when they knock off the competition they *get* the space. If Stavros had a legitimate claim against me, killing him would accomplish nothing. The man has heirs."

"You know for a fact he has heirs?"

"I know a sister. And there have got to be brothers. You ever meet a Greek who didn't have brothers?"

"You say you know his sister?"

"To say hello. She has a restaurant I eat at."

"I see. Young woman?"

"Thirtyish. Why?"

Ossian chimed in again. "She married?"

"I don't know. I don't think so. Why?"

The cops exchanged a glance. I knew what they were groping for—a new motive that sprang from an affair between a middle-aged writer and a hot-eyed Greek. I found it while they groped. When the affair went badly, the woman's brother, Nicholas Stavros, demanded . . . What? One, that the writer marry her; or two, that he never see her again; or three, that he support her baby. Something. His leverage was to threaten the writer with a lawsuit and when that didn't scare the writer he chased him to L.A. There followed an angry confrontation and a— probably—unpremeditated murder. I had that written in the nanosecond or two the cops hesitated. I had an unfair advantage over them; I did this for a living. It was time to bring these two back to reality-based.

I said, "Look, all you guys really want is to nail down where I was at about twelve-thirty, right?"

Dunleavy seemed relieved to be pulled from speculation. "And a half hour before and after," he said. He didn't have to check his notes. "That's probably after breakfast and around when you were out at Venice, right?"

"Roughly."

"Strolling on the beach, one-on-one with the sun. You mix it up with anyone?"

"As a matter of fact, yes." I was surprised to see that they liked this answer. "I picked up a woman. Or maybe she picked me up. A roller skater, pretty, young." Dunleavy was jotting all this down. "Now you're going to ask me her name."

"You could write all my lines, Mr. Saldinger."

"That's good. Jenny. An office worker. On unemployment. The downside is I never did get her last name."

"Or where she lives?"

I shook my head.

"You don't get much you can use picking up girls, do you?"

"Enough. The upside is, I'm meeting her for dinner. Seven-thirty at Musso and Frank."

That did it. Dunleavy shut his notebook and apologized for taking so much of my time, especially since I probably wanted to get ready for the date. I agreed not to leave town in the next twenty-four hours and to let him know in the morning how to get in touch with Jenny. He gave me his card. He, on his part, would check at Rascals' Retreat, just in case someone *had* remembered me there. We parted in a spirit of good fellowship and eased tensions. Dunleavy had gone through the motions, but I decided he had never really believed I had anything to do with Stavros's death. He was ready to direct his energies elsewhere.

Just before the two left I asked Dunleavy how

many police had been assigned to the case. He said he thought six.

"Six, eh? I like that," I said. Naturally he didn't know where I was coming from.

Once they were gone I called Waxroth and the Blaus at their offices. It was after six and they had all left for the day. Calling the Blaus at home would make me appear too anxious, and Wolf wouldn't be home; Phoebe Waxroth was not a person you went home to until you had exhausted all other options. Too late, I remembered to turn on the TV. There was no remote control; anything portable in the room would have been liberated by guests. I flipped from one six o'clock news to the next in search of the Stavros murder. I was too late for the hard news. They were all on weather or sports, another instance of life failing to imitate art: four out of five television dramas would have popped Stavros onto the screen as soon as it warmed up. I turned the set off and went to take a shower.

The bathroom was one more reminder that I was not staying at the Beverly Wilshire or the Bel Age. Never mind the absence of milled soap, shampoo, conditioner, or shoe rag. I would have settled for a showerhead with more firepower than the one in my West Seventies brownstone. There was plenty of self-pity in my role of self-sacrificing divorced father, but there was also a measure of truth in it. The showerhead in my lost home in Irvington—now there was a showerhead.

While I dressed I sneaked a look at myself in the closet mirror. I hadn't socialized much this past year, never with any enthusiasm, certainly with no one as young as the date I had stirred up for tonight appeared to be. Did I look my age? And since Jenny wasn't a development exec deciding whether I was too old to relate to his core audience, did I care? In L.A. forty-four conventionally went with twenty-two, and either one could be the man. And thanks to the divorce having taken fifteen pounds off me, and the Desert Palm's low-wattage lighting, at the moment I could have played thirty-five.

I put on a necktie and immediately took it off. I opened my collar and slipped into the other jacket I had come west with, the unconstructed, carelessly wrinkled linen one Jenny hadn't seen. A what-the-hell look, calculatedly uncalculated. The idea was to downplay the evening and not act the way I was feeling, as if I had won an evening out with the Homecoming Queen. What I should have been feeling was regret over Stavros's untimely and probably brutal death. I couldn't seem to summon up much of that.

CHAPTER FOUR

The hotel was throwing long shadows across the inner court when I made my way down the lash-up of stairs and ramps to ground level on my way to the Palm's garage. I was crossing the pool area when a voice behind me called, "Yo!" I turned to see a figure loping toward me from the office. I assumed I had gotten a phone call after I left the room. But as the figure emerged from the shadow of the building, I saw he was too stocky for the desk man. He said, "Nearly missed you, huh?"

"Al Vecchi," I said. "What, did Kornbluth send you?" Seeing him brought back the scene I had been trying all day to forget. I felt a sting of anger. I supposed it would fade when he announced the purpose of his visit—to deliver, I assumed, an expression of concern and support from the network for any awkwardness Stavros's death might be causing me; plus, it was probably too much to hope, a personal apology from Kornbluth for that tacky game-playing in his office.

But he said, "I haven't seen Kornbluth since this morning. I came over to see how you're doing. After the news. I expected this place to be swarming with cops."

"They left. There were two." I relished passing along this tidbit. "There are six on the entire case."

He took the news in stride and slid off it. "On a case like this six would be a swarm. It isn't exactly the Martin Luther King assassination. But I thought if the police did come on heavy I might get them to ease up. As a professional courtesy."

"Is this service an unadvertised network extra? Thanks, I wasn't hassled. Just the reverse. The police couldn't have been more courteous. Look, I appreciate your stopping by, but I'm expected down on Hollywood Boulevard at seven-thirty—"

"I'll walk you."

"You'll *walk* me?" It was only a few blocks, but if anybody I had ever done business with saw me walking into Musso & Frank from the street entrance, my price would plummet. Plus, I didn't like the idea of a possible network informer tagging after me and then running back to Kornbluth to report. Then a thought struck me. "How did you get here?"

"I walked. I'm staying in Hollywood, maybe a mile from here. The Hollyview Motel?"

I had never heard of it and I had no regrets. I said, "Don't you have a car?"

"No. That's why I figured to dress a little warmer." He spread his arms and I saw now that he was wearing a machine-made Norwegian sweater under his windbreaker. A line of reindeer his barrel chest had stretched like taffy was galloping into an armpit. Vecchi's nose, it struck me, was not that different from the reindeer's. It was a nose with a life of its own. I followed it to his eyes. They were alive, and younger than his years.

"Who made your deal with the network?" I asked.

"I did."

That figured. And on deeper reflection I decided he didn't fit the profile of an informer. I said, "Al, you're going to a lot of trouble for me . . ."

He said, "So how come, huh?" He took a beat. "You were mousetrapped this morning. So was I. Nobody told me up front why I was invited to that meeting."

I took a moment. Then I said, "Tell you what. You're not doing anything, drive down to the restaurant with me. You can fill me in on how Stavros was killed."

"You don't know how he was killed?" He was walking alongside me toward the garage and he turned back admiringly, his eye following the contours of the Casbah. "I like the look of this place."

That figured too.

"Stavros was staying in a hotel called the Grandee," Vecchi began as we eased out of the garage. "You know it?"

I did, a high rise on the Strip, four hundred rooms with identical Spanish-style furniture. The entrance, anytime I walked by, was choked with luggage coming off or going on the buses that brought tourists in on package trips to the Universal Studios tour, Disneyland, the Hollywood Wax Museum, Frederick's—the real Hollywood insiders rarely get to see.

"When did he get to town?" I asked. I was turning south toward Hollywood Boulevard.

"Couple of days ago."

"Go on."

"I can see you're expecting a story. It was a one-sentence crime. Around twelve-thirty, I think, someone pitched him through the window of his room on the ninth floor of the Grandee into the lunch-hour crowd on Sunset Boulevard. I hope before their lunch."

"God. It was twelve twenty-seven."

"They told you that much, eh?"

"And they're sure he didn't do it himself? It wasn't a suicide?"

"You're right, pending investigation, this kind of death is usually called 'jumped, fell, or was pushed.' But this one they didn't have to think about. The windows at the Grandee don't open—to make the air conditioning work better, maybe promote the spread of Legionnaires' disease. Just kidding. Jumpers look for a place where it's easy to jump. I never heard of one who was so hungry for it he had to back into the john for a good enough running start to throw himself through a plate-glass picture window. By the way, two passersby were cut by falling glass."

"God," I said again. "What do you think this is about?"

"I only know what I heard on TV. Stavros's wallet was missing. But there was no forced entry. If I had to make a guess, I'd say the stolen wallet was a cover, that someone he knew, someone real mad at this little guy, gave him a good hard shove. It would have to be hard, with his whole body behind it. Someone who had to be your size at least—five ten or eleven and, what, a hundred and seventy pounds?"

"A hundred and seventy-five."

"By the way, that picture of you must have been taken ten years ago. A typical publicity shot."

"Stavros had a picture of me in his room?"

"Easy does it. The cops didn't tell you? The picture was on the TV. The reporter said Stavros was believed to be in town in connection with a dispute over an upcoming television series to star Trig Bascomb, and so forth and so on. The movie star connection was what the TV was mostly hitting."

"Don't give me and so forth. What did they say?"

"That Stavros was threatening to sue the supposed writer, Byron Saldinger, as well as the network, Bascomb, the whole world. For plagiarism. No news there, it's been in the papers. All Stavros had to say was 'Trig Bascomb' and he got the interviews, right? The whole thing is being pumped up by the media because Bascomb is still news. By the way, he looked good in the clips they ran, except for going a little soft along the jawline. Come to think of it, that must be why he had to hold his nose and jump off the silver screen into this shit business you're in."

"We're in," I said.

When we pulled in to the Musso parking lot, it was barely ten to seven. I didn't know why, but I invited Vecchi in for a drink. I did know why. He might help bridge those awkward first few minutes with my date. "Jenny, this is Sergeant Al Vecchi, NYPD, an old friend. You must remember the Edgar Allan Poe Murders?" It could propel us into that story, keep her from having time to dwell on why she had ever agreed to this date. I was that insecure.

The place was already nearly full and I hadn't made a reservation. I had forgotten, as I often did, that restaurants in L.A. peak at least an hour earlier than they do in New York. I swept through both rooms to make sure Jenny hadn't arrived before us, and then Vecchi and I squeezed into a spot at the bar from which I could keep an eye on the front of the restaurant. We ordered, a Beefeater martini, up, for me, and a bourbon on the rocks for Vecchi. He looked around approvingly at the room, and at the vibrant, noisy crowd. "Like one of those old German places used to be near Times Square," he said. "Last of them must have died thirty years ago, may they rest in peace."

"Yeah, it has a New York beat," I said. "I made it my restaurant when I first came to L.A. I'd eat at the counter, missing New York, and pretty soon I found I was rubbing shoulders with below-the-line movie people I thought had died when knickers and golfing caps went out. Cameramen, production managers, location scouts who had worked on legendary films of the twenties and thirties—*The Awful Truth, The Scoundrel, The Big Parade.* It was like having dinner with the men who copyedited the King James Bible."

"How long ago when you first came out here?" Vecchi asked.

"Over twenty years. I thought I was a boy wonder but I found out boys younger than me had run whole movie studios." I could see he wasn't really interested in any of this. "How long were you on the cops?" I asked.

"Long enough for the pension. Twenty years. I started late."

"How many commendations did Kornbluth say you had?"

"He gave a number? I don't have a number." Our drinks had arrived and he was looking at mine dubiously. A mixed drink. But he said, "Here's looking at you."

"And you." We drank. "Al, tell the truth. In twenty years—and whatever the number, I know you were highly decorated—how many times did you fire your gun?"

"At a perpetrator? You know the paperwork you have to do after?"

"So, how many times?"

"In twenty years? None." Darkly, "There's ways to collar a perp without bouncing slugs off bystanders and sitting still for questions from inquiry boards."

I said, "You and Kornbluth bounced a few rounds off me this morning." I had waited for the drinks to make this calculated segue. "How long did the meeting last after I walked out?"

"Just long enough for everybody to take a guess at how much of a headache the Greek was going to be."

"Come on, Al. Kornbluth had to ask you for a cold reading on me."

"Yeah, he asked."

"Would it be a problem for you to share your verdict with me?"

He let me dangle before answering. "I didn't give one."

"Why not?"

"Insufficient evidence." Beat. "And even if I had an opinion I wouldn't give them the satisfaction."

"So it's okay with you that you might be having drinks with a plagiarist."

"I've drunk with pimps and cat burglars. I once drank with a man who burned down his girlfriend's two-family house because she told him he was putting on weight. A plagiarist is high society."

"Any of those good buddies you mention drink martinis?"

"Listen, nobody's all bad." He drained his bourbon while I stole a glance at my watch. "Stop look-

ing so anxious," he said. "Your lady friend is only
ten minutes late. Not a record."

He might as well know. I said, "She's more than
my friend. She's my alibi for the time of Stavros's
death. You must know the way we do it on television.
If you really need the alibi, the alibi doesn't show."
He gave me a stare of disbelief and I turned in embarrassment to the bartender and signaled for another round. I was nursing this funny premonition I
blamed on television immersion and I said, as casu-
ally as I could manage, "Maybe I'll just take another
quick look."

I left on a slow circle of the room and Vecchi
called after me, "I'll take this round."

I had picked the wrong place to meet this woman.
With two rooms, and both a street entrance and a
parking entrance, there was a slim chance of our
missing each other, so this time I searched more
carefully. The restaurant was in full swing. The diners who had finished their day's work and were just
here to socialize sat back easily in their seats. At the
few tables where there was pitching, or deal-making,
or ass-covering, all present leaned forward. At a back
table I spotted Sheila Bannister, Kornbluth's second
banana, at dinner with a girlfriend. She fiddled with
the menu and held her drink up to her face. Either
she didn't see me or she didn't want me to see her.
It wouldn't have been worth my while to approach
her. Without Kornbluth's permission she wouldn't
give me anything but the time of day, and only a
rough approximation of that.

I collared the busy maître d' at his lectern near
the front door. "My name's Saldinger. Did a lady ask
for me?"

"I'm sorry, sir . . ."

"When she does I'm at the bar, and we'll be two for dinner. Saldinger."

"Mr. Saldinger! I'm sorry. Yes, the lady was in twenty minutes ago. She left this for you."

It was a tightly folded note with "Byron Saldinger" on the outside in a bold, loopy hand. Inside the folds it said,

Hi! I would have called if I knew where you were staying. It turns out I have a family emergency so I'm afraid I'm going to have to skip dinner. And I was so looking forward to it, really! What a shame . . . But don't you think we're bound to run into each other again one day? In New York, if not here. I just feel it. Meanwhile I'll think of you when I see your name on TV. I'm sorry . . . Please forgive me.

Fondly,
Jenny

P.S. Would you believe it? The job I went on the interview for? I got it. Didn't I tell you this was a lousy month for Cancers?

CHAPTER FIVE

When I got back to the bar I had Jenny's note in my clenched fist. Vecchi said, "This the first time you been stood up? Join the club."

I said, "It's not that, Al."

He said, "The alibi. So you'll call her tomorrow."

I made an effort to keep it light, as though I were playing the patsy in a Feydeau farce. I explained that I had no phone number for Jenny, no idea how to find her—no last name, no address, no occupation, no clever identifying marks; that all I knew about her, in sum, was that she was a pretty girl with a great figure. In L.A. that would make her stand out from her peers the way formal wear does a penguin.

Vecchi found my quandary professionally challenging. Couldn't I remember something more . . . ? I summoned up one last scrap: she was on unemployment and about to go off it. Could I do anything with that? Or with the likelihood that she might go roller-skating again in Venice? To make a search for her at the beach pay off would require a

Vecchi-sized police task force armed with stacks of eight-by-tens. I could give him nothing to work with.

By the time we left the bar I had drunk more martinis than could have had a therapeutic effect on my system, which seemed to be made up entirely of nerve endings. It had been many months since I had consumed this much alcohol. I was guaranteed a night of wired off-and-on sleep. We ate at a rear booth, near the door to the parking lot. Vecchi worked his slab of roast beef and pressed me to recount my meeting with Jenny stroke by stroke. I picked at a crab Louie. When I had exhausted all I remembered, he got down a nearly final chunk of beef and said, "When I meet someone I say, 'I'm Al Vecchi.' I don't say, 'I'm Al.' You didn't think it funny she didn't give her whole name when you gave yours?"

"First name only is more common here than in the East," I said. "Anyway, many women are cautious. To keep the heavy breathers off their phones."

"But she said yes to dinner so she must have decided you weren't a weirdo. She could have given her last name then, or at least signed it to the note."

"She was kissing me off in that note. She had second thoughts about meeting me and she was making sure I couldn't find her."

"A good-looking stud like you? She probably figured you for hung like a kosher salami."

"But with twenty years on her."

He began probing the rib for the last scrap of beef while he silently rooted through my story for some shred of a clue. He came up with both. "She thought a skater swiped at her with a box cutter? Come on."

"Anything is possible on the Venice beach."

He chose not to debate the point. He abandoned the rib and picked up the note. He studied it, then turned it over.

I said, "No, Al, it wasn't scrawled on the back of a letterhead from 'Jones and Company, Jenny's Last Employer.' It's a page off a notepad."

"Written on with a ballpoint pen." He had turned it to the front again and was angling it this way and that, his face close to the paper. He caught my look. "I'm looking for an impression from the sheet above."

"That works? You've done it?"

"No, but I saw it on TV. Some crap show like the ones you do."

"Not one of mine. It's an old gimmick, plus I don't think anybody believes it happens."

"Yeah? Is that so? I may have something." His eloquent nose was right on the paper. He worked the page against the light. "Wait a minute." He tilted it again. "It's a list. A shopping list. Potatoes . . . beans . . . cabbage . . . carrots . . . bread . . . pasta . . ." He put the paper down. "I got most of it."

"Perfect. I find the store that sells that stuff and I hide in the back till the girl shows."

"Okay, it's not much. But it tells you something. The girl may be hard up for money. There's no meat on this list, no fruit, no sweets."

"She may be on unemployment. But we already know that, don't we?"

"A second opinion never hurts."

"And you've opened up the possibility she's a vegetarian, like everyone else in southern California. Look, I know you're trying to help. Don't think I'm not grateful. But this subject is starting to bore me. Alibi or no alibi, I don't think the police are really

interested in me. Can we ease into something else?
Do you eat dessert?''

He may have seen that I was trying to cover my
doubts, but he backed off.

I took advantage of the break for coffee to start a
rambling lamentation over my kids. The ache of sep-
aration was always worse when I'd been drinking. My
complaint was that every second weekend with Benjy
and Jane didn't do it for me. I needed them around
in a less ceremonial way—fewer trips to the circus,
more fights over where are your gloves. I wanted to
look in on them at night when they were asleep and
so defenseless I felt I ought to stand guard at the
door to hold off a nasty world. When I saw in
Vecchi's vacant eyes that I'd slobbered long enough,
I signaled for more coffee.

Vecchi saw his chance and bore in again. He
pressed me to go through my entire day, exactly as I
had with Dunleavy. He listened closely to the dull
recitation and when I finished he asked if I had
made any credit card calls. I knew what that was
about—the time, as well as the place where I had
made them, would show on my phone bill and
might be enough to vindicate me. But I hadn't
made any calls. He had a final question: exactly how
had I asked for my eggs to be cooked at Rascals'
Retreat and with what kind of toast? I said to forget
Rascals' Retreat, that avenue was hopeless, and anyway I was there too early in the day for that meal to
work as an alibi. But Vecchi insisted. "You never
know," he said, and he wrote my answer in a slow,
careful hand in a well-thumbed notebook probably
left over from his days on the cops.

I said, "Why are you going to all this trouble for
me?''

"It's what I do," he said. "Procedural. I'm good at it and I like it."

"So how come you took retirement?"

"That was a mistake. I thought maybe I'd try something else. But once I was out I discovered police work is all I'm any good at."

"You're lucky to have found a way to stay involved." My questions had depressed him and I was trying to make up for that. "Advising the network's writers on police procedure? That must give you a certain satisfaction."

He shook his head in disbelief. "Did I tell you to lay off the martinis?"

At not yet ten-thirty in the evening, the solid citizens had vanished from the streets and Hollywood Boulevard was in the hands of the Cong—loitering bikers, cruising low riders, transvestite hookers, and the usual mix of pushers, weirdos, and sickies. I was expecting to drop Vecchi at his motel, but he opened the car door at the first traffic light and started to climb out. I said, "What are you doing?"

"I just wanted to make sure you're sober enough to drive," he said. "I'm walking back. A walk before bed relaxes me."

"Here?" I said. "Walking through this will relax you?"

"Through what? Traffic's down to zip." He didn't have the least idea what I was talking about. So I promised to drive carefully, thanked him again for his support, and watched him march off briskly down the avenue, totally unconcerned, into the heart of darkness.

I made my way, carefully, back to the Desert Palm, carded the garage gate, and watched it groan and clatter open. Even in daylight I hated that dank garage. Driving in now, I counted only one dim bulb burning of a possible four. The gate clanged shut, completing my sense of having entered the dungeon of the Château d'If. Out of New York habit I locked the car, although its theft would be Dollar Rent-A-Car's headache. As I made for the door to the camel market, a voice reached out from behind me. "Would you be so good as to hold the door, please?" A chirpy female voice, English, nervous.

I turned to face two women. Slim and seemingly very young was all I could make out in this light. And fidgety. They had climbed out of a compact and were hurrying toward me, high heels clacking on the cement floor. "Coming! So good of you," the other one chirped. Also English.

Closer, they were more wiry than slim and not quite as young. Thin lips, sharp noses. But nice-looking. "Thank God you came along," the first said gratefully in a low voice as we left the garage together. "We might have ended up sitting in that car all night, don't you think, Cissy?"

"Or longer," said Cissy. "I'm Cissy Bray and this is Pam Walker. We're from London."

They were the Pigeon sisters, was my first thought, from the second act of *The Odd Couple*. I introduced myself and asked what the problem had been. Cissy said when they drove in, someone had been—well, loitering was the only word for it—near this door and they had been nervously debating what to do about it when I appeared. Now there didn't seem to be anyone, so it must have been a guest or maybe their imagination, but this was such a nervous-making place, not at all what they had expected right in the very heart of Hollywood, which is the reason their travel agent had recommended the Desert Palm, although they had since heard that moviemaking was everywhere *but* in Hollywood and was that true?

I said except for postproduction. They said they hadn't come six thousand miles for postproduction, but anyway the Desert Palm was almost worth it for the professional discount, despite the disappointing absence of tinsel in Tinseltown. By this time we were grouped in a pair of lounge chairs at the pool, me in one, the Brits squeezed in the other. I asked what their union affiliation was. They were British Equity, production dancers, and they were here to test the waters for film and television work. If there wasn't any, they would move on to investigate the Las Vegas hotel shows, although, Pam understood, they might have a problem there in the breastworks department because of a preference for American quantity over British quality.

"Speak for yourself, luv," said Cissy confidently; she was the livelier of the two, with merry eyes and a firm chin. "And what do you do?" Meaning me. "I'll wager you're a screenwriter."

"What's that?" said Pam, suddenly alarmed.

There had been a distant sound, something between a footstep and a thud.

"For Heaven's sake, calm down. We aren't the only ones staying here," said Cissy. "Do you mind if someone drops a shoe?"

"Outdoors?" asked Pam. But she did seem overly jittery.

"Outdoors, indoors, does it matter? We are under the protection of this gallant screenwriter, Mr. Byron Saldinger." She paused. "Byron. How dashing."

This didn't seem the time to reveal that Byron was a consequence of Myron not carrying enough weight on the screen. I offered an alternate, equally shameful confession. "Actually, I'm a television writer."

"Oh," said Cissy, disconcerted. "Well . . ." She recovered quickly. "Byron, we have a lovely bottle of gin in our room. Thank God. Because we're just back from dinner with old friends, two English-women who were imported here years ago like prize poodles to be secretaries to a pair of film executives who like their phones answered with what they imagine is a certain elegance, although in London the instant these women open their mouths they give themselves away for what they are, the daughters of a barrow boy and a turf accountant. We four dined in a town called Santa Monica in a sort of pub—darts, Guinness, and so on—frequented by English émigrés looking for a bit of a home feeling among the palms and balmy air."

"Torquay on the Pacific," murmured Pam.

"They were downing their pints along with mashed avocados," Cissy continued. "So depressing. All by way of saying we are very much in need of a nightcap and why don't you join us?"

Pam jumped in before I could reply. "Oh, Cissy, I have such a splitter. I'm sorry, Byron, could we put it off for another night?"

To my relief, from that point the festivities pretty much wound down. Considering how much gin I had already consumed, and how much more might be required to fuel the fantasy, remote as it was, of an invitation to three-way acrobatics with these chirpy dancers, the impossible dream seemed hardly worth pursuing. With repeated promises to meet again, and several hearty good-nights, we climbed to our rooms. They were separated, it turned out, by only one unit, although the ramps, stairs, and plat-forms of the Casbah made them seem streets apart.

I had more than the usual difficulty getting my door open. The martinis wouldn't quit. By the time I figured out which key went in which lock, and then failed at various combinations of right and left turns, the Brits, with a final "ta-ta," had long since retreated into their room. When I got in mine, I left the door open so I would have enough light to find the switch.

I felt a slight breeze from inside the room brush past my face. I thought the windows had been closed when I left here this morning. Had the maid opened a window? In most hotels they only close them. Experiencing a slight chill the breeze did not cause, I scanned the windows. Dimly, I made out the contours of a broken pane. Adrenaline surged, and I darted forward reflexively, sensing danger but not sure from which direction it might come. I turned.

And found myself face-to-face with someone in deep shadow behind the door, a man about my size, who had been waiting for me to close it. He plunged toward me and my blood froze. I managed to scramble backward a couple of steps, barely out of his reach. I took in a heavy jaw, deep-set eyes, and the dull glint of a short-bladed knife, half-raised. But the edge of surprise had been blunted when I turned; his probable plan to grab me from behind with one arm while the other with the knife found its mark would no longer work. He exhaled a grunt of disappointment. My heart was pounding.

I had backed up until I was caught behind the knees by the bed and I fell back on it. Before I could move he was directly above me. He braced one arm against my shoulder and leaned over me to bring the knife straight down. My body raced ahead of my mind; fear had energized me. My bent right leg, foot cocked, was probing wildly for his crotch. Instead, my heel caught him just below the navel. I dug it in. With my back braced against the bed I managed a mighty shove, straightening the leg and locking it before he could drive home the knife. He staggered back against the wall.

In the seconds it took him to catch his breath, I sat up and managed to pull out my wallet and throw it at him. "Here," I said; my mouth was bone dry and my tongue was so thick I didn't know if I was making myself understood. "My money. That's all of it." I had the sensation I was watching the scene from another planet.

The wallet bounced off his chest and fell to the floor. He didn't take the time to bend for it. Instead, he changed his grip on the knife and set himself to come at me again. His flat, stupid face was without emotion. My body was coated in sweat; it ran in rivulets from my neck. My feet were on the floor, but I was still half on the bed and close enough to the night table to grab either the phone or the lamp. The phone wouldn't have stopped him, but I should have thought at least to knock it off its cradle. He was coming now and all I could think of was I needed something massive. The lamp was a wrought-iron monstrosity. I managed to get both hands on it. I felt the cord pull from the wall and the iron slipped a bit in my sweaty palms. I tightened my grip and felt the strain in my shoulder as I swung the hunk of metal at the knife arm with all the weight I could get behind it.

He turned just enough so that he caught the blow on his upper arm. It slowed him long enough for me to get to my feet. He was on me before I was erect, breathing, "You fuck, you fuck," and smelling of dead cigar and body odor. I managed to check the knife with my forearm, but he was raising it again as I tried to sidestep and grab his wrist. The bed was pressing me from behind and I had no room to maneuver. He kicked the ankle of the leg I was balanced on and I pitched sideways.

I grabbed for the bed and got hold of a handful of spread and felt that come down with me. Falling, I had the sensation of losing control over my body, over my life. I fell until I cracked my temple against a corner of the night table. Nausea washed over me as I dropped heavily to the floor. Above, I saw the knife starting to come down.

And then my kids were running toward me across undulating dunes on the Bridgehampton beach. Appearing, disappearing, appearing, disappearing. In full color.

And then deep, sweet sleep.

I came to out of another dream, this one in black and white. Helene and I were sitting in a rowboat on a mirror-flat lake. I was trying to row but the oars kept slipping in the locks. Finally I lost them and they fell noiselessly into the lake. I could see them through the clear water sink slowly to the bottom and settle in the sand. How was I going to control the boat? It was at that point I sensed a pillow being slipped under my head. The room racked into focus.

Not the room so much as a figure looming over me. "Are you all right? Shall I call for a doctor?" That chirpy English voice. Cissy.

She went to turn on the lights, then came back to lean over me again. I felt warm and relaxed, as though awakening from a healthy nap. I decided that her breasts, swinging free behind the scoop-necked dress, would definitely pass the Las Vegas chorus-line test. And then my throbbing head and a wave of nausea reminded me where I was and what had happened.

"Where is he?" I asked. The adrenaline was starting to pump again. I tried to sit up.

She was looking at me with sweet concern. "It's all right, he's out cold." I must have looked as if I needed further reassurance. "I never thought I'd have the nerve to do anything like that," she said. "But when I saw that hideous knife . . . Well, actually, I didn't think at all, I just did it. Thank God the bottle was practically full. What a sickening sound . . ."

She was holding a liter of Bombay gin by the neck and she caught my gaze shifting from her to it. "Just because Pam didn't fancy a nightcap," she said, "was no reason I shouldn't come here and have one with you."

I managed, "I couldn't agree more." The throbbing filled my head and pressed against my skull. Warily, I looked around. My assailant lay in a motionless heap near the bathroom door. A trickle of blood had matted his dirty blond hair at the back of his skull and was oozing thickly down his neck and over the collar of his western shirt. Cissy had done considerably better with the gin bottle than I had with the lamp.

I said, "Where's his knife?"

She said, "Don't worry, I threw it out the door before I phoned. The police are on their way. I was waiting for you to come round so I could help you out of here, you poor dear." I had to remind myself that I had pegged her as a twit out of a Neil Simon play.

I said, "He may have another weapon. I'd better have a look." Even with Cissy's help I had trouble getting up. I did it very slowly. The room lurched before it settled. Another wave of nausea washed over me, but the fear had ebbed. I said, "Why don't you wait outside?"

I coaxed her gently toward the room door and walked unsteadily to the heap in the corner. That flat, ugly face with the big jaw and low brow no longer looked menacing. Stupid was the best description for it. I bent to him—more nausea—felt his jacket pockets for metal, then under the jacket for a shoulder holster, then at his waist and in the small of his back. Nothing. His body was hard; he was a cat burglar who kept in condition for his trade.

I ran my hands down his legs. Behind me I heard Cissy call softly, "No . . ." and my hand met his, alive now, at his ankle. With a single motion he rolled away from me and pulled a gun clear of an ankle holster. A .25, probably, but big enough. Now he was half up, propped on an elbow. The deep-set eyes were alert; they darted around the room to see what he had missed while he was unconscious.

"Okay, back, back," he said, then pointed the gun toward Cissy, who stood petrified near the door. "You. Shut that door." And to me, "All the way back."

Cissy obeyed as I backed off unsteadily, hands over my head, until I was stopped by the wall. The room rocked again.

He came slowly to his feet, his free hand moving up the bathroom doorjamb to steady himself. He was in worse shape than me, but he managed to keep the gun raised.

"Over there," he said to Cissy, and motioned with the gun. "With him." She hesitated, reluctant to leave the door; her hand was still on the knob. His eyes narrowed. "Move, you bitch." He knew who had delivered that blow to his head. Cissy scurried to my side.

He was still unsteady on his feet but either unaware or unconcerned that blood was seeping from that head wound. He stood silent for a moment, apparently thinking. Cissy had long since dropped the gin bottle. Her shoulder pressed against mine for reassurance. She was trembling. Or was it me?

"Down," he said. "Get down on the floor, both of you." In unison we started to obey, but not fast enough for him. "I said move it. Flat out, face down. Hands behind your head. Get the hell down there." His voice was getting stronger.

We lay down, side by side, hands behind heads, noses buried in the musty, threadbare carpet, the legacy of countless shuffling bare feet. I supposed he was making sure we stayed this way until he had climbed back out the window he came in.

Then, as his other option crept into my consciousness, I felt my heart beat against the carpet. He wouldn't dare.

I could sense him bending to pick up my wallet. Now he was walking, heavy steps. But not toward the window. He was coming toward us. I saw his shoes, heavy work shoes, well worn. Now he was standing over me. My pounding heart was louder than the throbbing in my head; when I spoke I felt it was drowning out my voice.

"We called the police," I said. My tongue was so thick I could barely form the words. "If I were you I'd get out of here. As fast as I could."

He stood over me, not moving, a heavy shoe pressed against my rib cage. That dull mind was laboring toward a decision. Finally he knelt, and I felt the gun barrel press into the base of my skull below my clasped hands. Shit, shit, was all I could think,

was this it? I refused to believe it and I made no
move.

Next to me Cissy must have sensed what was happening. She was crying softly. Muffled, racking sobs.

"You've got the money," I said. "Don't do it.
There's no reason to do it."

He wasn't listening. Still pressing the barrel firmly
against my skull, he moved it around, adjusting the
angle for the shot. I had waited too long; it was too
late for any kind of action. I shut my eyes. My body
was a block of ice, my mind flashed images so
quickly they didn't register. And then I felt the pressure ease. He had pulled the gun away at a sound: a
fist had struck the front door. A drumroll of fist-
pounding followed, and a voice called, "Open up!
Open the door!"

In the room there were heavy footsteps and then a
sound at the window. At the door, the rattling of
keys. My blood began to flow again. I waited a moment and looked up cautiously. The window was
wide open and Cissy and I were alone in the room,
her face still buried in the carpet.

"It's all right," I said. "He's gone." I cupped the
back of her neck with my hand and held it reassur-
ingly for a moment. Then I got up and went unsteadily to the door.

I let in not the police but the night desk man who
had fumbled through registering me the night before. He was wearing the same pizza-stained T-shirt.
I would have embraced him anyway in relief and
gratitude, but he swept past me into the room.

"You reported a prowler?" he asked. "Where?
Are you sure? Because the cops are on their way and
they get pissed as hell at false alarms."

CHAPTER SIX

The two cops who eventually showed up made a routine search of the shrubbery and grounds under my window with some help from me and the night desk man. My assailant was long gone, but we found plenty of places for foot and hand holds on the outside of the antique building. It would have been no problem for an experienced cat burglar to get up to my window. I gathered that this was not the first such incident at the Palm, not even the first this year.

The cops offered to call for an ambulance to take me to a hospital to have the bump on my forehead examined. When I declined, they arranged for a pair of detectives to come and pick up Cissy and me and take us to the police station to look at mug shots. They assured us a patrol car would be stationed near the Palm for the rest of the night. And they reminded me to cancel the credit cards that had been stolen with my wallet. They left with our assailant's knife in a plastic bag.

Once they were gone, Cissy and I had that long-delayed nightcap, two thirsty gulps each, directly from the Bombay bottle held in shaky hands. By then Pam had joined us in her robe to be supportive of Cissy. Thoroughly rattled by Cissy's account of our misadventure, she took a swallow too. Other guests in various stages of dress milled about examining my wound and shaking their heads. None of them had much to say except a permanent resident, a retired day player, who declared in a cracked baritone that for many years every day on this block had gotten uglier than the day before.

When the detectives showed up for us, Pam wanted to come along to the police station. But she wasn't dressed and the detectives didn't want to wait, so we left her. Cissy and I sat in the rear seat of the beat-up detective car, and the detective who wasn't driving regaled us with bone-chilling stories of neighborhood crime. Eventually he ran out of steam and fell silent. I turned to Cissy. She looked ten years older than when we met a couple of hours ago. I said, "You saved my life." It sounded ponderous and I wanted to take the heavy edge off by adding something like, "You shouldn't have gone to all that trouble." I couldn't get the words out. Instead I put a hand gratefully over hers.

Eventually she said simply, "I did, didn't I?"

I said, "I don't know how to thank you. Now or ever. But I'm certainly never going to forget you." I felt thoroughly ashamed of my brittle early reading of her.

Cissy was uncharacteristically quiet the rest of the journey. When we got to the police station, the detectives led us to their gritty squad room, gave us their set speech on what good citizens we were, and sat us at a large table with piles of thick loose-leaf albums of mug shots. They asked us please to examine them carefully. In answer to my question before they left us alone, they said that yes, if decent prints could be lifted off the knife, they would be faxed to Washington. I knew that even one could do the trick.

The pictures were uniformly depressing. Armies of men stared out at us through smudged plastic covers. They had hungry eyes, angry eyes, haunted faces. Most were Hispanic or black. The whites were either too young to be our man, too old, had too much hair or not enough. None came close to that flat, dull face neither Cissy nor I was likely to forget. And still the detectives kept returning to shove more books at us. The sheer weight of the desperate, the walking wounded, the clearly deranged formed an assault on our defenses. It affected Cissy even more heavily than me.

After a while the detectives gave up, collected the books, and thanked us for our cooperation. They said if we waited out front they would bring the car around and drive us back to the Palm. We made our way back to the front door, and I suddenly found myself facing Dunleavy and Ossian, who were coming in. The sergeant looked fresh after a long day on the job, every silvery hair neatly in place.

"Mr. Saldinger, how're you doing?" He was less surprised than I was by the chance meeting, and I quickly understood why, as his gaze settled on Cissy. "You've come in with your lady friend. Good."

I introduced Cissy the best I could—awkwardly, since I didn't remember her last name—and then explained, as the detectives listened with blank faces and Cissy stood by, understandably bewildered, that this was not the woman who was the witness to my morning at the beach but a fellow guest at my hotel, where we had just been robbed and assaulted. And all the rest of it. Dunleavy stared at me and slowly shook his head.

"You're not having much luck today, Byron," he said finally.

I hate when cops call me by my first name. I said, deliberately, "About my witness, Ed, I'll call you first thing in the morning."

"You do that," he said. "Oh, and you were right about Rascals' Retreat. We found the people who were on duty this morning. Nobody remembered your being there."

It was another night of sleeping badly, and jet lag was the least of it. I got out of bed twice for aspirin. If everything seems worse at three A.M., and you've just had a brush with death, a severe bump on the head doesn't help. I put to temporary rest one or two of the things troubling me, but aspirin did nothing for the nagging fear about my economic situation. With Stavros's murder escalating the talk of a plagiarism scandal, the *Corrigan's Way* project could be well on its way to unraveling.

I found myself awake at four-thirty and I put in a call to Jane and Benjy. It was seven-thirty in the East and they would be getting ready for school. The call proved less than nourishing. Helene put them on quickly enough, but talking to them didn't give me a feeling we were in what the specialists call "quality time." The children's heads were elsewhere—on breakfast, on would the rain stop, on who lost the toothpaste. They would have stayed on the line with me, they meant well, but I could tell they were relieved when I let them go.

Naturally I was in a deep sleep when the phone

rang at ten after seven. I flailed for it like a fish on a line and was rewarded with Werner Blau exploding into the earpiece: "Don't you ever walk out of a meeting on me."

Werner wasn't interested in my views on the subject; he had called only to tell me Trig Bascomb was now ready for his script meeting with me. It would be at Trig's house at ten A.M., and it was essential that I for Chrissake get there on time and make nice, because yesterday's publicity about the murder on Sunset was making Bascomb extremely edgy. I was to listen to what he said, agree to all his notes, and offer no arguments. I was—did I understand clearly? —to make nice. I asked Werner if he would be at the meeting and he said he would only get in the way, and anyway he thought I knew he didn't go to meetings with actors unless he absolutely had to, but that he would consider sending Seth.

Early in the morning, before his day's aggravations piled on, was the only time I had ever found Werner to be expansive with me, so I took advantage of his call to address my major concern—how reliable Bascomb might be in a crisis. If a growing scandal should cause him to fall out, what did Werner think of Casey Train as a fallback replacement?

"Train's an eight o'clock actor," he snapped. "Mike, don't make me review the bidding. *Corrigan's Way* isn't *Gone With the Wind*. Without Bascomb it's just another property and we're out in the parking lot holding it in one hand and our dicks in the other. So please reassure Trig about the death of the Greek. Make sure he understands there's less there than meets the eye, and anyway, you don't know any more about it than the police." Beat. "You don't, do you?"

"No. Werner, what about Kornbluth? How's he taking the Stavros business?"

"How do you think? He's having an out-of-body experience. If Oscar doesn't prove himself in the upcoming season he'll be ankling the network for indie prod. And he's not going to make his bones with a series starring a widely popular movie actor. If *Corrigan* works, his secretary could have developed it. If it crashes, Oscar's a schmuck who couldn't get on the chart with a sure winner. Before the industry will acknowledge his genius he needs a hit that, I don't know, pairs a galactic detective with a one-legged black psychic. You and I and *Corrigan* are a pothole on his road to success. I gotta go."

He hung up before I could ask how Kornbluth reacted to my storming out of his office yesterday. But the answer came a moment later. The phone rang again. This time it was Wolf Waxroth. No hello, just, "Who was that on the phone?"

"Werner called."

"Don't waste your time with Werner. You two are selling, you're in the same boat. Worry about the rocks the boat can hit—Kornbluth, Bascomb, the heirs of that Greek they scraped off Sunset yesterday. Believe me, there'll be heirs. They'll come up from the cracks in the sidewalk. Mikey, level with me, you don't have any special knowledge of that unhappy business, do you?"

"No. None."

"Good. And if the police start to hound you on this, you'll call me?"

"Absolutely," I said, and thought, *But will you take the call?* Wolf took calls only from clients who made more than he did; everyone else went on his callback list. What I said was, "What about Kornbluth yesterday morning?"

"When you bolted from his office? Brilliant. What you did was menschy. He complained, sure, but I saw the respect. He's worried you've got something up your sleeve. As of now, you're one up."

"No bull?"

"On your next deal? You know that the gonifs who bought the network are trying to hold the line. But you're up a minimum of ten percent, I guarantee." No wonder Blau hadn't brought up Kornbluth's reaction; he would have had to compliment me, and Werner Blau complimented no one. But before I could bask in the glow of my inadvertent triumph, Waxroth was saying, "Of course, provided everything goes all right . . ."

This caveat turned out to be only partly to cover his ass. Gravely, he went on to tell me that Kornbluth had called him after the news broke of Stavros's death. Oscar's concerns were my concerns —that adverse publicity for the network, or a nervous backing off by Bascomb, could bury the project.

"Will you be at Bascomb's?" I asked.

"I'll try," he said. "Gotta run."

I gave up on sleep. Instead, I called my bank in New York and had them wire me some money care of the Desert Palm to replace what was in my stolen wallet. I fought with the showerhead and got dressed. The bump on my head looked worse than it felt at the moment. I figured by now the Brits would be up and I would invite them to breakfast. I would have preferred having Cissy to myself, but something told me that during the day the two were basically joined at the hip.

The night before, when Cissy and I were dropped off at the Palm by the detectives, she had tilted her head up and with slightly cracked lips planted a sweet kiss on mine before she slipped away wearily to her room. Nerve endings long dormant in me had tingled pleasurably, and when I went to bed, determined to get some sleep, I tried to fix that kiss, of all that had happened that day, in my throbbing head. Now when I phoned her room I was disappointed but not really surprised to find the pair already out. I supposed that coming from London they would be more screwed up by jet lag than me.

As soon as I left my room, I saw Cissy below, standing just outside the office. She looked as if she had dressed for a job interview. Neat little form-fitting suit, matching shoes, contrasting blouse. At eight-thirty in the morning. I hurried down. When I got close I could see she hadn't slept. "Oh, Byron, you're up," she said, and appeared relieved. "I was going to call. Pam and I are off."

"To a casting call?"

"No, we're leaving L.A."

"For Vegas? So soon?"

"For London. We're on a ten forty-five A.M., so we've got to hurry. Passport control and all that. Pam is settling our account."

"But . . . when did you decide to . . . ?"

"At five o'clock this morning. When I stopped shaking sufficiently to dial the airline." She was reading the disappointment in my face. "I want very much to go home and so does Pam."

"But . . . I thought . . ."

"Yes, we did think we might have gotten some work here. And anything in show business would definitely have paid better than London. Everything's bigger here, and better. Including crime. We have lots of crime at home but it's smaller, you know what I mean? More manageable, more in keeping with the pay scale. I never want to be scared like that again. The way I was last night. Lying with my face in that filthy carpet. Never in my life. I won't ever forget it."

"I'm truly sorry, Cissy."

"Me too. Next time you're in London you will look me up?" She mustered a smile. "I'll be third from the left in some chorus or other. The girl with the definitely adequate bosom." She laughed. "Perhaps you two could get to know each other."

"No question, you'll see me again," I said, and wondered if my voice carried conviction.

We were saved further awkwardness. Pam stuck her head out the office door. "Cissy, the luggage is in the car. Do hurry. Bye-bye, Byron. Wish I could say it was lovely meeting you."

She gave me a little two-finger wave and ducked back in the office. Cissy brushed a warm cheek against mine, held it for a moment, and was gone.

That made the second woman to vanish on me in the last twelve hours. It was a record I expected to stand for the rest of my life.

CHAPTER SEVEN

Bascomb's home address and phone number in Bel
Air were in my pocket address book. Not because we
were in any regular communication; I had met our
star only once. But I had learned early on in the
business that the first thing you did on a project was
take the home address and phone number of everyone involved, because before its air date you were
going to need at least one of them urgently some six
A.M. or on Christmas Eve. Every few years I did a new
address book and dropped the names of co-workers
I had once seen or spoken to every day for months,
had sworn eternal friendship to, but had never had
occasion to be in touch with since.

My previous meeting with Bascomb had been at
his agent's office in Century City to discuss my ten-
page presentation for *Corrigan's Way*, a document
consisting of two pages of useful information and
eight of snow. Someone had obviously briefed him
on my credits and he had flattered me more than
necessary. I liked him for going to all that trouble.

He told me he had been attracted to the Corrigan concept because of the character's "vulnerability." I nodded vague agreement and made a mental note to reread whatever bullshit it was I had written about my aging hero; I didn't recall that particular trait.

Like most early creative meetings before the concept is hardened into contract, this one had been full of good feeling and incipient male bonding. All present had been in agreement on the creative direction of the series. Based on my experience of previous such meetings, I knew this good fellowship would evaporate when we got down in the trenches about two weeks before the start of principal photography and began disemboweling each other, but I enjoyed basking in its temporary warmth.

Bascomb hadn't seemed very much the movie star except for being that camera-aware kind of painfully thin that makes you ashamed of even the bit of flesh between your thumb and forefinger. Mostly he let others do the talking and he listened with focused energy, turning the famous crinkly eyes on whoever had the floor. In his last couple of pictures he had still been playing late thirties, but I guessed he was close to fifty; the crinkles were cast in cement. If the show went five seasons—from my lips to God's ear— he would be in his midfifties toward the end and probably showing it. But we were safe with his character, Corrigan; old was no drawback. It might even be a plus. That may have been why Bascomb's agent brought *Corrigan* to his attention.

When he cut out of the meeting a little before it broke—nobody leaves before the king—Bascomb looked my way from the door, one thumb hooked over his harness-leather belt. "You've nailed the character, Mike. That's a skin I can get inside of. Just

build on it. And don't be afraid to have fun." It was
a typical good early meeting.

Almost as soon as I drove through the Bel Air
gate, I got lost, as I usually did, in the maze of poorly
marked wandering roads that had been laid out, I
supposed, to prevent robbers from making quick
getaways from the homes of the obscenely rich. I
had allowed plenty of extra time to find Bascomb's
house, but I was a couple of minutes late when I
finally announced myself at the talk box on the
fence outside what looked like a Mississippi Delta
plantation house. The gate swung magically open
and I was reminded of the legendary note from the
Bel Air mommy to the teacher: "Please excuse
Johnny's absence yesterday. The electric gate
wouldn't open."

I drove in past a gatehouse designed to simulate
slave quarters and was brought up short in the semi-
tropical vegetation of the driveway. The Eumenides
appeared to be in hot pursuit; a police car was
pulled up between a couple of hibiscus trees.

Bascomb himself answered the door in baggy
swim trunks and a T-shirt, relaxed and smiling, just
folks. He grabbed my hand and I said, "Is this a bad
time?"

He didn't know what I meant until he followed
my gaze. "The cop car," he said. "Liberated off a
picture I was on years ago. Not bad for scaring off
the amateur burglars and kidnappers." He had a
couple of children by his current wife. I saw now
that the car was not much more than a rusting shell.
"That's a nasty bump," he said. "You run into a
door? Or is it a domestic problem?"

"A little of each. It looks worse than it feels." It
didn't feel great at the moment.

Having demonstrated that he was interested in me

aside from what I could do for him, he led me swiftly through the antebellum-type mansion, but not so swiftly that I failed to notice the impressive assortment of late-twentieth-century paintings—Rothko, Frankenthaler, Roy Lichtenstein, and so on. We left the house through a French door to the pool patio, where a squat Henry Moore bronze commanded the scene. It contained several holes of the magnitude I was prepared for Bascomb to punch in my script. We settled on the patio furniture and Bascomb asked if the help could rustle me up some breakfast.

"Thanks, I just had some," I said. If he was going to offer breakfast he should have made it part of the invitation. My defenses were up.

But a moment later he disarmed me with "I always forget to ask, because I had to give up breakfast myself. It was that or lunch. At my age the camera is a son of a bitch." Score one for Trig's vulnerability. But what about that folksy western twang? I had never noticed it before, and if memory served he had gone to an Ivy League college and been discovered in a straw-hat production of *The Male Animal.* Score one, maybe, against Trig. And I had better, I decided, stop keeping score.

Bascomb's script was on the patio table and I took mine from a manila envelope. "Is it just the two of us?" I asked. The fewer the critics, the sooner I would be out of here. This terrace would be baking hot in an hour, and that was likely to be the least of my problems.

"Yeah, the kids are in school and Wanda's visiting her mother in Toluca Lake. And I figured, you and I are going to be working together, let's get to know each other. Without agents or producers or network hacks backseat driving. I called them all off half an hour ago." He looked toward the pool. "Oh, Vince is here."

As if on cue, Vince rose above the lip of the pool, hoisted himself out, and came dripping toward us, a well-muscled thirty-year-old about Bascomb's size, and with his coloring. If he wasn't his stand-in he was a relative.

"Vince is my stunt double, stand-in, good friend. Vince, this is the man I pointed out on the news last night. When they showed those clips of me in connection with that hotel murder?" There was the faintest hint of distaste in his voice. "He wrote the fantastic script for the TV pilot we're prepping. Byron Saldinger. I forget what they call you. Byron?"

"Mike," I said as Vince's wet hand engaged mine in a contest of wills. "Nice to meet you, Vince."

Vince nodded; he could live with that. He dropped into a chair far enough off so he wasn't part of this story conference but close enough so he could hear everything that went on. I wondered if they might be lovers—were Bascomb's three wives a smokescreen?—and decided I didn't much care one way or the other. I made a point of opening my script. I wanted to get on with this before the discussion segued to the dead Greek on the TV news shows and all the baggage that would go with that.

"So," I said, "let's see what we can do about your problems with the script."

"Hell, I don't have any problems," he said in a voice that foretold trouble. "It's a damn good script, well crafted, and you've got me down so right I could have written it myself."

Yes, I thought, and you *would* have written it yourself if you had the time and were willing to stoop to this kind of work, which you believe, but are too much of a gentleman to say, is about on a par with washing windows. Whatever was bugging him, if I didn't flush it to the surface we could be here dancing all morning.

I said, "Then, pending a director's notes and whatever changes are called for by casting and locations, you're ready to go with what we've got?"

"Mmm," he said, and I couldn't tell whether that was a yes or no but my money was on no. "From a structural standpoint, the way you've written it, there's nothing wrong with the script *itself*. Scene for scene it works."

"Yes?"

He deepened the crinkles in his eyes in the trademarked Trig Bascomb way. "Mike, I've got to tell you, and this is no reflection on your work, there are things here that will have to go."

"Such as?"

He riffled through his script. "Page thirty-one? I don't do this kind of scene."

I found the page and scanned it for clues. "I'm not sure I know what you mean."

"Scenes where I buy clothes. I don't do them."

I had a sudden rush of blood to the head and I took a long beat before I replied. "Trig, this scene is our shorthand for Corrigan's acceptance of his change of career. The clothes he casts aside and the things he picks to replace them tell us a lot about his ambivalence. It's comedic, sure. But it's a character scene. And it's visual, cinematic."

"I like comedy, Mike, I'm not afraid of comedy. And I can see it's visual, and I know it's cinematic. But I don't do scenes where I buy clothes. Period. Page fifty-two."

I turned to it. My hand was trembling.

Bascomb said, "Here it is. I don't do scenes where I cook dinner for the girl."

I said, nice and easy, my voice cool and neutral, "This is a scene—probably the warmest in the whole piece—where Corrigan begins to build an emotional bridge to his new environment. The cooking is a kind of penance. With the help of this aware but wary young divorcee the scars left by the years in the inner city may finally begin to fade. She doesn't know what he needs—she doesn't really know where he's been—but by the time she leaves that kitchen she knows something more is going on in that man's head than an urge to jump on her bones. This is the scene"—I hit this hard—"where Corrigan finally shows his vulnerability."

"Yeah," he said, "I got all that subtext. The problem is, Mike, I don't do scenes where I cook dinner for the girl."

"Trig—"

"And why a divorcee? To me that's shorthand for a woman who cut off some poor guy's balls in the settlement. Divorcees do nothing for me. 'That bitch' is the first thing comes into my head. Everybody's head. Why fight that? Why not make her a widow?"

"I can do that," I said. "That's not a problem. But about this scene, Corrigan cooking dinner—"

"Find something else."

Find something else. I had already *discarded* everything else. I said, "Is it okay if I ask why you don't do scenes where you cook dinner for the girl?" I was still trying to keep it conversational rather than confrontational but I could hear the edge creep into my voice. "I mean, this isn't even *scenes* where you cook for the girl, it's one scene. Two and three-eighths pages. Trig, I really like this scene. So do the Blaus."

"I do too. Nice scene. But I don't care if it's a quarter of a page. It's out. Okay?"

I had no idea why I kept pressing, but I couldn't seem to stop. "Your message is coming through, Trig, believe me. I'll go any way you like. But if we can keep this dialogue going another minute, I'd like to make just one more point. And that is that the viewers would love you in that scene."

"Viewers." He spit out the word and a violent shove from his foot sent a patio chair spinning away. "For twenty-four years I acted for audiences. Now I've got viewers."

"The same people, only they're in their underwear." I was too stubborn to let go but maybe I could lighten it up. Bascomb had built a head of steam and I had to be careful; I needed this job. "Trig, you can get closer to them when they're at home. The loyalties are different. Maybe stronger."

"Look, my friend, I've managed my career for twenty years. During those years all kinds of well-meaning people have advised me to do this, do that, play this, play that. In the end it's Trig Bascomb who takes his mark on the set and it's Trig Bascomb who has to answer to the camera. And the public."

It was a speech he had doubtless made many times, but now that he had managed himself out of films and into television, it had lost its punch. And about television I knew better than him. I could help him; help myself. The cooking scene made Corrigan believable and accessible. It was the kind of scene that gave him durability, and in durability lay the pot of gold. I took one more cautious shot at saving the cooking scene.

I said, "Trig, I don't have to validate your ticket. You've proved yourself every which way in this business. And putting aside your art, the women love you, the men don't feel threatened, and you've been eminently bankable. So what's left? Maybe you're at a point in your career—why not?—where you can surprise your fans and maybe yourself by stretching a little, taking a chance or two. What do you have to lose? Look at Paul Newman, look at Shirley MacLaine, look at Jack Nicholson. Taking chances has given their careers an added dimension, a shot in the arm. What the hell, why not do it? Cook dinner for the girl.''

Slowly, he closed his script. "Saldinger, I appreciate your sincerity, but I didn't bring you here to debate this scene. The subject is closed.''

He held up a couple of fingers, spread them wide, and wiggled them. Vince rose slowly from his chair and moseyed over and stuck a cigarette in the V. There followed an extended lighting ceremony. After the first drag—Vince was moseying back to his seat—Bascomb said, the words curling out with the smoke, "But listen, the worst thing for a writer is having to write something he doesn't believe in. I know, because the worst thing for an actor is having to play it. I had to put up with that my first few years in the business. Never again, thank you.'' He took time out for a second drag while he pretended to ponder the situation. Then, "Mike, you know what would make this go better for both of us? You could use some help.''

What I definitely didn't want was "help.'' I couldn't afford "help.'' "Help'' would ask for a share of the writing credit and the Guild would have to conduct an arbitration. By no stretch of my paranoia would the arbitrators approve a second writer's claim to a slice of the *story* credit; but two off-the-wall arbitrators on a panel of three was all it would take to award my "help'' shared *teleplay* credit, and I'd be saddled with a thirty-five percent partner on royalties, residuals, profit sharing, the works. I said,

"Thanks, Trig, I really don't see any problem with this. Believe me, if I didn't think I could handle it, I'd be the first to holler. The two scenes troubling you? When I look at them from your perspective, I have no doubt I'll find a way. Ideas will percolate."

Bascomb leaned toward me across the table. "You can't be sure, Mikey." I had stirred up the hornets and they weren't ready to settle back down. "And if it turns out you need somebody to help get you over the creative hump," he went on, "I was thinking, isn't this right up . . . You know, the guy who created all those series? Vince, what's his name again?"

Vince's voice floated to us effortlessly. "Rutherford Cole."

"Right. Isn't *Corrigan's Way* right up Rutherford Cole's alley?"

"Absolutely," I said. "Rudd Cole. Definitely his kind of show." I kept my surprise choked back. Better to go with the flow until the hornets were dozing again. "I didn't know you were that well plugged in to the television community."

"That's Vince," he said. "Vince worked as a day player on action shows."

I said, "But not in a while, right, Vince? Rudd Cole has been out of television for years. He made his pile and he'd had it to here. He's working on a novel. Look. Trig—"

Bascomb said, "How well are *you* plugged in, Mikey? Is New York out of the loop? I hear Cole is back in development."

I put on a wide-eyed look. "Is that a fact? Where did you hear that?"

"I looked up his agent."

I said, "His agent is my agent." What was that son of a bitch trying to do? "Wolf Waxroth."

"That's the man. We talked."

I said, "It's coming back. Wolf did mention he'd put Rudd in a development deal." I laid it in. "He tied him to one of the majors in an exclusive."

Bascomb nodded agreement. "Where he's getting no action. If we wanted him to lend us a hand here he could take a suspend and extend on that deal."

"Waxroth said that?" Probably. "Suspend and extend" would be his phrase, not Bascomb's.

"Don't try to pin me on details. I pay a manager to handle the nuts and bolts. Just believe me, if we want this Cole we can have him."

"But not just yet," I said. "Not till I've delivered every draft of this mother the network calls for in the contract." I should never have gone up this path —Talent talking business.

"So deliver, my friend," he said. "Time's a wastin'."

Did that signify the meeting was over? Bascomb tossed his script carelessly toward a chair, so I guessed it was. I said nothing; I had already said too much. I shoved my script back in the manila envelope and breathed in and out evenly in an effort to get my blood off the boil. Bascomb's face was a mask. The eye crinkles were an inch deep.

I had damn well better try to make nice again. I said, "I'm glad I had this chance to get your input in person, Trig. There's no substitute for face-to-face. I understand your concerns, believe me. I'll shoot the changes back to you from New York. In the end we'll have a better show."

"Yeah?" While I was working at making nice, he was turning sulky, moody. Something.

I said, "Nothing ever falls into place until the star locks onto the character."

"You're going to lock me on, Mikey?"

"I'll do my best." I was trying to dance to his tune but I couldn't feel the beat.

"I'm rooting for that," he said, and paused. "Too bad your inspiration flamed out."

"Come again? I don't know what you mean."

"Not what. Who. The guy who broke the sidewalk on Sunset yesterday. Stavis. Stavros."

"What about him?"

"Mikey, just between us girls, I promise it will never leave this terrace, didn't this Stavros grease your creative engine just the least little bit?"

"No."

"Well . . . he's gone now, so I guess we'll never know."

"We'll know," I said. "What counts is what's down in black and white, not what Nick Stavros shot off his mouth claiming he wrote."

"You mean," he said, "I shouldn't pay any attention to what he told me?"

"You met Stavros?"

"We talked. On the phone."

"Why?"

"He called me. Called my agent. From New York. I called him back."

"Why?"

"This was a guy claimed he created the character I might be playing. Playing—who knows?—for years. I was curious, so what? He said he was coming out to L.A. and he wanted to see me. I said absolutely not."

"That's something."

"So then he jumped in with his side of the story. He talked a blue streak. And I have to tell you, Mike, he was making a damn convincing case when I was finally able to break in and cut him off."

"Was that smart? The network lawyers will tell you you shouldn't have talked to him."

"No, let me tell you where maybe I wasn't smart." He bit down hard on the words. "Getting involved in a project where I have to look at myself on the six o'clock news, this fading movie star so hard up for work he had to help screw some poor wimp of a writer out of his property. Let me tell you, Mike, there's only one time I want to see myself on the six o'clock news. When I've got a picture that's just opened. Not coming out of divorce court. Not after a restaurant punch-out where Vince has to peel some crackpot off me who thinks I jumped his wife. And certainly not, definitely not, when the smell coming into the room is from me, because I'm suspected of stealing some wimp's legitimate property."

I was beginning to understand why he had had this bug up his ass all through the meeting. I said, "I'm sorry, Trig. But don't hold me responsible when a nut case like Stavros elbows his way into your life. Not my fault. And Trig, I don't care how 'convincing' a case he made. I don't care if he told you he wrote the Declaration of Independence and you saw him with the quill in one hand and the wet parchment in the other. He'd still be a goddam liar. Now if you'll excuse me I think I'd better go home and work on your scenes." Bascomb started to get up and I added, "Don't bother, I know the way out. First left past the David Hockney."

It was a good enough exit speech that I would only have undercut it by waiting for him to reply. I made a beeline for the terrace door, throwing back over my shoulder, "Nice meeting you, Vince."

CHAPTER EIGHT

My concern that the Desert Palm was not noted for dancing attention on its clientele was borne out by the day clerk's martyred look as he handed me a stack of messages. It read, People who get this much phone action should stay at a better hotel. He said, "Maintenance fixed the window was broken in your room." His tone implied that the little business of last night had probably been my fault too.

I shuffled through the message slips as I climbed to my room: Werner Blau; Jasmine Cole; Oscar Kornbluth; Seth Blau; Sergeant Dunleavy, LAPD; "your son"; Al Vecchi; Oscar Kornbluth. Kornbluth got the award for quantity; I was hoping he would also win for quality. There was nothing from Waxroth; if Wolf was trying to sell me down the river he might have suspected by now that I had gotten wind of it.

I dialed the Westchester number first. Benjy would have been home from school nearly an hour and waiting with the fidgets for the callback. But it

was Helene who picked up. She was businesslike but
in no way adversarial. More or less the perfect ex-
wife. She even managed to avoid letting me know
that my call had interrupted her at something or
other. "Benjy did want to talk to you," she said.
"About school, I think, but he's gone out to play. It
was nothing important, he's just not used to your
being so far away these days." She was reminding
me that my once-frequent L.A. trips had all but
dried up. "How's it going?"

I said, "Too early to tell." At daytime phone rates
I wasn't going to walk her through the convolutions
of the *Corrigan* situation or my entanglement with
the police. She would be solicitous, sympathetic,
supportive, and I would get no nourishment from
any of it. I restricted myself to, "Would you just tell
Benjy I called and that there's a pretty good chance
I'll be back to take him and Jane for the weekend?"

She said, "Oh, good, that'll free me up to put in
some serious library time." Okay, so she did manage
to slip in a reference to her academic workload. I let
it hang. Damned if I was going to ask, "How's the
thesis coming?" That she would have to volunteer.

She didn't. She said, "Oh, did a Sam Wilson, or
Witson, get in touch?"

"No, who's he?"

"I thought you'd know. Something work-con-
nected, it sounded like. I think maybe he was offering some."

That sounded vaguely promising. "I don't know
why he'd call me at the house." I couldn't quite
bring myself to say "your house." It was, at least
legally, our house.

"People still do. You're in the book. I told him
how he might find you."

"Thanks. I have to go."

"Good-bye, Mike."

We hung up. Fifteen years.

My next priority was to get on Waxroth's callback list. His secretary, Winnie, was her usual chipper self during our thirty-second warmup. We covered my flight out and her cat's third visit to the vet in as many weeks. When I asked for Wolf she said, "Right."

I counted to ten—I had figured on eight—and she came back on and said, "He's in a meeting. He'll get right back to you." Why did they all do that? If he was in a meeting she knew it before she put me on hold. He had guessed the reason for my call. I would go to the bottom of his callback list and "right back to you" would mean a minimum of thirty-six hours. I said, "I'll be here about another twenty minutes," and hung up.

And then I thought that maybe I could learn something about Waxroth's maneuvers from the other end. If Jasmine's call was another shot at inviting me to dinner, I would take up the offer. I couldn't picture Rudd ducking me if I asked him face-to-face what our agent was up to. Would Rudd Cole try to undercut me on my one job? On any job? Jesus. And then I remembered his shooing me out of the office when he got that call yesterday, and how sick he looked after it. That call had come late enough in the day so that Stavros's death might have been on the radio and the smell of trouble already assaulting Waxroth's sensitive nostrils. Had that been Wolf on the phone laying out a fallback position to Rudd? No, this was paranoia time. I refused to entertain the possibility.

I called the Coles and got passed through two not quite English-speaking servants before Jasmine came on the line. Yes, she had called to urge me

again to come up the hill for dinner. Any evening,
they weren't all that social these days.

. "Is tonight too soon?" I asked. "If the network
releases me I'm going home tomorrow."

"Perfect. Rudd will be thrilled. After you left yesterday we agreed we don't see you nearly enough.
Myron, what was that all about yesterday?" she went
on without so much as a pause. "The man killed on
Sunset? Your picture on the five o'clock news? Is
that anything to be concerned about?"

"I don't think so. I'll tell you both about it at
dinner." If I *saw* her at dinner. If she stopped running to the kitchen long enough to listen. We said
good-bye.

I shuffled through the remaining message slips.
Waxroth had earned some fraction of his commis-
sion this morning with the advice that I give the
Blaus a low priority since we were in the same boat,
selling. I tore up the slips from both Blaus, the better to concentrate on the buyers, and put in a call to
Kornbluth.

"Yes, Mr. Saldinger," his secretary said, and
sounded relieved. "We have been trying to reach
you, he does want to talk to you, but he's at a screening. Where will you be in an hour?"

"I'm not sure, I'd better call you. Would you happen to know what it's about?" Any little clue would
help.

"Yes, it would be in reference to *Corrigan's Way,* I
believe." She was a regular fount of information. I
thanked her and hung up.

That left Dunleavy and Vecchi and I knew why
Dunleavy had called. He would want to know why I
hadn't shown up with the woman who was my beach
alibi. I ran an explanation past myself and didn't
much like it, so I ducked Dunleavy and called Vecchi

at the Hollyview. He wasn't in and they seemed reluctant to take a message; I got the feeling it was house policy. But the woman on the switchboard did volunteer that she remembered Vecchi going in and out a couple of times this morning. She couldn't help but notice, because he had passed straight through the office, right out to the street, walking. Did I think his car was possibly stalled out there somewhere on Highland and he was too shy to ask for help from the management? I said no, I thought he was just, you know, walking.

As I hung up, there was a knock at my door. It turned out to be the walker in person, no windbreaker, no Scandinavian sweater, just a sleeveless pullover over a polyester sport shirt. I wasn't sure why, but I was glad to see him. I said, "Al, you're going L.A. on me."

"You mean what I'm wearing? Sportivo, eh?" He did a turn for me. "Your phone was busy so I knew you were in. I figured I'd take a chance and come over. Who cracked you in the head?"

"Tell you in a minute," I said. "What were you doing in the motel? Aren't you supposed to be at the network, reading police scripts?"

"I'm doing that," he said. "But at the motel. And one or two a day is all I can handle. It's not the reading—you notice how there's hardly any words on a page of script?—it's keeping my teeth from grinding when I read about, for instance, a detective on the job without a partner, or a pair of cops who move in on an armed suspect without waiting for backup."

"It's a shorthand, Al. Authentic can be boring."

I was impatient to fill him in on what happened in this room the night before and I plunged ahead before he could sidetrack me. He gave me his full at-

tention and stopped me only twice. The first time
was when I proudly described how I had at first managed to fight off my knife-wielding attacker with the
kick that threw him back against the wall. Vecchi
said, "That's exactly what I mean. How TV sends the
wrong message. Those guys who stage the fights in
the shows?"

"The stunt coordinators?"

"They go for that. The kick in the groin from the
guy who's flat on his back. It always sends the other
guy staggering back across the room. It's flashy,
looks good. Instead, you could have ended the fight
right there, fixed your man so he wouldn't come
back at you."

"How would I do that?"

"You're down on the bed, right? He's over you
with the knife raised, like this. His face is exposed.
One free hand is all you need. You go straight for his
eyes, deep thrust, a finger in each. Not as visual,
maybe not so good for TV, but you'd be surprised
how it does the job. Sorry, I didn't mean to inter-
rupt."

I managed to resume my narration. When I got to
how Cissy put the burglar's lights out, Vecchi was
definitely impressed. "With a gin bottle? My kind of
woman."

I said he would have had to fight me for her but
that we were both out of luck. And then he let me
finish the story. By the end his face told me he
hadn't been prepared for it to turn that ugly. He
took a moment and then he said quietly, "I guess
you know he would have shot you both if it hadn't
been for the knock on the door. It's what these
bums sometimes do in liquor store and bodega
holdups. Grab the money, get the clerk down on the
floor behind the counter, and feed him a round in

the back of the head to take care of the witness problem. It's a junkie crime. How much did he get?"

"Just what was in my wallet. A few bucks and two credit cards I've already reported. He was lucky I showed up when he was in the room, because there was nothing worth stealing here except what was on me."

Vecchi was already somewhere else. "And you couldn't make him from the pictures they showed you at the precinct house . . . ?"

"No."

"Funny. He seemed real set on putting you away. Like he *could* be made easy. On parole, say, with a fixed address. Or otherwise well known to the local police. And I guess you've thought about was this somehow linked to the Stavros murder?"

"Sure, it occurred to me. But how? I don't know, it seems like a reach. He was just some punk, and they've had break-ins here at the hotel before. What do you think?"

"Too early to say." He reviewed the event in his head and gave me a nod of respect. "You had a busy day." And then he turned to new business. "Breakfast at Rascals' Retreat. You were waited on by Janet Fross."

"Wait a second. The police checked. Nobody remembered me."

"Nobody did. Still, a regular waitress, Janet Fross, took care of you. That's what I came over to tell you."

"How did you . . . ?" I was beginning to feel a bit Watsonish to his Holmes. Except that among other differences he was a good five inches too short for the part.

He said, "I was there this morning. I told them I

was a cop—nobody doubted it for a minute—and I went through the waitress checks. They're time-stamped and spiked by the cashier. You paid your check at eleven fifty-three A.M.—eggs easy over, whole wheat toast, tomatoes instead of hash browns, decaf. Exactly what you told me, and written down by Janet Fross for the kitchen.''

I said, ''I appreciate your going to the trouble, but if the police think I was the one who did Stavros, that check isn't much of an alibi. I would still have had more than enough time to get from Rascals' to Stavros's hotel room to help him through that window by twelve-thirty.''

''No question,'' he said. ''But let me ask you this. Does a man planning to do that kind of work at twelve-thirty have that kind of breakfast at twelve? Not on your life.''

I said, ''That's a matter of opinion. Let's see how it plays to Dunleavy when I tell him I can't produce my twelve-thirty beach alibi.'' A thought hit me. ''Al, how did you get to Rascals' Retreat?''

He said, ''You know what a cab costs in this town? I'm holding the receipts for Kornbluth. It's a legitimate expense. If I save his writer from a murder rap I save him from having to lay out for a replacement.''

The phone rang. It was Dunleavy's partner, Detective Ossian. He asked, in that uninflected voice civil servants put on when they have the weight of the law behind them, if it would be convenient for me to drop around in the next half hour to the police station where I had been last night. He and Dunleavy had been expecting to hear from me and they would wait. I said I'd be there in fifteen minutes. He said under no circumstances was I to disappoint them.

I thought I would get some comfort from having

Vecchi along, and it didn't take much to get him to agree. I figured he had already decided to be a buffer on all matters between me and the police. Even if he hadn't, my hunch was he'd have preferred watching the action at a car wash to going back to the scripts Kornbluth had laid on him.

We liberated my rental from the Desert Palm's dungeon, and I drove us through moderate midday Hollywood traffic along the route Cissy and I had taken to the station house with the detectives. Meanwhile Vecchi entertained me, probably with the intention of taking my mind off the coming interview with Dunleavy, by reflecting on the walk he had taken back to his motel after I dropped him last night.

"There's a type of creep you see in New York along the Deuce, you know where I mean?" he was saying.

"West Forty-second Street."

He nodded. "If this type of creep happens to go west, he gets off the bus, rails, whatever, heads like a ground-to-ground missile straight for Hollywood Boulevard, looks around, takes a couple of deep breaths, grins from ear to ear, and says, 'It's good to be home.' Why? Why here?"

"I don't know," I said. "Fading movie theaters? They've got as many here as on Forty-second, and they're bigger."

"You could be right. We'll know soon enough. The theaters on the Deuce are being rebuilt, dolled up. The bums won't be able to hang out anymore. We're being followed."

I didn't get it. "Hollywood is following New York in rebuilding its theaters? I haven't seen any signs of that."

"No," he said. "I mean we're being followed right now. In the mirror, the blue midsize, two cars back. Take this right."

"Are you sure?" I made the turn doubtfully; Vecchi may have been starting to relive his glory days. Who the hell would take the trouble to follow us? I said, "I hate this kind of crap."

"Hugger-mugger with cars? Isn't that what you TV guys love to write? Chases, surveillance, repos, getaways?" His eye was on the intersection through the rearview mirror. "Yeah, here he comes."

"I don't write them, I don't like them. You see one, you've seen them all." I was still checking the mirror. "Three heads, two in front, one in back?"

"That's the car. I think they were waiting outside your garage. Take this left." As I turned he said, "You're making a mistake if you don't write scenes like that. I've been reading them for two weeks. They run two, three, four pages, hardly any words on a page. Or wait—does the writer get less money for those than for other kinds of scenes?"

I said, "It isn't like buying chicken parts. There's one price for the whole job." The blue car was still with us. I said, "Do you have a gun?" I knew that retired cops usually continued to carry their smaller-caliber off-duty pieces.

"Yeah, in New York," he said, "where it's licensed. And how was I going to get it on the plane?"

I thought, This is perfect. I said, "So what do you want me to do, lose them?"

"Lose them! Take it easy, let's find out who the hell they are, why someone is following you."

"What do you mean, me? Why not you they're following? Someone you put away years ago who's been nursing a grudge." Denial had sent me rummaging through stale TV plots. "Have they sprung the Edgar Allan Poe killer?"

He didn't dignify that desperate question with a reply. "Take the right," he said. "Not this one, the secondary street ahead. And do what I say."

The blue midsize was hanging back a couple of blocks, so I had time to make the turn, let Vecchi out just inside the corner, at his request, and then pull into the narrow driveway of a pinched little Spanish-style stucco villa farther along what had turned out to be a drowsing, lower-middle-class residential block of similar Spanish-style stucco villas. I hated this car stuff as it was developing in the round even more than I did on paper. And even more when an ancient woman in hair rollers pulled aside a lace curtain in the house to stare out at me through narrowed eyes.

A moment later the blue midsize rounded the corner. I was waiting with my car in reverse and my foot on the brake. I slid it to the accelerator, jammed down hard, and shot straight back into the street, braking when I had pretty effectively blocked passage. The blue car stopped a few feet from me, remained there for a beat while the two men in the front seat looked to each other for a decision, and then began to back up. But now Vecchi was standing in the middle of the street a few yards behind them, legs apart, barrel chest thrust forward, defying them to run into him.

The midsize stopped, and a man jumped out of each front door. They were rugged, mid-to-late thirties, dark-complexioned, and angry. Fists flexing, arms cocked, they moved toward the unyielding Vecchi. The younger one said, "What the hell you think you're doing, you want to kill someone?"

"It's an idea," Vecchi said. "I could start with you.

Don't you know better than to play bumper tag with a cop?''

"You're a cop?" the younger one spit out, still advancing. He seemed to be spokesman for the group. He groped for a line of attack. "The hell you're a cop. Let me see some I.D.''

By now I was approaching from my car and what flashed through my head was the bandido who claimed to be the law in Huston's *Sierra Madre:* "Badge? Badge? I don't need no stinkin' badge." But Vecchi pulled out a leather folder and flipped it open to reveal a gold NYPD shield, I supposed the one he retired with. The younger man looked confused. "That's a New York badge," he said.

Vecchi said, "I'm here on a job. You have a problem with that?"

I had reached the group, and the older, taller of the two men planted himself in front of me, dark eyes blazing, jaw firmly set. The backseat passenger was getting out of the car. A woman. She had strong, striking features, high cheekbones, and jet black hair that splashed carelessly across her shoulders. I couldn't remember where, but I had seen her before, and more than once. The younger man was still pressing Vecchi. "Who the hell are you, anyway? If you're a cop, what, are you arresting this guy for something? You got ex-tadition papers to New York or something?" He turned to the woman and pointed at me. "Christine, this is him, right?"

Christine. Of course, Christine Stavros, of Christine's. I had never seen her outside her environment, the restaurant, where she seated patrons with a reserved smile, always dressed in something figure-revealing that had just come out of the dry cleaner's bag. Now she was rumpled and frazzled, but still striking.

I said, "Christine. I'm sorry about your brother."

The younger man echoed scornfully, "He's sorry!"

Christine glanced at me and away and said, "Yes, that's him. Byron Saldinger."

Now both men came at me—they had to be brothers, as well as *her* brother, and Niko's—and each grabbed an arm. I tried to pull free while Vecchi came up growling, "What the hell is going on?"

If people were at home in any of those little stucco villas, aside from the old woman behind the lace curtain, they were not about to come outdoors merely to see why two cars had stopped in the center of Fuchsia Drive, one at right angles to it, and disgorged five people who were now in an angry confrontation. They would need a better reason than that to violate the unwritten L.A. residential code: no resident may expose himself to public view outside his house except for the sole purpose of walking to his car. I said to Vecchi, "That's Stavros's sister. I guess she's come to take the body home. And these are his brothers, right?"

"Two of his brothers, Phil couldn't come." The older one was speaking for the first time. He didn't relax his grip on me. "I'm Alex, that's Connie."

Vecchi was looking at Connie. "And what's your name?"

I said, "Al, that's Connie. The woman is Christine."

Connie said, "And who the hell are you?"

"Sergeant Al Vecchi, NYPD." And then, grudgingly, "Retired."

"So I was right," Connie said. "You're no cop."

Sorting out the introductions had drained the confrontation of some of its heat, and the brothers now gradually loosened their grip and finally let me

go. I turned to Christine. "If you want to talk to me,
you don't have to trail me all over the city."

Connie said, "She don't want to talk to you, she
wants us to break your neck."

Vecchi said, "Okay, Connie, lighten up." It was as
though he had been dispatched here by 911 to settle
one more messy domestic dispute.

I said, "Christine, why would you want my neck
broken? You don't really think I stole a story from
Niko?"

Alex, the older brother, was the only member of
the family present with an accent, but he may not
have been the oldest of the siblings if Phil, the missing one, was named for Philip of Macedon, father of
Alexander the Great, and Alex was subsequently
named for him. Alex said, "Yes, you stole what came
out of Niko's head, from his brain. The dirtiest kind
of stealing, to take from a man his imagination."

I wanted to say there is very little call for imagination in television, but out of respect for the dead I
said, "Look, I'm not getting into that in the middle
of the street. But I'm not a thief." That had almost
come out "I'm not a crook," and I shuddered at the
echo.

Connie took over. "I say you're more than a thief.
The only way to bury the truth was to kill Niko. So
you pushed him out that window. Like this." Suddenly he had me by the shoulders and was propel-
ling me backward against the side of his car. I
started to push back, and we were in a kind of dumb
grunt contest when Vecchi came up and separated
us by slamming his arms down against ours to break
our grips.

"Cut it," he said. And, to Connie, "You want to
ask this man questions, wait your turn. The Los Angeles police are first in line."

"That's where you're taking him? To the police?"

"And we're late," Vecchi said. "You want me to tell the sergeant how come we're late? How we were sandbagged on a public street?"

Alex said, "Aaah, let's go, Connie. We don't need this." He had his brother firmly by the elbow and was hustling him toward their car.

Over his shoulder Connie hurled back, "You think you can walk away from this? From murdering my brother? I know where to find you, Byron Saldinger."

I said, "Why don't you have your lawyer talk to my lawyer?" I didn't have a lawyer, the network was handling my action.

He was resisting being boosted into the car. "Forget the lawyers! Christine knows what you did, you thieving murdering bastard! You think we'll let you get away with making a stench that rises to heaven from my brother's grave?" Right 'in the middle of Fuchsia Drive he was improvising on a theme from Sophocles.

Alex somehow managed to get him in the passenger seat. Christine was still in the street, looking lost, a Fury more to be pitied than feared. I felt for her. She had always seemed a decent person, and we had treated each other with respect. I tried to compose a look of both sympathy and reassurance. Could a man who asked regularly for double vegetables instead of potato be the kind of person her brother was describing?

"Christine . . ." I began, reasonably.

But she turned her troubled face from me and climbed into the car. Alex quickly backed up and they disappeared down the cross street.

Vecchi and I walked back to my car and climbed in without speaking. I started the car, turned its head forward, and drove it slowly out of the block. Once all five of us New Yorkers were gone from there, Fuchsia Drive could return to its usual unpeopled quiet.

CHAPTER NINE

Ossian folded his *Hollywood Reporter* and slid it into a desk drawer when Vecchi and I came into the otherwise deserted detective squad room. He then poked his head through the doorway of an inner room and announced, "Ed, he's here." He turned back to me and added, "I thought you said fifteen minutes."

I said something about a traffic tie-up, and then Dunleavy was in the room, moving quickly, looking impatient. To Ossian he said, "Okay, you want to get them organized?" Ossian left the room and Dunleavy glanced at Vecchi. "You brought your lawyer," he said. "Good."

I explained that this wasn't a lawyer but an associate of mine at the network, Sergeant Al Vecchi, NYPD, retired. Dunleavy nodded, then took a closer look. "Vecchi. Not the Vecchi who made the collar in the Raymond sisters' case?"

"That too," I said.

Dunleavy acknowledged respect with a raised eyebrow and a look of envy, and there followed a few minutes of spirited shoptalk between the professionals. At the end of it Dunleavy said it would be perfectly all right for Vecchi to stay, since everything at this point was voluntary and informal, he was just exploring every avenue. But didn't Al think I should consult a lawyer?

Al said, "Not necessarily."

I added that in the unlikely event I needed a lawyer I would hire one, but until then I'd rather the money went toward a couple of years of child support. And what progress, I wanted to know, was being made on last night's brutal assault on me and the young woman visiting from England? I figured my best defense was an offense.

I was right. Dunleavy apologized for having no news on the assault. The detectives on the case—he explained carefully that the case wasn't his—were stymied, with no hard leads to follow. The assailant's knife hadn't yielded a single usable print—the Englishwoman had effectively smudged the handle when she picked up the knife—and the knife itself was an old one of no particular distinction. And, of course, Cissy and I had not been able to pick out the perp from their extensive library of police photographs. Although our assailant had behaved as though he had done this sort of thing before, it was possible he had never been arrested. Then again, he might be from out of town. Or, Cissy and I could have slid past his photograph in the books we waded through the night before.

Still on the offensive, rather than convinced, I said, "And you believe it's no more than a coincidence that I was attacked the same day Nicholas Stavros was murdered?"

Dunleavy said, "You mean, is there a killer out there who goes after anyone who claims he created

Corrigan's Way? That maybe he's the real author of
this script, out for revenge? No, Mr. Saldinger, that
might happen in LaLa Land but we're down here in
the real L.A., where a lot of crimes are committed
every day for the usual reason, a quick buck. Meanwhile the case I'm assigned to is not your random
mugging, unpleasant as that was, but the Stavros
murder. And in connection with that I asked you in
this morning to find out—''

"Right, you wanted to go over the story of my alibi
out at the beach yesterday."

I had jumped the gun. Dunleavy shot me a calculating look. "We'll get to the beach in due time," he
said. "Right now I'd like your permission to run an
informal lineup, see if we can clear away any confusion there might be over, you know, identification."

I said, "Wait a second . . ."

He was moving right along. He said, "You understand I'm doing this for your own protection and
you don't have to agree to it, it's purely voluntary.
But I assumed you'd want to go along with me, so I
took the liberty of bringing in three employees of
Stavros's hotel who were on duty when he was killed.
We want to make sure—as I say, for your own protection—none of them remembers seeing you enter or
leave the hotel around that time."

I said, "Wait a minute. For my own protection,
how?" I didn't like what he was springing in the
least. "If one of them identifies me, I'm a murderer.
If none of them does, it only means I was maybe
lucky enough to slip in and out unobserved."

Dunleavy said, "Mr. Saldinger, I wish you
wouldn't take a negative attitude on this proceeding. I've gone to some trouble organizing it. Four
civilian volunteers have come in here to line up with

you. We've already wasted twenty minutes of their time.''

"For a lineup? You never told me—''

He never stopped. "With your cooperation we can eliminate an area of inquiry that's tying up resources and keeping us from widening our investigation.''

We were wading through mud. I said, "By 'a line of inquiry' you mean me. And if I go along with your lineup I waive my Miranda rights, don't I?''

"That goes without saying, but I was about to say it anyway. Yes.''

I didn't hesitate. I didn't like this at all, but on balance I thought it best not to appear evasive. I was going to raise suspicion enough when I admitted I had no witness to support my beach story. I said, "Sure, okay, let's get it over with. Right, Al?''

Vecchi said, "So long as you asked, no. You're making a mistake. I don't care if you can prove you were in Cleveland yesterday. I guarantee, one of those three witnesses is going to place you in that hotel. That's the way these things go.''

I said, "Damned if I do and damned if I don't.'' I took a deep breath and let it out. "Let's get it over with.''

When Ossian beckoned, we five "suspects" shuffled in self-consciously from the hall. Ossian had made me Number Four. We ranged in age from thirties to fifties and in height up to six feet. None of us had any outstanding physical characteristics. The others were neighborhood merchants and professionals, good citizens doing their bit to fight the area's pervasive crime. Each of them knew at least one of the others but not me, so they figured me for the possible rapist, murderer—they weren't sure what. While we were waiting for our act to be called, none of them had talked to me and they had carefully kept a certain distance between us.

I had written this scene more than once, although with the witnesses shielded behind one-way glass and a raised platform for the possible suspects. Dunleavy's theater of the absurd was more modestly staged in what was probably the police muster room, a good-sized space with shades now drawn over the windows. Our end of the room was well lit, the lights tilted toward us, making murky shadows of the witnesses and the police who were assembled to observe us somewhere out in the protective dark.

Waiting for instructions, our group stood fidgeting in silence, shifting weight from one foot to the other and working at making our arms behave naturally. I tried to avoid squinting into the lights. Drawing on my sketchy knowledge of Method acting, I decided I was waiting for a train, the 8:53 from Scarsdale to Grand Central. Bored and patient. Gregory Peck couldn't have carried it off under these circumstances and neither, I felt certain, could I or any of these men flanking me. We were all guilty as charged.

After a bit there was some hoarse whispering out front and then Dunleavy's voice. "Number Three? Number Three, would you please walk a few steps? Up and back in front of the others would be fine. Thank you." Poor Number Three did a windup march that related not at all to how anyone on this planet walks, and then he beat a hasty retreat back into the line.

"Thank you," said Dunleavy. There was more whispering, a somewhat more prolonged back and forth. "Number Four," Dunleavy said, "could I ask you to give us a smile, please? A smile and a nod?"

How the hell was I supposed to direct a smile toward someone who was at that moment fingering me? I separated my lips to show some teeth, at the same time widening my mouth and lifting it at the corners. I supposed that was a smile. Then I bobbed my head like a figure in an animated Bonwit Teller Christmas window and went back to waiting for the 8:53.

More whispering from out front. Then silence. And then, "Thank you all for your cooperation." Ossian ushered us out.

"Inconclusive."

Dunleavy delivered his verdict after he, Ossian, Vecchi, and I had reassembled in a corner of the squad room. Despite the word, it was clear he thought he was on to something. And having subjected myself to Dunleavy's puppet show, I had no intention of accepting "inconclusive."

I had to press hard for the raw data, but he eventually gave me a rundown. The hotel registration clerk had drawn a blank on our group, but he said maybe that was because yesterday had been a heavy one for check-ins and his eye had been mostly on his computer screen. The bell captain thought it possible he had seen Number Three entering the hotel. Number Three, it turned out, was a funeral director and a member of the Chamber of Commerce who had been at Forest Lawn Cemetery through the middle of the day. Forget Number Three.

Dunleavy had saved the best for last. The room maid claimed she had exchanged nods with me, or somebody very like me, coming out of the elevator on her floor at around eleven-thirty A.M., when she was going on her break. Dunleavy watched to see how I was taking this, and I returned his challenging look with a defiant one. But it was Vecchi who spoke.

"What did I tell you?" he said to me. "I watched you up there with those guys and I'd have fingered you myself, you looked that sinister. As it happens, Ed"—he and Dunleavy were on a firm first-name basis—"it couldn't have been Mike here the maid saw at eleven-thirty, because at eleven-thirty he was starting on his toast, eggs, sliced tomatoes, and decaf at Rascals' Retreat, near Doheny."

"We've looked into the Rascals' story," Dunleavy said. "Much as I'd like to believe it, I found no one there who could say Mr. Saldinger came in yesterday morning."

Very gingerly, so as not to seem to be putting Dunleavy down, Vecchi explained how he had gone about verifying my breakfast alibi. I could see that Dunleavy was impressed, but all he said was, "We'll look into that."

He moved on quickly to cover his disappointment. "Okay, let's say the maid was mistaken, and let's forget eleven-thirty. Rascals' isn't important." He had gone to considerable trouble to stage his lineup; it was a bust, thanks mainly to Vecchi, and he was trying to get in step with that. "The murder was at about twelve-thirty," he said. "Let's concentrate on that time. You say you were at the beach, and that brings us to the woman who saw you there." I could see he was beginning to feel in control again. Before I could organize a reply he said, "I'll save you the fumbling. You can't produce her."

"Not right now." He had caught me by surprise. "How did you know?"

"It was written all over your face when I asked about her. Not now. Last night, when I ran into you here." He turned to Ossian. "What did I say when Saldinger left with that English girl?"

Ossian jumped at the cue. "You said, 'This guy doesn't have a witness, he can't produce a witness.'"

I began the speech that I had rehearsed explaining how Jenny had blown our date last night at Musso & Frank. Her note was in my inside jacket pocket, ready to be produced at the appropriate point in the narrative. But even as I spoke I could hear how limp the story was, how unpersuasive the voice telling it. And the note, I now realized, could very well have been written by my aunt Bernice.

Dunleavy spared me having to lurch through the whole narrative. He broke in and said, "You're wriggling on my hook. If that means you're confirming 'There is no witness,' please save us both some time and say so."

"I have no witness at the moment. But I have Rascals', so does it really matter?"

"In the big picture? When we have the big picture I'll get back to you. Meanwhile I duly note your statement that you have no alibi for the time of the murder."

I said, "Fine. Are we finished here? Because I'm running late . . ."

"Wait," Dunleavy said. "There's one more thing I'd like to go over with you."

I said, "The network is paying for this trip and I was supposed to make contact with them an hour ago."

"This won't take long. Did you know the Stavros family came out here from New York?"

"I ran into them this morning."

"That so?" He was surprised. "I was with them

last night when they identified the body. Afterwards we had a talk.''

He took his time. He was letting me know he had retaken full command of these proceedings. "You told me yesterday," he went on, "that your contacts with Nicholas Stavros were limited to hello, good-bye, how's the veal. Stuff like that. Christine Stavros has a different memory of the relationship.''

"Does she?"

"She says you not only had plenty of opportunity to learn about her brother's television proposal, he actually told it to you—"

"That never happened."

"—in her restaurant, in enough detail for you to appropriate it for your own purpose. I'm no lawyer, but isn't proof of access to the original material one of the key factors in plagiarism suits?"

I kept my voice steady. "I can't help what Christine Stavros says. And why are we discussing that here? Doesn't it belong in a civil suit?"

"You may be right. If you are, forget I brought it up. I can reach you at the Desert Palm?"

"Or at home in New York. My agent knows how to find me."

"New York." He didn't like any part of that. "When were you planning to go back?"

"In a day or two. As soon as the network releases me."

He didn't like that either, so I pushed it. "Unless you're planning to have me arrested."

He said, smiling, "Now why would I want to do something dumb like that?"

The words didn't come easily.

On our way out of the building I asked Vecchi how I had done.

"I'd say it was a wash."

"Why is he hassling me?" I asked. "Does he seriously think I pushed Stavros out that window?"

"Probably not, but you're all he's got and he has to come to work every day."

"The crime is only a day old. His bosses can't be crowding him this soon."

"Dunleavy isn't the kind of cop who waits to be pushed. That hair of his—silver and black, brushed back real nice? That's not sergeant's hair, if you know what I mean."

I had long ago given up assigning ambition as a motive when I wrote cop characters, but life didn't seem to be giving much of a damn around here about imitating art.

CHAPTER TEN

On my way back to the Desert Palm I dropped Vecchi. From the street the Hollyview looked as if it might rent by the hour, with maybe a two-hour minimum to salve the management's pride. But the pained look on Vecchi's face as he got out of the car had nothing to do with the seediness of his lodgings. I don't think he even noticed that, and if he did, he wouldn't have much cared. What pained him was having to return to that pile of police scripts in his room. He told me that reading them was throwing his digestive system out of whack.

At the Palm the surly day man handed me a few more messages. Benjy had called to say, "Never mind." He and I would have to have a little talk about running up phone charges from Westchester. Seth Blau had called; that one I tore up. The last took me by surprise: "Wolf Waxroth returned your call." That was a first. And then I realized Wolf would have figured I'd be out—why would I hang around a shabby hotel room in the middle of the day?—but that he would win Brownie points for having made an effort to reach me. I phoned his office and Winnie said, "Oh, darn. He just this minute left for the acupuncturist. And then he's out at meetings the rest of the day."

Decks cleared, I braced myself and called Kornbluth's office. His secretary sounded relieved; she said she had been waiting to hear from me. Could I meet Mr. Kornbluth for a drink at Jimmy's, on his way home? I was surprised that he wanted to meet me for drinks; we didn't have that kind of relationship. "On his way home" let me know the meeting would be brief. But Jimmy's? Very upscale; his picking it could be a sort of mark of respect.

The plan suited me fine. Both the time and location fit in perfectly with my dinner date at Jasmine and Rudd's. Just in case there were not going to be any further script problems to keep me in town, I called the airline and made a reservation on the nine A.M. for New York. And then I lay down to sack out for an hour, hopefully two.

Kornbluth was already seated at a corner table in the well-populated bar. I was surprised at how comfortably he blended in with the secure executive types at Jimmy's, mostly people not on the make but who had made it. Oscar's job commanded power but not much money. Only his restlessly searching eyes and the tension in his awkward, Nixonesque body gave him away as still climbing. He sported the same expensive clothes and haircut as his betters, and I now noticed that even his chin seemed more firmly molded, more aggressive than when I first met him six months ago at the start of the *Corrigan* project. He was then the network's fairly new VP for Dramatic Development—not yet that well groomed, not especially articulate, and not even interesting enough when he did speak to generate the caution "He doesn't say much, but watch him."

Why he got the job remained a mystery, but now at least he looked and sounded the part. His tailor deserved some kind of prize for getting the jacket to hang decently from those tortured shoulders. And in his memos and phone calls these past few months I noticed he had gradually picked up the two dozen or so phrases he needed to sound like a development exec. If he could hold the job long enough, Mrs. Kornbluth, a nursery school teacher, would be dumped—the rumors had already floated back east —and he would become a seamless, nearly indestructible part of the creative community. But first he would have to commit no more than a minimum of really egregious errors through another full season. From that point on, as far as his financial security went, it wouldn't matter how badly he performed. If he had to be eased out of this job, he would be sent on his way with a handful of series development commitments from the network that he could trade in at an independent company for a producing deal with a guarantee of half a million a year.

A waiter appeared as I arrived at the table. Kornbluth said, "Mike, sit down, tell Rick what you're drinking, and then tell me how the hell you got that nasty bump."

I had almost forgotten the bump—it had stopped throbbing—but any sympathy I could drum up from Kornbluth was welcome, especially in light of my inexcusable departure from his office the day before. So I began a long-form account of last night's mugging. When I read the impatience building in his eyes and saw the tic at the corner of his mouth accelerate, I abruptly aborted and accepted his pro forma expression of concern. It was his meeting. I waited for him to open it.

He chose not to until we were halfway through our drinks. He rambled on amiably about the season, pretended to take me into his confidence about a couple of programming strategies, shared his opinion of the Blaus (low personally, high professionally), and then settled into an account of where his enthusiasm really lay—in his extraordinary rise to the top as a time salesman for the network's Boston station when he was only twenty-five. The story was well larded with his views of the psychology behind that success. "You have to think of the prospect as a gazelle," one part of it went, "and yourself as a lion with four ravenous cubs back at the den." Yesterday's friction between us had been either forgotten or filed, so I chose not to remind him that *lionesses* hunt food for the cubs, lions only for themselves. But maybe that's what he meant. The tic was assuming larger and larger meaning in that face.

Oscar may have forgotten the friction, but not what had caused it. When he finally got around to substantive matters, we were back to Nick Stavros. He said, "That man's death yesterday coming practically right on top of us talking about him—I can't tell you what a shock that gave me. First from the personal perspective, and then because of the possible business consequences. It's changed the entire equation on this project. And the pressure has become unbelievable. Not from upstairs or our outside lawyers. From New York. I mean heavy."

New York meant corporate headquarters, now manned by business school zombies set loose on the network by the drug conglomerate that had recently acquired it in a distress sale. "I don't have to tell you

how bottom-line crazy the pill pushers are," Kornbluth went on. "A Trig Bascomb show they understand. It's meat and potatoes to them. If they lose
Bascomb because of adverse publicity, or if they
have to give away a piece of the store to Stavros's
heirs, they'll foam at the mouth. Believe me. And
you know whose ass will burn."

"Mine."

"Get in line. You'll see the smoke from mine in
Burbank."

I said, "Are you and I about to review the same
Stavros material we went over yesterday?"

"No, Mike. This is entirely new." He pulled a manila envelope from his briefcase. "It's the basis for
the concerns I expressed in my office." He laid it
between us on the table. "Stavros left this with me."

I didn't reach for it. He would have to put it in my
hand.

I said, "When he came to see you yesterday morning? Before our meeting?"

"That's right."

"Oscar, when I fly west, jet lag keeps me awake
the first two or three nights. It's a bitch, except that I
do my clearest thinking, such as it is, lying there in
the dark. And you know what hit me at something
like three this morning?" I didn't wait for him to
rise to the rhetorical bait. "When I signed in for our
meeting yesterday," I said, "I looked in the book to
see if Waxroth and the Blaus had shown up. If Nick
Stavros's name had been in that book, it would have
hit me between the eyes."

"What do you think, he never showed? You think
I'm jerking you around?"

"You tell me."

"Of course I'll tell you. Why do you think I asked
you here? So shut up and listen, because I've got to

run in a few minutes. I've got a three-year-old daughter I haven't been home to say good night to in three weeks."

Once he was satisfied he had my full attention, he modulated his voice. "Maybe half an hour before our meeting yesterday? I got a quiet call from Chuck, the security man down in the lobby, the one who signs you in. Someone named Nicholas Stavros was at the desk, there was no pass for him, but he claimed I'd absolutely want to see him. Stavros. In person. I told Chuck to have him wait, I'd be right down."

"Why?"

"Why not send him up, or why see him at all?"

"Both."

"Why not send him up. I thought the lawyers wouldn't like that—his signing the book, going into offices, establishing some kind of record of a connection with the network. I didn't know how much of a crazy we were dealing with. Why see him at all? See above, I wanted to know how much of a crazy we were dealing with."

"You wanted to know how much of a threat he was."

"Why not? So I break off a meeting and go down to the lobby. I'm looking at maybe a dozen people sitting around. Stavros jumps up and yells, 'You looking for the man who created *Corrigan's Way*? At your service.' Right away I could see he was crazy enough. Keyed up, anyway. Who knew what kind of scene he might make? I steered him back to the supply room. I locked the door and sat him down. And he tossed this at me." He tapped the manila envelope. "A photocopy, he said, of his series proposal for the show he claimed was the spit of *Corrigan's Way.*"

I said, "What I've been asking for? What your lawyers have been asking for? How come he decided to cough it up now?''

"Why else? He wasn't getting anywhere without it. And I think there was something else. My assessment? He wanted an excuse for a personal confrontation. He wanted to be a presence, someone to be reckoned with. He didn't want to deal through a bunch of middle men. I think that's why he held off bringing a lawyer into the picture. And he was right, he got to meet the network VP for Dramatic Development. Eyeball-to-eyeball.

"Anyway, he handed me this manila envelope. A carbon of what he said he wrote six months ago, which would have been about the time the Blaus approached Bascomb with your *Corrigan*. He said he sent the ribbon copy back to himself by registered mail.''

I reached for the envelope. Kornbluth put his hand over it and drew it back. "Uh-uh," he said, "I don't want you to have it."

"Why the hell not?"

"You can take my word for it. There are elements here that are close—eerily close—to *Corrigan*."

"Why should I take your word for it? Let me see the piece of shit."

"Mike, stay with me for a minute. Stavros asked me to take his proposal back to my office and read it when I could grab a few minutes, but before the day was over. After I had read it, he said, he felt sure I would want to get in touch with him at his hotel and agree to cut a deal. A gentle deal. He said right now what he was basically looking for from the network was recognition for his work."

"Bullshit."

"But if he didn't hear from me he was going straight back to New York and turn over the date-stamped registered original to a lawyer. After that, he promised, this was going to be mostly about money. Lots of it."

"Are you telling me the original hadn't gone to a lawyer?"

"You picked up on that, eh? That came from his wanting to go head-to-head with us directly, to stay in control. But there's more. The original isn't even in a bank vault."

"How would you know that?"

"It came out during his riff about lawyers. Lawyers, courts, banks—he didn't trust any of them. The true peasant mentality says never let anything valuable get out into the system. My mother says her grandfather kept his citizenship papers and his marriage license rolled in a suit of long underwear. Unwashed, for added security."

I said, "So what you're getting at, you believe the original of this so-called series proposal . . ."

"It's called *Boynton's New Life.*"

"Jesus. It's your belief it still resides, possibly unknown to his family, somewhere in Niko's apartment?"

"I'd bet on it. Not the 'unknown' part. The family may know. But with his body still warm, putting their hands on it isn't their highest priority."

By now I had seen where he was headed. I said, "And if this document was found and destroyed, you would be relieved of the mother of all headaches."

"And you. In terms of career, the possibly terminal headache."

"So what these drinks are about, you're looking for me to go dowsing for Niko's manuscript. Breaking and entering his apartment and committing a felony."

"You can't violate him, he's dead. It's a victimless crime. But one that could save our asses." He looked at me, clear-eyed. My eyes were mostly on his tic. "Have you ever wondered how I got my job, Mike? A bland sort of nebbish like me?" I wasn't going to answer that one.

He said, "I'll tell you. I had a little bit of luck and a whole lot of ambition. I've got a mighty engine in that department. Let me share a confidence with you. I lied, cheated, and back-stabbed to get this job. Plenty. But I'm such a dull, colorless, thoroughly *uninteresting* person that it doesn't matter whether you pass that tidbit along or not. Hardly anyone will listen, and those who do will either forget it at once or conclude you made it up. Stavros's apartment? I'd do it myself without a minute's hesitation."

I could almost believe that. I finally understood the tic. I said, "Be my guest."

"No, it's more up your alley. In the first place it has to be done fast, before the heirs get the body home and buried and turn their attention to looking for the evidence they need for what could be a fat lawsuit. You'll be back in New York tomorrow. I'm releasing you to go home. You've had your script meeting with Bascomb, that was the important one. It went okay, I hear. My line notes will follow by FedEx."

"What about Vecchi's notes?"

"You two can get together when he goes back east."

"What's 'in the second place'?"

"Mike, I'm a fan. Your scripts are clever. Inventive. You've got the mind-set for this kind of thing. You'll know how to do it. You've probably done it more than once on paper, so now you'll put it on its feet. You're the perfect analgesic for our collective headache.''

"Let me read Stavros's photocopy."

"No." He was putting it back in his briefcase. "You'd just be looking for excuses not to do what I'm asking for. You'd say this is different in Stavros's outline, that's different. You'd find a way to say his piece isn't nearly enough like yours to be worth the trouble."

"I'd be damned surprised if it was."

"You see? I'm not saying you're a plagiarist—you're too inventive, you don't have to steal—but we've got a problem here and I don't want to get into nitpicking with you over how close this bit is to yours, how far that bit is. We're in a shadow area and you have to trust me on this. I want you to eliminate the doubts, once and for all. So this thing stops hanging over us."

"No. I won't do it."

"Why not? It makes sense."

"I can think of a couple of good reasons aside from it would be breaking the law. And it would be breaking the law, Oscar."

"It's an empty apartment. If you don't get in, no harm. If you get in, who'd know? What are the other reasons?"

"Suppose I lucked out and got in. What are the odds that I find the damn thing?"

"Very good, if it's there. And he gave me the strong impression it's there."

"There's the other reason. Even better."

"Tell me."

"There is no date-stamped ribbon copy. Stavros was sucking wind. I'll bet on that one."

"You could be right. If you are, what could be better? All is well. Our worries are over."

"Except for the small fact of my having been busted for a felony."

"It will never happen. You're too smart."

"Let me see the photocopy."

"No. I'm not going to give it to you. You're looking to weasel your way out of this. I can't take that chance. I want you so scared that doing it is the only way. I want you to *have* to do it."

"I don't think so, Oscar. I don't think I can."

But something in my voice may have reassured him. He dropped the subject, paid the check, and we went our separate ways.

CHAPTER ELEVEN

Some small surprises were waiting at the Coles'. One of the servant corps met me at the door and actually asked, as she led me back to the living room, if I would "care for a drink of any kind of whiskey?" I said very carefully, without a hope that the request would be honored, that a gin martini would do me fine, straight up, with a twist, if that was okay. She indicated she would pass the order along to *Okusan*, whom I knew to be, having inquired on a previous visit, "the honorable person of the interior," or the lady of the house.

The second surprise came when we passed the entrance to the dining room. I could barely credit my eyes. The table was set, actually set for a party of six with a lace tablecloth and an array of gleaming flatware and Waterford wine and water glasses. The centerpiece was a spare, architectural flower arrangement that included only three skimpy blooms but, I had no doubt, an abundance of tradition.

Rudd was alone in the vast nouveau-pioneer living

room the Coles rarely used. He was wearing a jacket and the gas fire blazed behind the ceramic logs. Both facts confirmed that, indeed, other guests were expected. Rudd hesitated, then stood up to greet me. He shook my hand and asked about the bump on my forehead, which by now I had forgotten I had. I was tired of talking about the damn bump, but I cranked up to tell the story of my mugging one more time.

The story was more than Rudd had bargained for; I could see that my brush with death shook him. He listened gravely, without interrupting. When I was finished he masked his concern for me, as he did about almost everything, with a brittle observation. "Could that so-called mugger have been a television viewer," he mused, "expressing his gratitude for the many years of pleasure you've brought him?"

We moved on to the Stavros murder. Rudd said he had heard about the Greek's violent death in a phone call no more than an hour after I left him. I meant to ask from whom, but he had already begun to speculate about the motive for it. He often did that with crimes reported by the media, and his hunches were often right. "When I was in the slammer . . ." he began.

It was the way he began many stories, and it never failed to grab the attention of people who didn't know him well. The facts were hard to believe now, but when Rudd was eighteen and nineteen he had spent more than a year in an Iowa state prison on an assault charge. In a free-swinging brawl over the affections of a girl—a baseball bat and a tire iron had figured in the proceedings—Rudd sustained a broken wrist. But he managed to hospitalize his rival.

Rudd always maintained that there had been no assault, just an ordinary street fight between equals, but that the other youth's father was politically connected and saw to it that Rudd had the book thrown at him. And yet he wasn't in the least bitter. He had only positive memories of his prison experience. Prison had awakened his appetite for reading, he maintained, and prison had plugged him into the skewed stories and characters that had established his early reputation. And if things should ever go bad for him, he maintained, he could always get a job in a laundry.

It was hard to dismiss Rudd's explanation of Stavros's death out of hand. It went like this. All the flak Stavros had thrown up about my plagiarizing him was a scam dreamed up for him by a friend or associate with more savvy than he had. But once the network began to take the scam seriously, and the smell of a major cash settlement was in the air, Stavros had tried to squeeze out his mentor and partner. The latter wouldn't go, and in an outburst of temper over the division of the prospective spoils, had pushed Stavros out the window. "An impromptu defenestration," Rudd called it.

Once he had unburdened himself of his plot he asked, "What's the police theory?"

I said, "The police don't have a theory. That's why they're on my back."

At that moment Jasmine entered, willowy in a trousered green silk hostess outfit that made me think of a blade of grass in a summer breeze. Jasmine could do that to me. She was bearing on a tiny silver tray what had to be a martini in a frosted glass, a long twist of lemon peel floating on the surface. She said, "Good evening, Myron, I'm so glad you were able to join us. Isn't this what you drink? It was made with Beefeater and Boissière."

That was the way I made them, and it couldn't

have been better—cold, jolting, and with enough vermouth to take the edge off the gin but not so much as to give the drink a winy taste. One to six? I was sure she had taken the order from her memory and not from her servant, and had mixed it herself. And I was grateful that although Jasmine had glanced at my purple forehead she seemed to have decided that perhaps it would be indiscreet to mention it. I told her I had never seen her look lovelier. Then I confessed to having seen her dining table and I apologized for having invited myself on a night when they already had plans to entertain other people.

"Not at all," Jasmine said. "The others were invited after you. We don't see you that often, or Sarah often enough, so we thought it would be nice to bring you two together. I hope you agree."

I said that, no question, Sarah did make it an extra-special occasion for me. Jasmine said she had a feeling that might be so, and then she excused herself to go back to the kitchen and her dinner preparations.

Sarah. I had seen very little of her in recent years but we used to see each other a lot, and giggle a lot, in my apprentice years with Rudd. It started with a magical drive to Ojai, which had served as the setting for Shangri-La decades before in the film version of *Lost Horizon* and seemed exactly suited to that purpose on the day we were there. Sarah, her brothers, and I had a picnic lunch on a picture-book hillside, and for dessert stole oranges from a grove that was heavy with fruit. The oranges turned out to be not nearly as good to eat as to look at, and we took the lesson to heart. The boys I hardly remembered at that age. Sarah had been about ten. That would make her, my God, about thirty.

I said, "How is Sarah? She still with the actor?"

Rudd said, "That ended seven or eight months ago. After six years. As you know, I never much liked him and I'd have been delighted, except he was the dumper, she the dumpee." He flushed, remembering that he was also describing my situation.

I said, "That's always rough."

He remained silent. I said, "I hope she looks on it as a learning experience. In any case she'll do better next time. She'll have plenty of choices. Sarah is an authentically beautiful woman."

Rudd was still brooding about the actor. "Wes found her perfect for the role of live-in girlfriend. When marriage loomed, with the prospect of children who might look like—who knew what?—he went into another casting huddle, this time with his mother and father. And he allowed himself to be outvoted." There was an unaccustomed quaver in his voice as he said softly, "No, Sarah did not take it at all well."

"A good thing she has those script assignments," I said. "Work is the great healer."

Rudd's take on that was to ask if I needed another drink, and then the subject of the discussion herself appeared from the entrance hall and made a bee-line for me.

"Saldinger, you rat," she said. She hugged me and held on tight. She smelled delicious but she felt thinner than I remembered. "We miss you," she said. "Why don't you move back here and take your punishment like the rest of us?" She didn't wait for an answer but released me to go to her father and kiss him. She was really beautiful, that particular kind of beauty you often see in mixed-race women— nature showing off its awesome possibilities. She still looked no more than twenty, but she was very thin. And strained, or tired. Something.

When we had settled on couches at the gas fire, Jasmine appeared briefly to kiss her daughter, hand her a vodka tonic, and deposit on the coffee table a platter of abalone ceviche. We knew it was abalone ceviche because she told us so and Jasmine would never lie. She insisted, as though to an inattentive class, that we try it at once. When we did, and voiced our approval, she nodded agreement and vanished again.

Sarah said, "You got my note about your divorce?"

"It helped. Thanks. I just wasn't in a frame of mind to get into a correspondence."

She said, "I know. I guess it doesn't help to say I liked Helene."

"I got left. There really isn't a whole lot you can do about that. Except move on." I had made my point and I got out fast. "I hear you've backslid from short stories to scriptwriting. How's it going? God, I can remember when you wrote with crayons."

"No, you don't. I was well past crayons when you came along. Mike, the kindly old uncle thing doesn't work for us anymore. I doubt there's fifteen years between us. That's practically the same age once both parties are past eighteen."

Rudd said, "Sarah's a little blocked on the writing. She can write, she's proved that with her stories, but she doesn't accept that TV writing is a craft that takes some time to learn, like hanging wallpaper. She's having trouble lining up the seams."

"Look, why don't you go on making elegant metaphors," she said. "I'm going to the kitchen and visit with Mom. I know I won't see her at dinner." I felt for Sarah. She was anxious and depressed and not having much success at covering it. Rudd's worried eyes followed her out of the room.

By my quick count of place settings, other guests were coming. It was unlikely Rudd and I would be alone for long. This was my one chance to ask him what exactly was going on between him and Waxroth and Bascomb—if I could bring myself to break in on his troubled thoughts. As it happened, I didn't have a chance to do that; the doorbell beat me to it.

Rudd looked at his watch. "Good, we gave him a dinner invitation forty-five minutes ahead of yours. Showing up an hour late for that makes him practically punctual. Perfect."

And a moment later Wolf Waxroth came bouncing into the room. The bounce went out of him when he saw me; I was clearly a surprise. But he rallied. "Mike. Rudd. What more could I ask?" he said. "You two under the same roof. You understand if this same roof collapsed on our heads television would suffer a blow it might take a generation to recover from." He broke out a grin he hoped was totally disarming. "I am speaking, of course, of the loss of the industry's premier talent agent." He looked at each of us to make sure we understood he was kidding. "Where is our hostess? I have to extend Phoebe's regrets. We were climbing in the car and she was hit by one of her migraines. Believe me, she wouldn't be fit company."

He brushed aside our murmurs of sympathy and moved on. "That's a nasty bump, Mike. If it hasn't been looked at you should by all means see someone. You want me to call Kalbfleish? I wouldn't send you anywhere else."

"I don't need a doctor, Wolf. It's under control."

He said, "I tried to reach you all day. Where were you?"

"Trying to catch up on my sleep. I told the hotel to hold my calls."

"That explains why Winnie couldn't get through," he said with relief.

Good old reliable Wolf, he told the truth only as a last resort. Even if a lie served no immediate purpose, it always served the purpose of keeping the skill honed. Wolf was not yet forty but he had been a boy wonder at twenty-two and he still cultivated that image. The secret of his continuing success was that he bounded out of bed every morning glad that he was alive and a talent agent and an accomplished liar. In no particular order.

"Before the ladies join us, Wolf," Rudd said, measuring the words precisely, "would you run through once more, so both Mike and I understand it, the proposal you laid out to me on the phone yesterday?"

Wolf turned an unattractive shade of green. "What do you mean, proposal? Who was talking proposal? Believe me, all I was doing was preparing us for contingencies."

"What kind of contingencies?" Rudd asked. I now understood that he had asked Wolf to dinner for the dual purpose of embarrassing him while he let me know what I already knew, that our friendship came before our agent. Rudd was already too late for purpose one. Wolf no longer looked green. Faster than a speeding bullet, he had his story fully in place.

He said, "What happened when I heard the Greek went out that window was my heart stopped. Some tragedy. The minute I got wind of it I knew what would stick in Bascomb's head when *he* heard of it. One thing only, I guarantee. If Mike should find himself tied up by the criminal investigation—"

"You mean if I was arrested."

"However they did it. Bascomb would worry about how that might derail *Corrigan,* or hold it up —about the project's survivability in a scandal. At that point he might well consider jumping ship himself. But meanwhile he would make sure to protect his options. He would send up a geshrei—that means a howl, Rudd—a geshrei for a standby writer. And that's where I beat Trig Bascomb to the punch." He spread his arms to indicate the inevitability of his logic. "I called him and proposed Rudd."

That wasn't the way Bascomb had told it to me. It was possible they were both lying, but there was no profit in getting into a you-did-I-didn't. That wasn't the important part. I zeroed in on the important part. I said, "You're telling me you sold him Rudd as a replacement for me on my own script?"

"Don't get your balls in an uproar. We're talking an 'if come' deal. Rudd signs to take over the script if you're suspended under the morals clause of your contract, and Bascomb sleeps easier because now he's got this top-flight replacement waiting in the wings. But here's where this is so beautiful it brings tears to my eyes. *I never deliver Rudd.* Mike, would I do that? To you? I stall with, Rudd's got to finish this thing he's on; after that I tell Trig there's that other script he's got to polish. And so on. I say, Trig, give Rudd a week; now give him a few more days; Trig, he'll be right with you; soon. That way, Mike, I keep you covered until you're cleared to go back to work. Guys, would I come between two tight friends? Am I that suicidal?"

He gave us each an open, innocent grin. He knew he had carried it off. Not great, but well enough not to be challenged. I had learned long ago to respect Wolf Waxroth's intelligence. And my gut feeling was that he did believe he could come between Rudd and me and that he did believe he could deliver Rudd. What gave him that confidence?

Totally at ease now, he was asking, "Isn't somebody going to offer me a drink?"

Jasmine's dinner included five or six dishes I had never seen before, several of them featuring different kinds of seaweed, most of them not all that bad. The best thing about the dinner was that the hostess actually perched at the table for a few minutes. Not to eat, although she did pick a bit, but to visit with her subdued daughter. It was obvious that Jasmine didn't see nearly enough of Sarah to satisfy her.

The second best thing about the dinner was that Wolf excused himself before coffee "to see if I can go do something for poor Phoebe." He had been in the Cole house for nearly an hour and a half, practically life imprisonment for Wolf. I could hear his motor roar as he spun out the driveway. That left the rest of us to visit and reminisce, family-style. Time had lent a sweetness to the ties we had been too busy to appreciate those years ago. Sarah continued to be subdued, but her mood brightened some under the gentle rain of well-worn stories Rudd and I told each other, mostly for her benefit. The rabbi story actually coaxed a bubble of laughter from her. I was surprised she had never heard it before.

Early in our association Rudd and I had developed a long-form series premise about a Rabbi Seligman in St. Louis, a wry, puckish eccentric who solved crimes as a by-product of his ministry. The project inched forward through a story proposal and two drafts of a two-hour pilot script, at which point we were summoned to the office of the senior executive overseeing the project at the studio where

Rudd had a development deal. Why the rabbi show got assigned to the only Irishman at the studio is one of those mysteries of command I will never understand. Anyway, Ed Burns said he had been wrestling from the beginning of this enterprise with a nagging doubt that had recently become worrisome. Where, he had been asking himself, did the rabbi develop the interest in, and the talent for, solving crimes? What was his backstory?

We explained in some detail the kind of probing, doubting, and questioning that rabbinical students are subjected to when they study the Talmud, and how that discipline might develop a taste and a talent for probing, doubting, and questioning the accepted wisdom in the solution of a crime. No, said Burns, that was all too lame. But he himself had come up with the perfect backstory and he promptly shared it with us: the rabbi's father was a cop.

We took a moment to pretend to consider this option before Rudd replied gently that no, a priest's father might be a cop but a rabbi's father was probably a rabbi. We were overruled. The pilot was shot, and it included several heart-warming scenes in which Rabbi Seligman went to his dad down at the precinct house for advice about the case. The series was never picked up, and neither was Rudd's option. But Ed Burns picked up a fellowship award from a temple in Sherman Oaks.

The party broke up at ten o'clock, and Sarah and I walked out to our cars together. Her parents stood watching in the doorway despite a stiff night breeze that blew up the canyon. Sarah's hair whipped across her face. When we were out of earshot she slipped her arm through mine and said, "Mike, can we have dinner one night? Just the two of us?"

Her thin arm was feather light on mine. "I'd like that," I said, "but it will have to be next time I come out. I'm going home tomorrow morning."

"Then how about—" Whatever that was going to be, she thought better of it. "I'm in the book, West L.A."

"I'll definitely call."

"I doubt it. But you should know, there is definitely a mysterious force connecting us. Maybe it's in our stars. Wouldn't that be delicious?"

"A mysterious force? What do you mean?"

"I don't know. Some kind of link. I've always felt it. Yesterday, for instance. I hadn't talked to Dad in a couple of weeks. You hadn't been to the house in a couple of years. And yet when I happened to phone, there you were."

So it had been Sarah on the other end of the line who had turned Rudd ashen when he waved me out of the office. She said, "Of course some of the connections between us are man-made. Woman-made, tonight. I said if Mom could lure you to dinner, I'd come too."

I said, "Are you confessing to entrapment? Forget it. This evening was the high point of my trip."

She said, "Now you're sounding like Wolf." She had no way of knowing the trip had been more valleys than peaks. She glanced back at her parents, reluctantly opened her car door, and climbed in. "Mom'll stand there till we're out of sight. Very Japanese, one of the last customs she clings to. We'd better go before they catch their death." She brushed the hair out of her face.

I had meant to say it before. "Sarah, Rudd told me about you and Wes. I'm sorry."

She said, "Don't be."

"Are you all right? I mean, with the world?" I hated to see unhappiness stamped across her brow.

She managed a smile, stuck her head out to brush a silken cheek against mine, and drove off.

CHAPTER TWELVE

It was still before eleven when I got back to the Desert Palm. There were no message slips; even the Blaus had given up on me. But I had ducked them long enough. I had better check in before they took offense. But I would do no more than check in; no further purpose would be served by making actual contact. So I called Seth, the bachelor of the pair and a relentless womanizer. The odds were he wouldn't be home.

I was right. I got a machine and I kept the message light and bright. "It's Saldinger, eleven P.M. Sorry to be so late getting back to you guys, the police kept me tied up until their casting officer decided I was probably wrong for the killer. I may get a callback. I guess you heard, my session with Bascomb could not have gone better, and all is well on that front. All he wanted was a couple of attitude changes, no problem. Except maybe *his* attitude. But not to worry. Let's see, Kornbluth is satisfied, and he's released me, so I'm on a nine A.M. to New York.

You can reach me at home tomorrow night if you want to go over the Bascomb notes. Or anything else. 'Night.''

Despite what I told Seth's machine I wasn't absolutely sure how the police felt about me and I didn't want to leave Dunleavy with the impression that I had slunk out of town. But neither did I want to get in a discussion with him about my leaving. I figured he would be off duty by now, so I called his office number. An answering machine wouldn't hassle me.

There was no machine; another detective picked up. I gave him my name and said if Sergeant Dunleavy needed me for anything I would be at my New York number starting tomorrow evening. That would sound reassuring. I left my home number and got off fast. There wasn't the remotest chance Dunleavy could get an arrest warrant issued between now and morning, even if he wanted one, since the nearest thing he had to evidence against me was that he had no other suspects. But just in case, I had carefully refrained from mentioning my flight or airline. Dunleavy should have no reason to feel betrayed. I had promised not to leave town for twenty-four hours and I was giving him an extra twelve.

I saved Vecchi for last. I needed him and I doubted he would be asleep. If he was, I figured he was used to being awakened at odd hours. He picked up on the first ring.

"Yo?"

I said I was going back to New York in the morning and I wanted some advice. He said, "Shoot."

"It's a technical matter, Al. I'd rather not discuss it on the phone."

"You want me to walk over?"

"No! Stay where you are, I'll drive to you."

* * *

He was waiting in the Hollyview office. When he spotted my rental, he came out and climbed in. "I can't ask you back to my room," he said. "It's a holy mess, the maid never showed. I guess now they wait for someone off the next vanload of undocumented aliens who'll work for their wages. You want to go someplace for coffee?"

"I'd rather talk in the car. Where we won't be overheard."

"Why do I think I'm going to like this?" he said. "Pull across the street."

I parked under a couple of yellowing palms that were beyond saving from asphyxiation, and launched into a detailed recital of my meeting at Jimmy's with Kornbluth. When I finished I said, "If I should decide to do what he asked me to . . ."

"The B. and E.?"

"Don't make it sound like you're reading it off my arrest sheet."

"Breaking and entering," he said. "What would you call it?"

"If I did it? An uninvited visit. More a rude act than a criminal one."

"If that helps, go with it. Who knows, if Stavros was alive and at home he might ask you in for buttermilk." He took a moment. "Let's look at the downside. Suppose you got caught? The worst wouldn't be the jail time. As a first offender you might even plea-bargain down to community service—maybe teaching kids from the South Bronx to write TV crime shows. Let me tell you, theirs would be more authentic than yours."

"So what's the worst?"

"Do I have to tell you? If you were nailed in the act you'd look to the whole world like a plagiarist who had stuck his neck out to find and destroy the evidence against him."

"Granted. But Kornbluth made a very good case on the other side. My accuser is dead. Now if I can get rid of whatever the hell junk he mailed himself to put me in this mess, that would end it. Once and for all. No doubtful evidence and no lawsuit."

"I can't argue that."

"So, Al, what I'm asking, if I do decide to do this —and I haven't decided yet—I would have to do it fast, before Stavros's family got back to New York and started sorting out his effects . . ."

"Do I know somebody who might help you open a door?"

"My question exactly."

"I could give you a name. Someone on the West Side." He took a moment. "But why would you stick your neck out until you had to?"

"What do you mean?"

"If I were you? First I'd read what Kornbluth has. See if it'll really stir up enough trouble to make going after the original worth the risk."

"I told you. Kornbluth wouldn't show me—"

"You told me. But if you're thinking burglary, you ought to start at Kornbluth's."

That rattled my teeth and I took a moment. "Another B. and E.? With three people at home? When I'm not even sure I can do Stavros's empty apartment?"

"Believe me, the risk here is much smaller. If Kornbluth catches you, can he holler for the police? The man who made you a burglar in the first place? Not without the police finding out what you came to steal. Kornbluth wouldn't want to get into that with them. Anyway, you won't get caught. Odds are he's still in the house he bought when he moved out here. He hasn't been in the money long enough to live in anything but a cheese box with no alarm system. And I can practically guarantee his briefcase will be in the hall closet. How about it?"

I said, "Are you talking about right now?"

"When else? It's close to midnight and he's got a very young daughter. The entire house will be asleep by the time we get there. How far does he live?" I started to open my address book and he may have noticed my hand shake. "B. and E.," he said soothingly, "is only a problem where people have valuable assets to protect. I can tell you, a lot of not very smart people make an okay living at this."

I said, "Suppose he keeps a gun in the night table? And fires in the dark?"

"Kornbluth? No way does Kornbluth have a gun."

The die was cast. "He lives in Encino," I said. "Twenty minutes."

"Was the briefcase locked?"

"No. He just snapped it open."

"Good." He was climbing out of the car. "I need three minutes."

"For what?"

"I have typing paper in the room. I'll get a few sheets you can switch with Stavros's papers in the envelope in the briefcase."

"How long do you think that deception will last?"

"Kornbluth isn't showing people what he's got. He has no reason to open that envelope. By the time he does he'll never know when the switch was made. And by then, who cares?"

He read the doubt on my face. Before I put up an argument he hurried on to his next point. "While I'm gone, you duck into the market at the corner for half a pound of ground chuck." I looked blank. "In case there's a dog."

"Al . . ."

"We're not talking attack dog, there's a little girl in the house. Maybe a family pooch."

Vecchi's eyes were dancing. I couldn't believe this. He was like a kid on his way to the circus.

CHAPTER THIRTEEN

On the drive to Encino I tried to get Vecchi to open up about himself. Partly I didn't want to think about what I was about to do, because then I might not do it. And partly I was curious about this short chunk of New York who had insinuated himself into my life. Until now we had talked almost exclusively about me and my problems.

And that, it turned out, was how it was going to remain. All that a couple of dozen questions from me yielded from Vecchi was that he was a bachelor (I had already guessed that), lived alone near Arthur Avenue in the traditionally Italian part of the Bronx, hung out mostly with cops and ex-cops, and made a pretty good zuppa di pesce—good enough to impress the women who drifted into his life and, apparently, out again. Further pressing revealed that in his twenties he had thought he would marry, but his widowed mother didn't like any of the women he brought around. By his thirties he had stopped bringing them around and stopped thinking of mar-

riage. His mother died about a year ago and he was
starting to think about it again. But not often. And
that was it. No surprises, and by then we were in
Encino.

The address we were looking for turned out to be
on the south side of Ventura, the pricey side, but not
so far up the hill as to be among the really substantial properties. The house was a neo-Deco ranch,
probably twenty years old—a transitional house for
Kornbluth if his career continued on its present up-
ward path. In two years he could be on the other
side of the hill and into the Beverly Hills school district. Heaven.

I drove slowly past the house while Vecchi gave it a
steely once-over, and then I turned a few corners
and came back at it again, this time even slower. The
plan was for Vecchi to slip out for a closer inspection
without my bringing the car to a complete stop. A
car parked on the street in that neighborhood
would raise more alarms than a loose tiger.

All the lights in the house were out; that was
something. Vecchi had fixed the switch on the car's
interior overhead light so it wouldn't go on when he
opened the door. He gave me a reassuring wink and
slipped out, surprisingly loose, between the Kornbluth house and the one south of it. His girth, it was
clear from the way he ran, was more muscle than
bloat. Bent double, taking cover from the heavy
shrubbery and looking like a heavy shrub himself,
he moved rapidly toward the rear of the target
house, Dunsinane Forest on the move. The package
of ground chuck was sticking out of his pocket. I
kept driving. I was to come back for him in five minutes. The street was quiet; in my present mood, eerily quiet.

Three or four blocks away a police car was patroling slowly. Both occupants looked my way as I drove past, a kid and a veteran. I made a point of looking straight back at them, self-righteously middle-class respectable. But I held my breath until they turned a corner. And I took care not to cross their path again.

At just about the five-minute mark, I was approaching the Kornbluth house and there was no Vecchi. I had no intention of stopping, but I slowed to almost zero. Before I was past, a large bush in the foundation planting stirred and parted, and disgorged Vecchi, who glided to the car and in. I never had to come to a full stop. It couldn't have gone smoother.

"Leave this for your maid," Vecchi said, and handed me the ground chuck. "I don't have one. There's no dog. What there is is double-hung windows, and hardly anyone ever bothers to lock all of those. I opened the one in the kitchen for you, left rear. Watch out for splinters on the sill."

I drove back down to Ventura and parked. Among the commercial properties on Ventura a parked car was no big deal. My understanding with Vecchi was that this was my B. and E. and I was the one who would have to do it. We switched places and Vecchi drove us back up the hill while I folded his blank pages and tucked them under my belt. My stomach was doing little flip-flops. At Kornbluth's house we repeated the earlier drill, only this time I was the one who slipped out of the slowly moving car and made a dash for the shrubbery. The smell of the damp grass was unaccountably comforting.

As Vecchi had promised, a window at the rear left corner of the house was open a few inches from the bottom. I raised it as quietly as I could—it stuck some—and hoisted myself over the sill and in. No splinters. I could see where people with no special skills might be attracted to this line of work. It was only when my foot touched the no-waxy-buildup kitchen floor that a wave of guilt passed through me for violating the law, the Kornbluths' privacy, and my own code of decency. What sustained me was my righteous anger at Kornbluth for having pushed me to this tacky behavior.

There was no dog, but there was a cat. He came in through the doorway to the pantry, stretched sleepily, stared at me, and turned around and went back to the pantry. So much for watch cats. I didn't want to leave heel scuffs on the freshly waxed floor—why punish Mrs. Kornbluth?—and I tiptoed through to the living-dining room.

This was not a traditional center hall house and it took me a minute to get my bearings. When I did, I headed for the large foyer at the front door, where I fully expected to find the briefcase, as Vecchi had predicted, in or near the entrance closet. It had better be there. No way was I going to violate the sanctity of the Kornbluths' bedroom.

But a little prowling in the dark revealed that there was no entrance closet. This wasn't the East, where every house needs a closet handy to the front door to stash winter outerwear. In this climate the architect had chosen to dedicate entrance closet space to a larger foyer. And no briefcase was visible anywhere in that flagstoned foyer.

I made my way back to the living room. By now my eyes had adjusted to the dark and I could see the furniture well enough. Probably too well. It was North Carolina standard, and pretty tired from having been lugged around the country during Kornbluth's meteoric career rise. The Kornbluths were waiting for the next move, the big one, before buying new pieces. Or, if the divorce came first, Mrs. K. and her daughter would have to make do into the foreseeable future with this junk and Kornbluth would furnish a little high-rise apartment in Santa Monica with some sleek Italian pieces that would announce his new life. Meanwhile there was no briefcase on any of this stuff, or under it, or beside it.

Kornbluth had brought the briefcase home, I was sure of that. Then what had he done with it? The drink at Jimmy's was less likely to have fired him up for homework than for still another drink at home. And he had told me tonight would be his first night home early in weeks, so it may also have provided his wife a chance to engage him in a serious discussion of the state of their marriage. That wouldn't have led to the clarity of mind necessary for a homework session either. All things considered, I doubted Kornbluth had really expected to open that briefcase and dig into some catch-up work tonight. My guess was he had taken his briefcase from the office for the sole purpose of scaring me with that show-and-tell at Jimmy's. So, again, where had he deposited the briefcase?

If there was a home office, the case could be on or near the desk, unopened, ready to be carried back to the network in the morning. I went back to the foyer. By now I wasn't even walking that carefully; I had noticed that the floor was a typical southern California poured slab, and absolutely creakproof. My likeliest route took me up a corridor toward what had to be the bedroom area. With only one child, Kornbluth might well have turned a spare bedroom into an office. There were many doors and several optional turns. A big house. The Kornbluths had bought it when things were still good between them. If he didn't move up, they must have figured, they could raise a large family here.

It was hard to keep my bearings. No walls were at right angles to each other, for no better reason, as far as I could see, than that the architect had wanted it so. By now I was less frightened by my surroundings than irritated by the capricious layout. But the door at the far end of the spur on which I now found myself would have to be the master bedroom. There were two other doors. One was open and I stuck my head in.

It was a sort of library-den-TV room. There was no desk. I circled the room anyway, making my way carefully around the cheap plastic toys scattered on the floor; I didn't want to step on anything that was going to honk. No sign of the briefcase. I was beginning to wonder why I had ever thought the damn thing would simply present itself to be taken.

Back in the corridor again, I considered the door opposite the den, only because it was closed. I turned the knob and eased it open a couple of inches.

And found myself looking into a cherubic face no more than a few feet from me in a bed along the wall. As soon as the door opened, the little girl's eyes snapped open too. She was looking right at me and I waited for the scream. Instead, she closed her eyes again and I closed the door. Heart in my mouth, I sprinted for the kitchen. It was going to take that kid about twenty seconds to decide that what she saw wasn't part of a dream.

The scream came as I hit the sill of the open window and caught a splinter. It was followed by "Mommy! Mommy!" I was out the window, had it closed, and was headed for the shrubbery by the time I saw a light go on somewhere in the house. I hunched down among the azaleas and didn't move a muscle. Four of five minutes that seemed more like twenty went by before the light went out again. Mommy, or Daddy, had finally convinced their daughter that she had been right the first time, I was only a bad dream.

Vecchi and I had had no way of setting a time for him to pick me up, since we hadn't known how long I would be in the house. He drove by once while the light was on, but I was afraid to make a dash for the car with one or both Kornbluths out of bed. That light must have caused Vecchi some sweat. But he knew to keep coming back until I showed.

Scrunched down among the bushes I had plenty of time to speculate about the little Mercedes two-door parked near me in the driveway, its nose close to the garage door. Kornbluth's, no doubt. His wife's car would be inside, probably a wagon that crowded her half of the two-car garage. His side would be too cluttered with the junk he had promised to clean out weeks ago to allow for the Mercedes.

Kornbluth's car. Was it possible, was it just possible, he had never bothered to take the briefcase into the house? It was, if our meeting at Jimmy's had been the sole reason for his having removed the briefcase from his office at the network. But would he really leave that richly tooled leather briefcase in the car? In New York, never. In Encino?

Vecchi was nowhere on the horizon. I scuttled the few yards to the driver's side door and peered in. The dark upholstery and dashboard absorbed what little light there was. I could make out nothing. I crept around to the passenger side.

Here too at first I thought I had drawn a blank, because the briefcase was nearly the same color as the upholstery. But then its outline gradually emerged from the background, like a photo print in a developer bath. The briefcase was lying on the front passenger seat. The door was unlocked.

A town of abiding faith, Encino.

PART TWO

L.A. TO N.Y.

CHAPTER FOURTEEN

The plane rolled on to the end of the takeoff line reasonably on schedule. *Boynton's New Life*—that grabby title had me green with envy—lay on my lap in a fresh manila envelope, still unread. My attention was on my mimosa, domestic champagne plus orange juice from concentrate, one of the amenities that came with the first-class ticket the network was obliged to buy me at about triple the coach fare. My seatmate was unfolding his laptop computer and organizing his spreadsheets; every so often on an L.A. trip I would be reminded that movies and television weren't the only industries in southern California. This corporate type had stared at the bump on my head while he loosened his necktie, but he had said nothing. He was not going to be a talker. Good. I could do without distractions.

I had sensed the night before that if I read *Boynton* then and was disturbed by its contents, sleep would never come. Even under ideal conditions I would have had only five hours of sack time. I had

decided not to open the envelope until I was aloft
and could give Stavros my undivided attention. And
I was sticking to my resolve. I nursed the mimosa.

A few minutes later we were airborne, and I
thought it best to wait until the FASTEN SEAT BELT sign
went off before opening the envelope. And a few
minutes after that, when the sign went dark, fate
intervened in the form of a service table a steward-
ess slipped between me and *Boynton's New Life*. I dutifully consumed every last scrap of a honey-drip-
ping, sickly sweet breakfast while *Boynton* weighed
heavily on my legs. When the dishes were cleared,
my seatmate did not take out the computer and
spreadsheets he had tucked away while he break-
fasted. Instead he cleared his throat, leaned toward
me, and spoke. "Any idea what the movie is?" he
asked gravely.

I said, "Sorry, no." For a moment I entertained
the wild notion of delaying my chore another couple of hours while I watched the movie. But only for
a moment. "I've got to work," I said, as if he or
anybody cared.

"Okay if I lower the shade?" he asked, and did so
before I could answer. The movie was beginning.

I turned on my overhead pinlight. I undid the
clasp on the envelope that held the pages I had
stolen and took them out. There were six. The first
consisted in its entirety of the following:

BOYNTON'S NEW LIFE
A Television Series
by
Nicholas Stavros

That title again. One of the ad agencies that make
preseason predictions on the new shows would no

doubt praise it for being on the cutting edge of the trend toward "dead-ass" titles. I stared at the page. Of course this was not "A Television Series" but, at best, a proposal for one. But I was nitpicking. Stalling, actually.

I finished the coffee I had been husbanding and turned the page. The work had been composed on a typewriter with a tired ribbon and down-at-heels keys. And the copy in my hands was a carbon. I hadn't seen a carbon in years. Not since my eyes had begun to dim. So on more than one count this would not be an easy read.

Stavros's spelling was shaky but no worse than his grammar. The voice was self-conscious. Or was that me? There was no style, just one word butted up against the next, something like laying sod. Nothing in the way this piece was put together suggested it was the work of a writer.

I read it through to the end as well as I could. Stavros had used the same sheet of carbon paper for the entire opus and I had to hold the last page directly under my pinlight to make it out. I stumbled from word to word and felt that to be fair I should read the piece a second time before I made any sort of judgment on it. This time I took notes as I read. Afterward I tilted my seat back, closed my eyes, and made a conscious effort to be objective. I didn't have to consult the notes.

I could see why Kornbluth hadn't wanted me to read this. It wasn't *Corrigan*. Close, but no cigar. I could point out areas of clear difference. Big chunks. And yet . . . and yet it was eerily close. There were enough—coincidences?—to stir the juices and raise a few questions. Would the answers come down on Stavros's side? I thought probably not, almost certainly not. But this was a subject on which nobody was going to ask me to be a judge.

I tried to tot up a score on the key points of similarity. Most of them were obvious. Boynton and Corrigan were both aging inner-city cops in eastern cities who had been worn down by their jobs—the escalation of random violence, the seeming hopelessness of fighting the drug scourge, corruption in the department, you name it. With the aim of escaping from this treadmill to oblivion, both took early retirement and moved to more wholesome environments in the West—Boynton to a cattle ranch a great-uncle had left him in Colorado, Corrigan to a heavily mortgaged fruit farm in Washington State he had bought years ago, sight unseen, as a refuge against the insanity of the inner city.

In Boynton's first season on the ranch, his cattle were decimated by anthrax, and he had to take on a little private detective work on the side to make ends meet. Corrigan had built his dream on an ad that had been more hopeful than factual. In his first month on his undernourished farm—no amount of sweat would ever bring that rocky hillside up to the promise of the ad—his pear crop was lost to a drought and he was obliged to take a job in the sheriff's office to meet the mortgage payments. Boynton's ranch was managed by a grizzled ex-uranium prospector. Corrigan's farm was supervised by a grizzled Tulalip Indian. Both Boynton and Corrigan got quickly involved with local women.

Plenty of similarities thus far, but so what? None of them were so rare they couldn't have occurred to two or more writers at the same time. And neither the woman in my proposal, nor any of my other running characters, *closely* resembled those in Stavros's. And the murder cases that pulled the two ex-cops reluctantly back to police work were in most ways different.

The only other major point of similarity between Corrigan and Boynton was the way the two men went about dealing with the locals and solving their cases—the play of big-city savvy, cynicism, and abrasiveness against the mellow rural background, and the consequences thereof. This interplay would be a major force in both series long after their pilot stories were forgotten and their running characters shuffled and reshuffled. It was the single element most likely to make either Boynton or Corrigan—whichever outline was recognized as having created that element—to be considered a valuable and unique property.

Was it valuable enough for a plagiarism action? Forget Stavros; had I devised anything unique here? Development ideas in dramatic television were as plentiful as locusts, except that they didn't wait seven years to descend; the plague was perpetual. And at this late date, were there any permutations in the character of the fictional detective that still remained to be explored? Hadn't relentless mining in this vein, to change the metaphor, just about exhausted the gold?

At this late date all that really differentiated one cop, private eye, insurance investigator, or D.A. from the next was the writer's skill of execution. And Stavros, from his arthritic outline, was an amateur, without even the amateur's passion. If he had lived in Idaho and hollered plagiarism from Boise, he would have been dismissed without a moment's hesitation as a paranoid crank. But he lived in New York, I ate at his sister's restaurant, and we had brushed against each other. Some judge, some jury—worse, the network or our movie star—might conclude that

I was a thief, that I had committed, in Alex Stavros's phrase, the worst kind of theft—I had entered his brother's mind and stolen his imagination.

I didn't want to think about this anymore—about what had gone before or what might lie ahead. I turned out my light, put on the earphones, and stared at the movie.

CHAPTER FIFTEEN

Burned out is the usual condition of L.A. in April, something like an Andalusian olive grove in summer. In mid-April, L.A. looks like a photograph in sepia, while New York is one in black and white. If I had come back to New York a couple of weeks later, the trees would have been newly in leaf with that cool green I forget I've missed until I see it again. Green forgives all; it would have softened the edges of the city's harsh verticals and masked some of the grit. On this ride in from the airport the city was raw. Or so it seemed through the down I was in.

My apartment didn't lift my spirits any. My thirsty plants drooped, my bag hitting the floor made a forlorn sound. There was no yapping dog, no kids scrambling for a hug, no shout of greeting or anger from the wife, no smile from the hired help, no smell of cooking or of life. After more than a year I still hadn't gotten used to the deathlike silence. Or this uncaring apartment. I slipped easily into my self-pitying mode.

The one sign of life was the answering machine blinking madly. I didn't take the time to punch up my messages. I shoved my bag in a corner and called the number Vecchi had pressed on me when we separated the night before. A voice boomed, "Axel Locksmith." I asked for Irving and the same voice boomed, "Irving here," and went into a coughing jag I thought would end only in asphyxiation.

When Irving rejoined the living, I gave him my name and told him Al Vecchi had suggested he might be able to help me with this problem I was having . . .

Irving didn't put me through a song and dance. He cut in with, "He called. From California. Some world, Al Vecchi in L.A. He said you're in a kind of hurry. Who isn't? I'm here till eight, what's the address?"

"My address? You want to meet me here?"

"After. The address of the place you're, uh . . . having trouble with the lock."

"Just a minute." This was happening faster than I expected, but the faster the better. I flipped through the phone book and found Nicholas Stavros, the only one in the book. I gave him the name, and the address on West End Avenue.

"That's good," he said. "That's very good." He didn't give me a chance to ask why. He asked for my address and when I gave it to him he said, "Stay home till I get there, boychik. Any time after ten." He hung up and I punched up my messages.

The first was from my kids. Although they hadn't a clue when I was arriving, they had called to welcome me home. They had argued and giggled into the phone at the same time and I couldn't make out much of what they said, but I was grateful for their enthusiasm.

The next call was from Sergeant Dunleavy, LAPD. He sounded for all the world like a jilted lover. Why had I failed him by leaving town without so much as a word? I was please not to disappoint him again, but was instead to keep him informed of all my movements whatsoever, as he might need my help in the course of his ongoing criminal investigation. Underneath the verbiage the tone was unmistakable: "Don't fuck with me."

I fast-forwarded through most of Wolf Waxroth. He had called to inquire whether I got home okay, did I have a pleasant trip, and to please call him if any problems developed. Who did he think I'd call? He's the one I give the ten percent to.

Werner Blau had called to remind me to shoot my script changes back to his office soonest, as he wanted to "crank up the preproduction machinery on this mother before somebody throws a wrench in it." That concern I understood.

The next message, essentially the same but softer, was from brother Seth. Neither Blau got into how I was supposed to make the changes they were panting for. I didn't have their notes as yet, or anybody else's. But I wasn't about to call the Blaus and start negotiating over delivery dates. Producers always wanted scripts soonest, but when you delivered them that way they wondered why you hadn't taken the time to make them better.

I didn't recognize the voice on the last message—female and melting: "I just wanted to say hi, and how really good it was to see you. And to remind you of your promise next time you come out." For a wild moment I thought it was Jenny, the girl at the beach. But even as I realized how unlikely that was, the voice was finishing the message, short and sweet. "It's Sarah Cole, Mike."

Sarah. I wasn't sure why, but I liked that even better. For some reason a story of Sarah's in a university quarterly Rudd once gave me popped into my head —a vignette of a young couple playing out a fight that would bind them in loving misery for the next fifty years. A portrait to remember, without a wasted word.

I called the kids. Benjy picked up, so I wasn't obliged to make civilized small talk with Helene. I told him I was back in New York and would pick him and his sister up for the weekend on Saturday morning, and to please tell Mommy. No, it wasn't necessary to get her to the phone. With my blessing she could stay at the library until her eyes turned to Jell-O. I refrained from sharing that sentiment with her children.

There would be nearly three hours before the earliest time Irving said he would show. I unpacked and took a shower and reminded myself again to get a new showerhead. I saw no reason to ape the charm of the Desert Palm.

I needed an excuse to get out of the apartment and I found one easily enough. I hadn't eaten since that sticky-sweet breakfast on the plane and there was nothing in the house but two bags of coffee beans in the freezer.

A few minutes later I was walking the three blocks to Christine's without having given the decision any more advance thought than that Christine was not likely to be back from L.A., and if she was, it was likely she would not have returned to work. At this hour I would have no trouble getting a table. It was after eight and the diners with tickets to Lincoln Center events would be long gone.

Christine's had been my safe harbor this past year.

Walking in there felt more like coming home than opening the door of my brownstone. The waitress who seated people when Christine wasn't on hand greeted me with a generous smile, and I got nods of recognition from others of the staff. Despite all that had happened this place still felt good to me. The room was too austere to be homelike, but on the other hand nothing about it offended. The food was never trendy and almost always better than it had to be at the price.

I signaled Beryl that I wasn't ready for a table, and I took a seat at the nearly empty bar. In the earliest months of the divorce I had done a lot of boozy thinking about my foundering life at that bar. More recently, as my drinking dropped off to the social level, it had been the site of an occasional creative flash that had moved *Corrigan* along. The pudgy bartender, Toby, greeted me in the rich bass-baritone voice he had long hoped in vain would catch the attention of the management people from the New York City Opera and the Met who occasionally came in to Christine's. In the course of a running update this past year, Toby had told me more than I cared to hear about his "I'm right at the edge of making it" singing career, including the character flaws of his ever-changing vocal coaches, the dates of his upcoming gigs in outlying churches and synagogues, and the progress he was making in matching his head voice to his chest voice. Toby was thirty-seven and mixed a perfect martini and I felt badly for his wasted life, most especially when my thoughts were on mine.

"I was thinking of you," he said. "Last time you were in you said you were going to L.A., and Christine is out there. I guess you didn't go."

"I just got back."

"That was fast. That's how Christine left here. Fast. She was a mess. Her brother died. The baby, Niko."

"I heard."

"Oh, sure, you knew Niko."

"I didn't know him, Toby. Only about enough to say hello."

"Any idea how he went? Christine was too upset to say much. You heard about it out there? Some kind of accident?"

"Something like that."

"Niko, poor miserable bastard. Did he ever have a happy day in his life? Nothing went right for Niko. Ever. That kind of loser, after a while the frustration —you know?—it shows in their face."

It was just starting to show in Toby's. I said, "I know what you mean."

Toby said, "You had to know him more than to say hello. Niko hated your guts."

"He had no reason to."

"He'd sit here at night when we were closing and I was trying to do the register, and I'd have to go through my figures three times because Niko'd be bitching in my ear about how you stole—I don't know, that TV idea he had. I tried not to listen. The Nikos of this town can bore you to death. Someone else is always the reason they fail, you know? I was surprised you gave him the time of day."

"That's about what I gave him. The time of day."

"After a while, right. After a while everybody caught on to Niko. But at first, when you'd be waiting at the bar until the place thinned out—"

"Toby, I never come in here until the Lincoln Center crowd is gone."

"*Now*. You learned. But the first few months you came in? It'd be early and you'd wait at the bar.

Back then you needed this bar. Not my opinion, you'd say so yourself. And while you were waiting Niko would zoom in on you, one pro to another, sucking around, trying to make shop talk. Mr. Show Biz. Pitiful guy.''

"That may have happened," I said. "Once. I don't talk television with people who aren't in the business. They always get around to what's Bruce Willis, or Carol Burnett, or Ted Danson, really like. How the hell would I know? I'm not sure what *I'm* really like.''

"Still, you're a minor celebrity here—''

"All the place deserves. It's a minor restaurant," I said. "Except for its major drinkmaster.''

He wasn't going to be sidetracked by flattery. "Mike, you talk to people. I don't know who in here first spotted your name on some TV rerun, but you get pointed out." He had been making a Beefeater martini for me, up, and now he set it before me and finished it off with a twist. "I've seen guys come up to you. They start by asking, like, do you know their cousin in L.A. in the business. You handle them nicely. You ask them what they do, turn them on to talking about themselves.''

"It works.''

"Not with Niko. He would never talk about that store in here. Nature's Buddy. Never. He really hated that place. You didn't see that?''

I was taking my first sip of the drink, a perfect, icy jolt I hadn't realized I needed. "No. I told you, I pretty much steered clear of Niko.''

"That store was just something to hold him until he made it big writing his movies or plays or something. To tell you the truth, I think Christine set him up in that store. Christine and her brothers. Did you know she has three more brothers?''

"I met a couple."

"No kidding? They never come in here. But I mean never. I think this place is too tony for them. They've got a diner up in the nineties, the Odyssey, the Cyclops—I don't know, one of those names the Greeks give diners. Green pepper in the chicken salad, that's as daring as they get. I can't say absolutely, but my hunch is they backed Christine in this place. Smart move. By now she must outgross them two to one. You know how much Yankee bean soup they'd have to sell? How much rice pudding? Their mistake was to back Niko. Nature's Buddy is a bomb." He took his first breath; it was all that diaphragm control. "He never complained to you?"

"No."

"Right, he didn't like to talk about the place. And with you the talk would be on writing. Two pros swapping notes on the creative process. Not to speak ill of the dead, but did he have a nerve? I had to fight to keep from laughing out loud."

"You may have thought it happened, Toby, but we never talked about writing."

"Listen, can I blame you for forgetting? Niko was world-class forgettable."

I said, "Do you mind? I'm going to take this drink to a table and order, because I've got a business meeting after dinner and I want to stay sharp. So if I ask you to do it again, don't. Okay?"

I signaled Beryl and had her seat me at a table toward the back of the room, as far from the bar as I could get.

CHAPTER SIXTEEN

Irving buzzed my apartment at ten-twenty and I went downstairs and let him in. The two-story climb left him winded and chalky-looking. He stood in my doorway until he had brought up a couple of ounces of phlegm, some of it, by the eloquence of his cough, from as far away as his big toe. He was a large man in every direction, a suitable repository for the booming voice and the search-and-destroy cough. He sized me up doubtfully while he lit a cigarette and his face regained what I supposed was its normal color, ash gray. I was not what he expected, but Al Vecchi had vouched for me, so he resigned himself to continuing to do what he had promised. I took his early arrival, correctly, as a sign that things had gone smoothly at Nick Stavros's building.

After very brief amenities he said, "First, you never met me, you never even laid eyes on me."

I nodded. "I don't even know your name."

"There you're right. It isn't Irving. Second, I'm going to give you three keys. When you're finished with them, throw them out in your garbage. Deep in your garbage, maybe in a grapefruit rind. You understand that what you're getting ready to do is illegal? Have you ever done anything like this before?"

"Not today."

"Okay." He didn't know whether or not to be reassured by my answer. "The apartment you're interested in is located in a twelve-story building. Prewar. The elevators are self-service, but there's a twenty-four-hour doorman, so coming in through the lobby is out. This first key will open the basement door. It's around the uptown corner from the entrance. Once you're in you'll see the elevators dead ahead. You should wait till after one A.M., when there's less likely to be action in the building. These are mostly business and professional people with families. They keep regular hours. You might as well know, the elevators are very slow. The apartment you want is nine E. Turn right when you get out of the elevator. This key opens the upper lock and this one the lower. Make sure you remember which is which. That's all there is to it."

I said, "Can I ask how you managed this so fast?"

He took a beat. "I could tell you I'm a genius. I am, but in this case you were lucky. Or Vecchi took an educated guess because this is my neighborhood. That building happens to be one where I've done a certain amount of legitimate locksmithing. The building works off a set of master keys. And that's all I'm going to say."

"Thanks, Irving. I really do appreciate what you've done. What do I owe you?"

"I wouldn't know how to bill for this particular service. Anyway, it's compliments of Al Vecchi."

"Is he . . . ?"

"Paying? No. Al is compliments of me. For good

and sufficient reasons too painful to go into. Suffice it to say I've owed him for five years. Good luck, and be real careful. I'd recommend sneakers." He took a final drag on his cigarette, pinched it out with his fingers, put the butt in his pocket, and clumped heavily down the stairs.

I waited until after twelve-thirty before going out and I didn't like the waiting. The night before, I hadn't had time to think; the decision to burglarize Kornbluth was followed immediately by the burglary itself. I didn't like dwelling now on what might go wrong. True, there would be no one home tonight, but there were also more ways of messing up. I ran them through my head once and shut the door on them when I felt my palms starting to go sweaty.

Only the hope of finally getting Stavros off my back could make me go through with this—although if he had been running a bluff, as I felt sure he had been, and I came up empty at his place, I would have taken this dumb chance for nothing. Big risks here; were the rewards worth them? I made myself stop analyzing why I was so hell-bent on the caper. I wanted my head clear for what lay ahead.

So I busied myself with picking a wardrobe for the night's work. I put on the closest I had to cat-burglar clothes—a navy turtleneck, jeans, black running shoes, and a forest-green wool cardigan. No outer garment. I didn't own one dark enough. Better underdressed and maneuverable than bulky and highly visible. I had a vagrant thought as I left the apartment: would Trig Bascomb agree to do a scene in which he picked out clothes suitable for committing a crime?

* * *

The night air had sharpened and I considered taking a taxi. Not to Stavros's building but somewhere close. There were plenty of cabs but in the end I played it safe, probably safer than necessary, and I walked. Columbus, Amsterdam, and Broadway were all pretty much deserted at nearly one in the morning on a weekday in April. I gave a wide berth to the few loners I passed. The odds were that some of them, like me, were criminals on their way to work. Crumpled newspapers blew past me, the tumbleweed of the Upper West Side.

I got to Stavros's building at a few minutes after one. It stood on a stretch of West End Avenue that was a bastion of bland middle-class respectability—not the sort of building a hotshot would-be writer would select for his bachelor pad but well in the ballpark for the owner of Nature's Buddy. Carved in stone and set amid Gothic doodads above the front door was its name, The King Arthur. I peered in the brightly lighted lobby as I walked slowly by, and I took in the lusterless marble walls and the furniture, lobby-medieval. The last thing I saw was the skinny young Hispanic doorman seated in a camp chair behind a sign that said ALL VISITORS MUST BE ANNOUNCED. He was wearing a jacket many doormen had worn before him, and he was reading the *News*. He looked both fit and awake. I walked around the corner in search of the basement door.

I had no trouble finding it. Tomorrow was evidently garbage collection day. The huge black plastic bags that would still be leakproof five thousand years after my series proposal and Stavros's had crumbled to a fine powder were piled high at the curb in front of a door marked SERVICE ENTRANCE. They formed a nearly ideal protective shield. I had key number one at the ready and I slipped quickly inside the door. Now that I was on the move, my nervousness was fading.

There were two elevator doors, but no visual display to indicate what floor the cars were on. The co-op board may have voted to save a few bucks here in the basement. I listened at both shafts and detected no movement, so I pushed the call button. There was a clank and then the whine of a descent that sounded very far off. Naturally. At this hour the elevators would be sitting at the floors of the residents they had delivered home for the night, most of them at seven o'clock, in time for dinner with the kids.

Irving had not exaggerated when he said the elevators were slow. Eventually the car thunked to a stop at my level and the door lumbered open. Not a lot of money had gone into updating this equipment. I got in and reached for the ninth-floor button. And decided not to press it. Why mark where I was headed? I punched ten. The door lumbered closed.

The car moved slowly enough so that I had time to read the initials delivery boys had scratched in the door panel. All of them. Above the door a device too sleek for the antique car announced the floors in oversized numbers that seemed to lap-dissolve from one number to the next. Probably one of the "modernizing" touches introduced when the building went co-op. The display stayed on 7 even longer than the near eternity it had spent on each of the previous numbers. And then it dawned on me that the car was easing imperceptibly to a stop. Here at seven.

The door lumbered open. A couple stood in the opening staring at me in confusion. I stared back noncommittally, my gut clenching. They were in their thirties, good-looking, dressed, probably, for a

dinner party, she in silk, he in his good suit from
Saks, the two of them more than slightly flushed
from wine. The woman said, "Oh. Are you going
down?"

I said, "Up."

The man said, "I told you you pushed the wrong
button." To me he said, "Sorry. We might as well
get in." He had his wife—date?—by the elbow and
he propelled her into the car. Wife. The door took
its time closing and we started up.

The woman giggled and carefully adjusted the silk
at her neckline. She said, "How is it out?"

I said, "Getting colder."

She turned to her husband. "I was afraid of that.
Aren't you dying to get on that plane?"

That was the entire dialogue while the car was
moving. After an eternity it eased to a stop at ten,
and I got out. The man called after me, "Have a
pleasant evening."

"Good night," I called back. Behind me the door
groaned closed. We've had our evening, Buster.
We're well into the night.

I waited for the car to start and then I found the
service stairs and made my way down to the ninth
floor. I had put keys two and three in separate pockets, along with a pair of leather gloves. There were
seven or eight apartments on the floor and not a
sound from any of them. By the time I found 9E I
had the gloves on and a key in each hand. I had less
trouble getting into this apartment than into my
room at the Desert Palm. I closed and double-locked
the door behind me and stood with my back to it
until, with help from a nearly full moon, I got used
to the dark.

I did a quick walk-through. The place wasn't
much. A box. Living room, bedroom, kitchen, prob-

ably the smallest unit in the building. Stavros had worked at trying to turn it into a bachelor writer's pad. It hadn't been easy. For one, he didn't seem to be much of a reader. I saw a solitary skinny book-case, and nearly half of that was taken up by thickets of men's adventure magazines. They might have been a cash outlet for his writing, possibly his only one. Of the books, several were of the "How to Write for the Marketplace" variety, and the rest were fiction classics probably bought for a college survey course, Highlights of the Nineteenth-Century Novel.

But elsewhere there were hints of a Renaissance man who may have tried to impress female visitors to the apartment. A coffee table held a chessboard with the pieces set up. They were the artsy sculptural kind that take too long to recognize to be of practi-cal use. I lifted one—a bishop?—and even by moon-light I could see the circle where the piece had kept the dust at bay. At one end of the living room, a tennis racquet, a hockey stick, and a soccer ball made a free-form arrangement. The sportsman at home. Nearby, an antique steamer trunk, circa the *Berengaria,* had a pipe rack on its lid loaded with clunky, gnarled specimens that Stavros had probably spent a lot of time cleaning when he was thinking about what to write. The currents had run deep with this guy. Above the leather couch a travel poster of Delphi commanded an entire wall, art's contribu-tion to the decor. The final decorating idea was nailed to another wall, a "School of Navajo" rug.

I pulled down the shades and turned on a couple of lights. I didn't feel the least embarrassment nos-ing about, the way I had at the Kornbluths' the night before. I already knew that the dead can't be libeled. I now decided that by extension neither can their privacy be invaded. The large metal office desk in the bedroom, topped with an ancient Royal standard typewriter and clearly the creative hub of the flat, would be the most likely location for a nine-by-twelve or thereabouts mailing envelope with U.S. Postal Service registration markings. I riffled through the detritus on the surface of the desk, a mishmash of unpaid bills and what appeared to be a number of stabs at the opening paragraph of a story. Then I checked the contents of the three desk drawers. Nothing.

Not what I was looking for, anyway. The drawers were stuffed with Stavros's manuscripts—complete and fragmentary screenplays, a novel, short stories. Action-adventure stuff. But I was surprised to see that the son of a bitch had really worked at writing. Worked long, and seemingly hard. I interpreted a twinge in the pit of my stomach as my first slight hint of sympathy for him. He had plugged into the writer's isolation and frustration at that typewriter. We were brothers of a sort. I shook off the feeling and went back to the search.

There weren't that many places to look—a walk-in closet in the bedroom, a smaller one in the tiny entrance hall, two chests of drawers in the bedroom, and the steamer trunk and a couple of drawers in a table in the living room. I rummaged through them all. I was able to do it quickly because I only cared about a large piece of registered mail. I was relieved when I didn't find it. That supported my belief that Stavros had been bluffing. I turned out the living room light. So far, so good.

But I had gone to too much trouble to give up this easily. If there was an envelope, the most likely resting place for it would be that desk in the bedroom. I went back to it to make a final check. Had I missed something in the clutter on its surface? This time I sifted through the layers of papers more carefully. Some of the bills were personal—clothes, apartment maintenance, more clothes, liquor store—and some were for merchandise delivered to Nature's Buddy. Most of the latter were marked "Past Due" or "Remit At Once." And every version I happened to put my hands on of that story Stavros had been trying to start was lousy. But at least he deserved credit for the effort.

Buried beneath the papers I now discovered three or four sticky-edged note squares glued to the desk top. Post-its with cryptic reminders to himself. None of them meant anything to me, but one held my eye. All that was on it was a hastily scrawled phone number with a 213 area code. Stavros had enclosed the number in boxes and circles. A number to be reckoned with. Or not; he may have been doodling while he talked to this person in L.A. I peeled the square off the desk and put it in my pocket. As I did, I heard an elevator clunk to a stop. On this floor, I thought.

It was too late to speculate on whether Stavros's neighbors already knew about his death. If they did, light leaking out from under his front door might get somebody's wind up. I doused the bedroom light as the elevator door groaned open, definitely on this floor. The corridor was surfaced in tile and now footsteps sounded sharply. And then came the sound of a key in a lock. In the door to this apartment.

Had Stavros lent the apartment to a friend when he left for L.A.? Damned if I was going to be trapped into huddling in the bedroom closet all night. As the first lock clicked open, I made a silent tiptoe dash for the hall closet. I pulled the door closed

behind me as I heard the second lock turn and then
the apartment door open.

I flattened myself against the wall behind a couple
of coats and a garment bag that rattled softly. I
waited for the hall light to go on; I would be able to
see the light under the door. But it didn't happen.
Nor were there footsteps. Whoever had come in was
standing near the front door, as I had, waiting to get
used to the dark. I sensed the continuing presence. I
was almost sure I could hear breathing. Time
passed, enough for me to become almost bored. I
wondered whether Niko's brothers would divide his
coats and suits between them, whether they could
even get them on. I doubted it; he had been smaller
than his brothers. A wasted life, and then he was not
much use in death.

Eventually the new arrival walked past my closet
toward the living room. I heard the shades rattle up.
A moment or two later the sounds became violent—
books pushed off shelves, drawers dumped and
thrown to the floor, pipes scattered, a rain of chess
pieces. And then fabric being torn, and what
sounded like the steamer trunk being ripped and
splintered.

The sounds took on a voice and form; they
seemed to be tearing open the night itself. As
alarmed as I was, it was dark enough and the intruder was busy enough back there that I felt it
would be safe to open my closet door a crack. Anything to shake my mounting claustrophobia. I
turned the knob and pushed gently. I was too far
from a window for the moonlight to reach me, but
neither could I see anything at this angle. I opened
the door a bit wider, to get my face partly into the
opening. There was a distinctive smell where the
man, it had to be a man, had stood for a time.

Cheap cigars and body odor. I pushed the door open still further.

I could see the wrecked living room with the couch tipped over and its underbelly slashed. Furnishings were strewn all over the floor. There were more sounds of upholstery being ripped. A moment later the intruder came into my field of view, his back to me in silhouette against a moonlit window. He was slitting the fabric of a chair with a knife and scattering the foam filling. He dropped the chair, went to the wall, and pulled down the Navajo-type rug. For an instant he turned his profile toward me. An instant was all I needed; there wasn't much surprise. I had already half-guessed from the smell. He was the thug who had mugged and nearly murdered me in my room at the Desert Palm.

I closed the closet door and waited until the sounds of pillage moved from the living room to the bedroom. Then I slipped out of the closet and eased through the front door. My heart was racing. I passed up the elevator for the service stairs, half-galloped down the nine flights and then the extra flight to the basement, and got the hell out of there.

The cold night air felt good.

CHAPTER SEVENTEEN

By the time I made my way home at two A.M. even the felons had abandoned the streets. But it would not be too late in Los Angeles to call Al Vecchi. I had a powerful need to talk to someone and he fitted the bill exactly.

The Hollyview switchboard picked up on about the twelfth ring. I had interrupted the operator at supper and she wasn't happy about that but she did put me through. Vecchi picked up on the first ring.

"It's me. Mike. Saldinger. Did I wake you?"

"No, what's up? You did it, huh? Wait, we don't need Eulinda on this. You home? I'll call you back from a pay phone."

He did, about five minutes later, and reversed the charge. He said, "Everything go okay?"

"You tell me. I got in, thanks to your friend Irving, and I went through the place from top to bottom. I didn't find what I was looking for. That part I like. Then I had to duck out of sight because someone came into the apartment."

"Jesus. Came in how?"

"Same as me. With keys. Is Irving running a sale?"

"Don't be funny. Who was it?"

"Wait a minute. The guy trashed the place. I mean, he tore the furniture open, he dumped the drawers, he emptied the bookcase. He was a lot more set on finding that piece of registered mail than me."

"Did you get a look at him?"

"Damn straight. Al, it was Mack the Knife. The guy who mugged me at the Desert Palm."

He took a moment before he said, again, "Jesus." Then he took another moment. "You know what that means?"

"Aside from I wasn't a random mugging victim at the Palm? I'm open to suggestions."

He said, slowly, "The guy who tried to kill you in L.A. shows up in New York with the keys to Stavros's apartment. Taken from Stavros's hotel room. By the man who killed Stavros."

"Exactly. Himself. This creep wants me and Stavros dead and he's halfway home. But why? For the original of Stavros's TV series proposal? Why would I have that anyway? None of it makes sense."

"You're sure you never saw the guy before."

"Just that one time when he nearly blew my brains out in L.A. But it stayed with me."

"It does that. But you know? This is not necessarily about that piece of registered mail. The Stavros proposal. Even if it exists."

"What do you mean? Why else would he search—"

"Listen to me. He was coming east anyway. Because you were coming east and you're . . . well, we know now you're unfinished business. He probably got a free ride to New York on Stavros's credit card. If he has his keys, he has his wallet with the credit cards. And maybe he figured since he was east why not use the keys to take an easy shot at whatever there might be of value in Stavros's apartment?''

"The way he savaged the place—''

"You know how burglars work. They don't take the time to look behind your stuff, or even in it, for the valuables. They dump everything on the floor and hope the goodies shake loose enough to pick up.''

"This guy's no burglar.''

"Maybe not primarily. But can you blame him for going for the easy extra?'' He laid it in. "On his way to settling with you? How safe is your apartment?''

"Very. I picked it partly because I thought I'd be leaving it empty a lot while I was away in L.A. It's the middle floor of a co-op brownstone. Five floors, five owners. There are no balconies, no ledges, and we all chipped in to have the roof alarmed. I lock my windows but I don't have to; this isn't the Desert Palm. It would take a professional acrobat to get at these windows from the outside. I have good locks on my door and the street-door lock is even better. We have an iron-clad rule in the building—no buzzing in of guests. You have to go down to the front door and eyeball anyone who rings your bell.''

Vecchi was unimpressed. "That should do it for tonight. He may figure something out later. Whatever his reasons, he means business with you.'' That was comforting. "In the morning I'll put you together with a detective in the two-four, you'll tell your story, and you'll get police protection.''

"How can I tell the story? I saw the man who's out to kill me, for Chrissake, while I was committing a felony.''

"I know, one I aided and abetted. My second in two days. Never before and never again. Meanwhile you won't tell it that way. You'll say the man who mugged you in L.A. with a gun and a knife has been lurking outside your building. That'll be enough to get some action. Now why don't you try to get some sleep?"

"Good idea. You've got me so drowsy I can hardly keep my eyes open."

"Relax. You're okay tonight, we'll have you okay tomorrow. Oh, before I hang up." He slowed down. "I've been meaning to ask about Stavros's story outline. Once you read the copy you took from Kornbluth you must have decided it was close enough to *Corrigan* that you had to go after the original, huh?"

"Al, what are you looking for? Doesn't that question pretty much answer itself?"

"Good night," he said, and hung up.

I didn't know what time I fell asleep. Add reverse jet lag to everything else that was keeping me awake. I remembered being wide-awake at 5:12 on my clock radio. The next thing I knew the phone was jangling and the clock said 7:52. I felt drugged. It was Vecchi.

I said, "Are you crazy? It isn't even five o'clock in the morning where you are."

He said, "No shit." Then, "Irving woke me."

I knew something was wrong but I wasn't ready to hear it. I said, "Doesn't he know from time zones?"

"He knows. He just saw the local TV news."

"And?" I braced myself for I had no idea what.

"The building you were in last night on West End Avenue? The morning doorman came on at six A.M. and found the night man in the lobby cleaning closet. His throat had been cut."

I said, "God. I saw him. A kid."

"Irving wanted to know what kind of maniac I sent him. It took some time to calm him down. Did anyone see you go in or out of that building?"

"On my way up. A couple in the elevator."

"Would they remember you?"

"They were drunk. But we exchanged a few words. I don't know."

He was silent for a moment. "All things considered, you know what I'm thinking?"

"That I should keep my head down."

"Check. You stick your neck out with the police, expose yourself to those witnesses . . ."

"And I raise a question the LAPD would start asking: did *I* kill Stavros and then use his keys to ransack his apartment and incidentally knock off his doorman? You're telling me to take my chances with Mack the Knife."

"You don't need cops. Your apartment sounds safe enough to me." He had played a different tune last night. "Basically," he went on, "what you want to do is stay home. If you have to go out, do it during the day. I don't have to tell you, on your block keep away from the building line on one side, parked cars on the other. Get in the habit of looking over your shoulder. Don't follow the same route twice. But if you can manage, the best thing is to stay in. I'll be back on Tuesday."

"Meaning?"

"I have no special plans. I can keep an eye on you until we figure this out."

Those words reassured me some. I said, "Thanks, Al. But meanwhile, who is this creep who wants to knock me off? Is he hired help?"

"That's the easy part. But whose?"

We had nothing else useful to say and we hung up. My thoughts were on that dumb . . . Mack the

Knife, would have to do, Mack for short. He had the keys to Stavros's apartment, so he thought he would have it easy. In and out. It had never occurred to him there might be someone on duty in the lobby. Dumb, dumb, dumb.

It was too early for the television networks' eight twenty-five local newsbreak, so I tried the two all-news radio stations. They were both on world affairs. In the few minutes remaining before the television news went on, I called Westchester. The kids would be at school, but I would have to let Helene know I wouldn't be able to take them to the city for the weekend.

I didn't look forward to this announcement and Helene didn't like hearing it. She sensed my evasiveness and she pressed me for a fuller explanation. The best I could do was dither my way through something about "a sudden complication in my life."

She blew up. She had plenty to say. She wound up with, "You knew I was planning a heavy session at the library. I particularly let you know that." Particularly. It was not a construction Helene would have used when I first knew her in her flirty, blond-bombshell, feature-the-cleavage days when she was saved from cliché only by a sense of humor that could buckle my knees with laughter. She said, "It happens the Columbia library will be open late both nights this weekend because it's an exam week at the college. I was planning to drive down and stay until closing."

"Friday and Saturday night at the library?" I said. "Where's the Professor?" "The Professor" was what I called her boyfriend, only partly because he was not yet a professor.

"Richard's out of town, but that's not the point," she went on. "I've got a tremendous nut to crack if I want to finish this thesis by December. I get absolutely no help from you. Are you deliberately out to sabotage me?"

I promised to drive up early on Saturday and take the kids for the day. And then about Sunday I'd have to see. That propelled her to further argument. From her angle I supposed she had a point; maybe I owed her a fuller explanation. Maybe she *deserved* the fuller explanation. It would scare her out of her drawers. But I glanced at my watch—it was 8:23—and I got off fast.

The murdered doorman in the solid middle-class West Side enclave was the lead story on Channel 2. The sequence followed a well-established order: EXTERIOR LONG SHOT of the scene of the crime, that stodgy lump of an apartment house, The King Arthur; ANGLE PANNING the body under a sheet being wheeled out to an ambulance on a gurney; HEAD SHOT, Detective Lieutenant Folsey (his name supered), the frightened neighbors behind him, admitting he had no leads to the grisly crime but that a thorough investigation was already under way; SINGLES and TWO SHOTS of the building's residents variously reporting that they were aware of nothing out of the ordinary occurring overnight on the premises, that this had always been a friendly, trouble-free building, that, in fact—who would have dreamed?— Osvaldo the doorman had hailed a cab for one of them that very evening. The residents described this young man as quiet, unfailingly polite, usually cheery, and a conscientious part-time student at Manhattan Community College.

That was it. No mention of the ravaged Stavros apartment. No one was yet aware it had been ravaged. That was a plus. The longer it took to discover a connection between the doorman's death and the Stavros affair the better for me.

The local news ground on while I continued to stare at the set. I was trying and failing to assemble a theme out of the events of the last few days. I was too close to them to have any real perspective. If I had been able to deal with this mess the way I sometimes dealt with a tangled script—put it in a drawer and take it out a week later to examine with a fresh eye— I might have had a better chance to make sense of it. At the moment the best solution seemed to be to dump the mess in a drawer and leave it there.

While I was chewing this over, something had hit me subliminally off the TV screen. By the time I directed my full attention to the screen, I was looking at an ECU of a cereal box in a breakfast-food commercial. That couldn't have been what had grabbed me. A moment later a wide shot followed. A pretty girl in a sundress on a rolling lawn was laughing as she spooned some soggy bran out of a bowl. A very pretty girl. Where did I know her from?

And then I knew. I wasn't the first person working in television who had thought she was a knockout. She was the wide-eyed, gosh-you're-a-TV-writer innocent, Jenny, my missing alibi for that hour at the Venice beach.

CHAPTER EIGHTEEN

An hour or so later I went downstairs in response to the frontdoor buzzer. Cautiously is how I went. First I checked the logoed truck parked out front through the door window and then the uniform of the Federal Express driver standing expectantly at the door before I opened it and accepted an envelope from him.

Back upstairs I opened the package. Werner Blau's secretary had assembled everyone's script notes: Trig Bascomb's reminder of the two scenes he absolutely wouldn't do, plus a few minor fidgets he had jotted down after I left him; Oscar Kornbluth's twenty-five or so line notes, half of them having to do with the jokes being "too good for the room," meaning he wasn't sure he understood them; Al Vecchi's five or six police procedural cautions; and a few cavils from the Blaus over "character arcs."

The Blau notes came with a scribble from Werner: "Can you send the revise Monday? I'd like to be in production with this yesterday. If you have to, forget everything else and just make Bascomb purr. The rest of this is busywork. It can wait till a director's on board.''

I took the package into my cubbyhole office and fired up the computer and brought *Corrigan's Way* into memory. Werner Blau was more right than he could possibly know. He would be wise to get the pilot rolling—major casting done, sets in work, director and DP off and running—before he was hit by this new scandal. An endless bank of headlines was already wrapping itself tightly around my chest:

MURDERED DOORMAN LINKED TO LA DEATH
Who Is Next In Bizarre Crime Spree?
Police Question Writer Accused of Plagiarism
Trig Bascomb Withdraws From Jinxed
TV Project

And so on. I was in no mood to deal with a real challenge—writing a scene, for instance, to replace Corrigan making dinner for the girl, or Corrigan shopping for clothes. The way to ease into the work was with Kornbluth's notes.

I read through them again. Those that didn't complain about the jokes were the usual mix, some up moves, some down, some sideways—mostly attempts to clarify further what was already clear or even blatantly obvious. (Why couldn't the killer's fingerprints be on the shotgun? Because, Oscar, then you wouldn't need the brilliant Corrigan to solve the crime; any hack could do it.) If I had buttonholed a viewer off the street—any viewer—he would have given me notes not a great deal worse. Or was I being negative because my mind was too full of other subjects to concentrate on the script?

Mack the Knife aside, the subject I most wondered about was a callback I knew wouldn't come for hours, maybe days. I had telephoned a college classmate, Hal Patch, the only person I knew who worked at an ad agency, and given him the name of the cereal in Jenny's TV commercial and described as much of the spot as I had seen. Hal said he would find out what agency had the account and he didn't foresee any problem in eventually getting the actress identified. Before he hung up, he couldn't resist asking if I had fallen in love with her because of the caring way she put the spoon in her mouth.

Stewing over Kornbluth's notes turned out to be counterproductive. After half an hour of false starts, I pushed back from the computer and refocused my gaze out the office window. My favorite urban landscape was the warren of back gardens between my row of brownstones and those on the south side of the block, and now the buds on the few trees in these gardens were fat with promise. Promises of things to come kept Mack the Knife in my thoughts as I scanned the scene. As yet there were no impatient gardeners out trying to turn over the thawing soil. There was nobody back there, not a living soul. Utrillo would have painted the scene that way, and I found myself in total sympathy with Utrillo.

A touch claustrophobic, I walked the long hallway to the bedroom and my other view—north across the street to mellow brownstone fronts with a few accents of early blooming bulbs in window boxes. At the moment the mellowness had been reduced by a fat-assed sanitation truck making late pickups. Its hydraulic jaws were choking back the contents of trash cans with a whine that set my teeth on edge. The empty cans bumped and clanged as they landed back on the sidewalk. And the drivers backed up behind the truck leaned on their horns in a mounting frenzy.

Those drivers said it for me exactly. Ordinarily I could spend days in this apartment if there was work to do, with no pull to leave it, usually without ever bothering to get dressed. But here it was not yet eleven A.M. on my first morning home and I was ready to sound my horn. This was going to be a very long few days.

By Friday afternoon, little more than a day later, everybody's notes had been duly addressed and changes made. The script didn't seem that much worse for my having laid heavy hands on it. I would read it through on the monitor Monday morning before printing a copy for Federal Express to deliver to the Blaus in Burbank.

Despite the many thoughts crowding my concentration, I had finished the revisions in reasonably short order. I credited that partly to never having left the apartment. There was plenty of coffee on hand and I had taken one delivery each—the deliverers carefully screened—from my regular pizza and Chinese take-out joints. Even more central to my efficiency, I had let the answering machine pick up my phone calls and I hadn't returned a single one.

The single distraction had been the speaker on the answering machine; I hadn't been able to resist keeping that on. Surprisingly few of the incoming calls unglued my concentration. There were two or three hang-ups, and those had certainly been attention-getters. Hal Patch had called to say he'd have the name of that commercial actress for me on Monday, but meanwhile—and here he erupted in a dirty chuckle—why didn't I start without her? And at four-fifty on Friday afternoon Sergeant Dunleavy,

LAPD, had called to ask why I hadn't been in touch, and to tell me I might be hearing from a Lieutenant Folsey, NYPD. That one took first prize in the blood-pressure-elevation contest. Happily, by the time it came I had finished the script.

The Dunleavy call sent me scrambling to the TV for the five o'clock local news on Channel 2. Sure enough, the top story was about a new development in the case of the murdered West Side doorman. We were treated to some familiar shots, now file footage: the fateful apartment house where the brutal crime had occurred; the gurney carrying the victim to the ambulance; and the stunned, head-shaking residents of the building. Meanwhile a reporter on voice-over gave us the new development—an apartment on the ninth floor of the King Arthur Apartments had been savagely burglarized, almost certainly on the night of the doorman's murder.

Next, in new footage, Lieutenant Folsey appeared on the screen to report that the burglarized apartment belonged to one Nicholas Stavros, who himself had been murdered in Los Angeles only a few days prior. The badly damaged apartment had been discovered by Stavros's sister, who had gone there to sort out the dead man's effects and had been admitted by the super. The department's ongoing investigation was now considering whether the unoccupied Stavros apartment had been merely a target of opportunity for a professional burglar who had been obliged to murder the doorman on his way in or out of the building, or whether there was some connection between the California crime and this one. "At this point in time" the police were leaning toward the latter theory, since there was no sign of forced entry to the apartment. Apparently there were no flies on the NYPD.

The segment ended with interviews with two elderly neighbors who had never dreamed that such a tragedy could strike a young man like—what was his name?—Mr. Stavros, who was polite and well behaved in the elevator, and always neatly dressed. But they supposed that was what today's world was coming to. There was no mention by anyone of plagiarism, or of the movie star Trig Bascomb, or of a strange man who was seen in the elevator quite late that night. I was thankful for small favors that were not likely to last.

The television news was followed almost immediately by an insistent buzz from my street-level door. I went to the intercom and asked cautiously who it was.

"Mr. Saldinger?"

"Yes."

"Police Department, Lieutenant Folsey. Like to talk to you for a minute. May we come up?"

He hadn't wasted any time. I said, "I'll be right down."

"No, we'd like to talk in private if you don't mind. We'd prefer to come up."

"I have to come down to let you in."

I did, and it was him, all right, as though he'd jumped off the screen, a thin, long-jawed man with dark, hooded eyes and pitted skin. I'd have cast him as an embalmer. A large black man was behind him. They were both dressed in civvies.

"You're thinner than on TV," I said as I opened the door.

"Everybody tells me," he said. "This is Detective Black." That's what he said. "Don't you have a way to buzz people in?" he continued.

"We prefer not to," I said.

"Good idea." As they followed me up the stairs he added, "That's a nasty bruise."

I had almost forgotten the bruise and this was not the time to reminisce about it. "Looks worse than it feels," I said.

When we entered the apartment I closed and locked the door. "Please, have a seat," I said. But they remained standing. Apparently the custom was the same on both coasts.

"You saw me on the news yesterday?" Folsey asked.

Was he testing me? "No," I said. "Were you on yesterday? I missed it. Just now, at five o'clock. A tragedy, that doorman. The story happened to catch my attention because I heard a name I'm familiar with. Nicholas Stavros."

"So you do know why we're here."

"Not really."

"Sergeant Dunleavy of the Los Angeles police didn't let you know I was coming?"

"There was a message on my machine when I came in this afternoon."

"So it wasn't only the name Stavros you caught on the news. You had just heard my name too."

He had come on as a little drowsy, but I would have to be careful with this one. "It hadn't stuck with me, Lieutenant. I'm better with faces than names."

"But you do know why we're here."

"Dunleavy just said to expect you." I was starting to learn how to handle these interrogations; you dragged your heels a little, just enough to break their rhythm. "He didn't say why."

He told me why. Then, "Nicholas Stavros's sister. You know her . . . ?"

"Mostly through her lamb stew."

He nodded. "The restaurant. She's the one filled me in—Christine Stavros—on her brother's murder in L.A. That hadn't come to our attention. It was Sergeant Dunleavy in Hollywood who brought up your name and mentioned that you came back to New York the day before Osvaldo Herrera was murdered." I may have looked blank because he added, "The doorman."

I said, "So you guys really believe there's a connection between Stavros's murder in L.A. and his doorman's in Manhattan."

He said, "What do you think?"

I said, "You're the detective."

"And you're the crime writer," he said. "You and this Nicholas Stavros."

"I can't speak for Stavros but I don't think of myself as a crime writer. I do many kinds of television writing. I like romantic comedies. It happens that cops and robbers is what the buyers want."

"Right," he said. "The demand is so great you and Stavros ended up writing the same story."

"I don't know what Stavros wrote. I haven't seen his story and I don't want to see it. I'm told there may be some coincidences—"

He cut in. "Was it a coincidence you got to L.A. the day before Stavros was killed, and to New York the day before his doorman had his throat slit?"

"Damn straight."

"Christine Stavros told me whoever sacked her brother's apartment may have been looking for the original copy of his television story. Do you have any reaction to that?"

"Yeah. If he found it he was in for a giant letdown."

"How do you know? You haven't read it."

"If Stavros was a writer there would be a body of work. At least a shoulder of work. Show me."

"I want you to consider this question carefully. You know, of course, you don't have to answer it. Were you anywhere near the King Arthur Apartments on West End Avenue between midnight and six A.M. yesterday?"

"This apartment is near there. Less than a mile."

"I'd prefer you didn't act cute."

"The answer is no. What made you ask?" The best defense was still an attack. "Did anybody report seeing me around there?"

"Not yet. Not you or anyone else. But we're hopeful. We're still questioning potential witnesses."

"Good luck, Lieutenant. And thanks for dropping by."

"Thank you for your cooperation, sir." He stuck out his hand and I automatically grabbed it. "You have sweaty palms, Mr. Saldinger."

"I'm not used to being questioned by the police."

"It gets easier. Good night."

Detective Black and I exchanged nods. They left and I locked the door behind them.

My situation being what it was, busywork was the only therapy available to me. Phone calls. It was three P.M. in L.A. and even the most dedicated lunchers would be back in their offices. I could pick up Brownie points by letting all concerned know that every script note had been addressed and appropriate changes made. "Appropriate" meant not every note got a change, but they might not notice that on the phone.

What I forgot until I called the Blaus was that today was Friday. Both Blaus had left for the weekend. Seth's secretary said he couldn't be reached; I assumed he was shacked up somewhere with a young hopeful. Werner's asked if I had Werner's number in Palm Springs. I had it, but I had no intention of using it. I left word for each of them that they would have a clean new script Tuesday morning, Federal Express.

Kornbluth was "in a meeting"; I told his secretary to check with the Blaus for a new script on Tuesday. Waxroth was "at a screening"; I alerted Winnie to bill the Blaus for "Second Draft, Revised." And at Bascomb's house someone answered in a low-pitched voice. "Yeah?"

"Trig?"

"Who is this?"

"Byron Saldinger."

"They left for the ranch with the kids."

"Vince?"

"Yeah."

"Would you tell him the changes are made and I think he'll like the new scenes."

"Right."

There was no danger of Vince running up my phone bill.

I finally got through to a person I called: Sergeant Dunleavy, LAPD. He did not greet me warmly. I told him I was just checking in, that I wanted him to know where he could reach me, that I'd basically be sticking pretty close to home for a while and, by the way, that I expected to be able to deliver my beach alibi woman early next week.

"That's nice," he said. He wasn't bowled over. "Did Lieutenant Folsey get you?"

"He dropped by," I said. "I'm still not sure why."

"Come off it."

"Sergeant, there are two thousand homicides a year in this city and I don't know how many tens of thousands of burglaries. And you want me to read something heavy into this one murder and burglary, both of which happened to hit West End Avenue? You're in the realm of pure fantasy."

"You're some piece of work, Saldinger."

I had taken my best shot; it wasn't much and I moved along smartly. "What about the Stavros case? Are you making any headway there?"

"You mean this totally unrelated matter out here? Not much. When I do, you may be the first to know. Oh, you remember Detective Ossian, my eyes and ears in show business? He says the rumor is your pilot is heating up either to go into production or into the dumper. Just remember to let me know if you're planning to come back out here."

I promised, and we hung up. I hate when civilians are more tuned in to my business than I am. Years ago it had been my misfortune to learn from the woman who was sheathing my pants in clear plastic at the dry cleaners' that the series I was supervising had been canceled that morning.

Phone calls out of the way, I became aware again of the walls. They had been closing in since I turned off the computer and now they were pressing against my temples. Could I take a chance and go out for something to eat? Any excuse to break loose for an hour. I dug out the field glasses I took to the track once or twice a year. It wasn't yet quite dark and I made a careful sweep of the street from the bedroom window. Almost at once I felt the gun barrel pressing against the base of my skull; the sense memory was that strong.

Mack the Knife was sitting in a white compact parked about four houses up the block on the opposite side of the street. He was wearing a tie and jacket that made him look as though he were going to a costume party. If he had parked on my side he would have been out of my line of sight. Maybe he hadn't been able to find a spot. Just as likely, based on his record, he had been too dumb to think of that. Whoever hired him hadn't shopped carefully. Or maybe price had been a factor. But dumb didn't make him any less dangerous. The next newscast I saw would almost certainly feature Osvaldo Herrera's mother weeping into a camera that had no business being there, while she tried in labored English to describe her loss.

I recognized the rental agency logo on the compact's bumper and got a pencil and paper and copied down the license plate. But that's all I did. My first instinct had been to holler for Folsey and bring the police charging in. To do what? Arrest a man sitting in a car who looked like someone who'd mugged me in another state? Not without a warrant, and where was the evidence for a warrant? Bringing in the cops at this point, before Mack could be nailed for good, could be counterproductive, even dangerous. I might succeed only in raising my profile and getting myself linked to the crimes at the King Arthur Apartments—breaking and entering, maybe murder. No, the time was not yet right for that kind of action. I wasn't sure when it would be. Meanwhile I could handle this.

So instead of going out I called down to Yang's for hot-and-sour soup and shrimp in black bean sauce. And in the process found myself some more busywork. Shuffling through my cash to pay Yang's deliverer, I came up with a piece of detective work I could do without leaving the apartment. Stuck to a ten-dollar bill was the little Post-it note with the hastily scrawled L.A. phone number I had found gummed to Stavros's desk. I wasn't hungry anyway, so I put the shrimp and soup in the fridge and dialed the number.

A voice said, "Pacifica."

I said, "Pacifica, uh, what?"

Irritably, "Tennis Club."

"Oh, sure. I forgot who I was dialing." Now what? "Could you tell me . . . how I go about applying for membership?"

"I'm sorry, sir, our membership list is filled, and at this time we're not taking new applications."

I couldn't think of anything else to say, so I thanked him and got off. Some instinct made me return to the bedroom window. Sure enough, Mack and the white compact were gone. To another location or out on the town, it didn't much matter. I'd have looked a horse's ass bringing in the police.

I called Vecchi and reported that Mack had been and gone. He said that sounded good. I asked him if he could somehow manage to get hold of the membership list of the Pacifica Tennis Club. He didn't ask why. He said, "I'll take a crack at it."

I went to sleep feeling I had maybe accomplished something.

The phone woke me at two-fifteen A.M. I hadn't been asleep long and it took me a few seconds to remember which coast I was on. Meanwhile a voice was shouting, "What, are you crazy? Are you *crazy?*"

It was Kornbluth. Was he referring to my having broken into his house and stolen his copy of Stavros's presentation? How had he found out?

It turned out to be an entirely different matter. He had just heard the eleven o'clock local news. The murdered doorman and the ravaged Stavros apartment had made it to L.A. as a curious follow-up to

the story of the corpse on the Sunset Boulevard sidewalk. "Are you out of your fucking mind?" he
screamed.

He had wrenched me out of deep sleep and I felt
a hit of nausea. I was tempted to strike back with,
"Oscar, what happened to your balls? You asked me
to do a job for you and I did it. You think knifing the
Guatemalan was excessive, huh?"

Instead, I said, "Relax. That wasn't me."

"Jeez." He was still hyperventilating. So much for
his mighty engine of ambition; it wouldn't pull
a walnut up Pikes Peak. He whispered, "Then
who . . . ?" And quickly dismissed that fringe question for issue number one. "Never mind. What
about the . . . ? You know, did you find . . . ?"

"No dice. No manuscript. What did I tell you? I'm
going back to sleep, Oscar."

But I couldn't.

CHAPTER NINETEEN

Mack the Knife was determined, but he was not relentless. When I peered out the bedroom window at eight in the morning, the white compact was nowhere in sight. And at this hour I could see every car on the block, thanks to alternate-side parking; the near side of the street was free of cars for street cleaning. Maybe this was Mack's first visit to the Apple and he had treated himself to a Friday night pub crawl and was still holed up in some fleabag sleeping it off. He was, after all, hired help and he wasn't being paid by the hour. I slipped quickly out of the building and set a brisk pace to the garage two blocks west where I kept my car.

The little Toyota was an expense I could have done without—the garage ran me more than my first Manhattan apartment—but it was the only practical way to pick up and deliver the kids on weekends. In five minutes I was on the West Side Highway, speeding north to Westchester along a sparkling Hudson and breathing easier. The early spring air was a tonic. Damned if I would let Mack take control of my emotional state.

But I wasn't keen on getting involved in another car chase and I did check the rearview mirror to see if I had picked up the white compact. I hadn't seen it at the beginning of the trip, so it was unlikely to turn up now. I checked from time to time anyway. I was reasonably alert considering the amount of sleep I had missed since going west nearly a week ago. Adrenaline was working its magic.

On the ride up I did what I usually did when I made the trip back to Irvington—picked through some corner of the rubbish of my marriage to see what Helene and I could have done, and when, to make things go differently. It was a wasted exercise. I liked to think that when Helene opened the door of the room I used as an office that day, her arms full of unfolded laundry, and said, "I'm leaving you for Richard Peevy and there's nothing you can do about it," it had come as a total shock. But the signs had long been there, and the inevitable had simply come to pass.

Helene's metamorphosis had taken longer than the one Kafka described, but it seemed to me almost as strange. The physical changes were the least of it —the cropped brown hair, the granny glasses, and the full figure behind that armful of laundry. This woman was as attractive, physically, as the slim blond bombshell of fifteen years ago and, hands down, a lot more interesting-looking. The more important change was in her aura—the scholar at home, the gravity bordering on pomposity. Bordering, hell; deep in the territory. I found it increasingly hard to remember the budding actress with dancing eyes and cascading laughter who led me through the maze of stage alleys and back lot streets at Universal one night to a production trailer parked on hard-packed dirt at the edge of the western street. I had picked the lock with her hairpin, and we had screwed on a pile of cowboy costumes that reeked of makeup while outside our aluminum wall a crew on overtime hammered, hauled, and shouted.

The screwing in those early days, those early years, had been pretty fantastic. That it would eventually wind down was probably a fact of nature. That Helene would gradually back off from me, or drift away, or turn to new values—however she thought of it—was less predictable. It was only in retrospect that a logical progression had become apparent there too.

Helene had dropped out of the University of Michigan in the middle of her sophomore year to follow her star to Hollywood. We fell in with each other midway through her sputtering career and were married in less than a year. Well before we were ready to have children, she faced up to something I had long ago decided she would have to discover for herself, that she was a monumentally bad actress. Refocusing her energies, and they were considerable, she enrolled at UCLA—we were still living on the Coast—and managed in less than three years to make Phi Beta Kappa as a junior, get a bachelor's degree with a major in cultural anthropology, and produce Benjy. And then she kicked back to enjoy Benjy. At that point we decided we would rather our son put down roots in the culturally richer soil of New York, and we moved east.

The East—my home, new to Helene—recharged Helene's batteries. In quick succession she had both Jane and an M.A. from Columbia. Eventually she was enrolled in a Ph.D. program. I thought I was delighted. My life companion had revealed new facets of herself. She was exercising her full potential, bringing surprising new riches to the relationship—doing, in fact, all the things that were slugged in approving headlines on the covers of the women's magazines I was stepping on all over the house. I cheered proudly from the sidelines.

After a while I noticed that my cheers were growing fainter. I had come face to face, no surprise, with a frontal attack on my male ego. I was of course dismayed to discover vestigial sexism in some cobwebby corner of my mind, and I made a conscious effort to knock off this crap and get with the program.

It wasn't always easy. One night when I was luxuriating at—admittedly—inordinate length in a steamy shower, my head foamy with lather, the Ph.D. candidate's hand snaked in and turned off the hot water. "There is a finite amount of energy on this planet," she said. But that was small stuff. Something more disturbing was afoot.

In the early years Helene and I used to watch my shows together when they aired, commenting, joking, criticizing—above the material but at the same time with it. For better or worse, this was the work that provided for our family, and very well, thank you. After a few years Helene had to start excusing herself from these viewings because of her heavy study schedule. And more and more I got the feeling that she was glad of the excuse. What hung in the air was that she was "growing" and I was not. Finally there came an evening when, as I turned on the TV, Helene said straight out, "Okay if I beg off, Mike? I really find it hard to relate to this stuff." This from a woman I had first seen work in a dinner theater revival of *Getting Gertie's Garter* and who hadn't been up to the material.

Three summers ago she had gone on a six-week field trip to Belize under the supervision of her Ph.D. mentor. The timing had seemed perfect. The kids were in day camp and I was hard at work on my last writing assignment before the big employment drought. With a little part-time help I was able to handle the children and stick to my deadline.

What happened in Belize while the rain drummed on the tin-roofed shacks in the steamy jungle where the quetzals flashed their plumage high in the big chicle trees I can only guess, but for months after Helene got back, Richard Peevy's name came up a lot in her small talk. Although he was six or eight years younger than Helene, Richard already had his doctorate and a teaching position at a small college in southern Connecticut heretofore unknown to me. He was untenured, but in my mind he would always be the Professor.

When the situation came to a head, it turned out there was a certain amount of hyperbole in "I am leaving you for Richard Peevy." She left me in spirit, but the Professor's salary did not quite support the Professor, so what comfort could it offer a Ph.D. candidate who had long ago adjusted to an income derived from "stuff" she found it "hard to relate to" and whose name she was too embarrassed to speak?

So until one or the other of them hit an academic jackpot, Helene continued to live with the kids in our house in Irvington, the entire package on me, and the Professor continued to live wherever un-tenured teachers at obscure colleges live. They saw each other weekends and whenever. And why was I working myself into a lather by once again chewing over this stale material?

I swung off the Saw Mill and made my way past

the skeletal trees to Route 9 and Irvington. I wished the green would come to these trees. Slower than waiting for the pot to boil, slower even than waiting for the movie to start when you're sitting in a darkened theater without a companion, is waiting for the leaves to open on an oak, a maple, and especially a hickory.

The children heard the crunch of my tires on the driveway gravel. They were already dressed for the outdoors and they raced out of the house to embrace me. The Labrador, Bert, bounced circles around us. The kids tried to outshout each other with news of the past week. The words tumbled out. You would think I had been gone a year. As always, I was in awe. The scars of the divorce had never seemed deep with these two and had soon faded. Maybe they were brilliant at covering their pain, having inherited their mother's doubtful acting talent and sharpened it to the tenth power. But I always suspected they had been wiser than me, and had seen down the track sooner and farther than I had, and prepared themselves for what was to come. I supposed they would be hell on wheels as teenagers. All I knew was that for most of this year they had been, against all expectations, a delight.

Eventually Benjy announced that Mommy wanted to see me before we left. That did not set my heart singing but I said, right, why didn't they wait in the car and get ready for the great adventure. What that was I had not yet figured out. I had better see Mommy first.

Helene was in the kitchen organizing her briefcase for a day at the library. She looked good, vibrant, and sexy; she usually did. She was wearing her hair even shorter lately, and that brought out the

good planes in her face. The tension lines at the
corners of her mouth could mean I was in for a hard
time or simply that she had had a hard week. For all
my bitching about Helene, my admiration for how
she handled the kids, the house, and the study load
was unqualified.

I said, "Hi, how's it going? What's up?"

She said, "Mike, what exactly is going on?"

I would have liked a hello. I said, "In what regard?"

"Rudd Cole—I haven't talked to him in years."

"What about him? And I doubt it's that long. Couple of years, at most."

"A couple is years," she took the trouble to point
out. "He called yesterday, out of the blue. Just to
chat. He wanted to know how things were, how I was
doing."

"And?"

"I told him I was doing all right. We had a mean-
dering conversation for about two minutes and then
he hung up. Perfectly pleasant."

"So?"

"I mean . . . why?"

"I don't know. Maybe he wanted to know how you
were doing. Devious, huh? Is that it? What you
wanted me for?"

She wasn't satisfied but she moved on. "No. You
had a call. Last night. Remember I told you when
you were in L.A. that someone had called here looking for you?"

"Wilson, Winton—something like that. About
work. You gave him Wolf Waxroth's number. I never
heard from him."

"Wilter. At least that's what he said last night. I
made him spell it. But I don't think it was about
work. This time we were on for a minute and he

didn't sound like any of the people you do business with. I didn't like the kind of questions he asked and anyway, he sounded, I don't know . . ."

"Dumb?"

"Dumb. Exactly."

"Let me revise what I said." I was on my way to a window. "I didn't hear from him in L.A. but he did sort of make contact there. And then again here in New York. I didn't expect him to track me to Irvington."

I got the kids' attention and called to them to come in the house and wait for me in the playroom. By now there was nothing for it but to tell Helene whatever I knew that would be of any help.

She had listened without interrupting and she didn't panic. We weighed various courses of action. Mack wasn't after the kids, or Helene, he was after me. But he might show up here looking for me and his history indicated that if they were in his way there was no telling what might happen. I wasn't going to take any chances. I didn't want any area of doubt. I wanted the three of them unambiguously separated from me.

Helene agreed with me that the safest thing would be for all of them to leave the house for a while. She wanted to find a place to stay that was close by, so the children could continue to go to their regular school. The nature of the discussion—parents at the kitchen table making decisions affecting the welfare of the family—was the kind that usually draws couples closer, binds them together against a possibly hostile world. We had had such discussions in the old days. It was disorienting to have one now.

It took Helene only two calls to find what was needed. The parents of Benjy's best friend had a

small apartment over their garage that was empty.
They would be thrilled to have Helene and the kids
for "a few days while some serious work was being
done on our plumbing." The kids were so excited
by this prospect—so this was the surprise adventure!
—that they forgot to be disappointed at not getting
to spend the day with me.

I helped them pack suitcases and load them in
Helene's station wagon along with the dog and the
parakeet, and then I stayed behind to make sure the
house was securely locked and the alarm system on.
Before I left I called the village police and alerted
them to keep a close eye on the house, as the family
would be away for a while.

Driving south on the Saw Mill, I kept one eye on
the northbound lanes. There wasn't much traffic
and I took a good look at every white compact I
passed. At first I was sure I saw Mack behind the
wheel of all of them. It always turned out to be
someone else. It was never even close.

If Mack still wanted me, and I supposed he did, he
would have to try to take me in the city.

CHAPTER TWENTY

Back at the apartment I found a phone message from Kornbluth, a gasped "Where the hell are you? Call me," left at six-fifteen A.M., his time. To have phoned that early on a Saturday morning he must have been in a state of high agitation, probably hyperventilating again. But I made coffee and drank two cups before I returned the call. Let the bastard sweat. He had put me through hell for a very doubtful reason.

Mrs. Kornbluth answered the home phone. She sounded nice, knew who I was, asked about the weather in New York, and called Oscar to the phone. He shooed her out of the room and closed the door before he spoke. I didn't even say hello. I plunged right into what I assumed he was after, an explanation of what happened "at that apartment the other night."

He didn't want to hear any of it. "Mike, I've got no time for small talk" was the way he put it. His harmless little B. and E. had mushroomed into a

murder, and he must have figured the faster he
backpedaled from it, the less likely he was to be
nailed as an accessory.

Oscar had his own angst-producing news. He had
heard from Trig Bascomb. Word had reached our
star late last night of the grisly crime in New York
to which his name had been linked. That made two,
and he had seriously blown his top. He was now
absolutely determined to blow the deal and ankle
our project, and he had so informed his lawyers.
The network's hastily devised strategy was to scramble into production before Bascomb's people had a
full head of steam. Bascomb would face a heavy
countersuit if he tried to pull out once they were
into principal photography. So the Blaus were busy
at this moment lining up a director. Sets were being
built over the weekend, and locations scouted, and
could I come back out on Tuesday, while they were
casting, to work on the polish, even though nobody
had yet seen the Second Draft, Revised? I said, you
bet.

The rest of Saturday went by without a reappear-
ance by Mack the Knife. He was again nowhere in
sight when I checked with the field glasses Sunday
morning. It was possible, of course, that he was
down there somewhere but not in my line of sight. I
had the compact's license plate number and I remembered the rental company name from having
read the logo off the car. I called the company's
Kennedy Airport number and fumbled through an
excuse about having left something in my friend's
car. It got me the information I wanted: the car had
been turned in at the airport the night before. Mack
had given up on me in New York and gone back to
L.A. For his convenience I would be flying west to

meet him. Perfect. Everybody knew my business before I did.

Meanwhile Mack's absence allowed me to read through the revised script on the computer screen Sunday afternoon, and make a few last fiddles, with a somewhat clearer mind. But not entirely. I had been having uneasy second thoughts about my decision not to call in the police when Mack was right under my window. That option was no longer open to me, but my silence had not sat well, even though I knew in my bones my family was now safely out of the equation. What if I went to the police now and told them everything I knew about Mack?

Free of script problems, my mind was uncluttered enough to consider the question, and I tried to put myself on the receiving end of a statement from me to the police. How much of it was believable? That Mack might be a hired killer, yes; the papers carry a story a month about ordinary citizens—ministers and housewives—who rent hit men, men very much like Mack. But who would profit from hiring this killer? So far as I could tell, only the person who hoped Stavros's death would end the charge of plagiarism—the same man, it might soon be discovered, who was on the scene when Stavros's apartment was sacked and his doorman killed. Me. All things considered, I decided to continue my present course of action—keep my mouth shut and wait for further developments.

After another day and a half in the apartment, the walls were closing in again. Now that it was safe to do so I had a powerful need to get out for a breath of fresh air.

I fell in with the strolling and window-shopping couples on Columbus. It felt good not to have to look over my shoulder. I noted with satisfaction that in the few days I had been out of circulation, the ice cream cone season had begun. Fruit flavors were much in favor.

Without realizing it, I wasn't merely strolling, I had a destination: I was standing in front of Christine's. Through the glass door I saw Christine herself, cool and poised in a cream-colored sheath that emphasized her dark good looks and her cascade of Anna Magnani hair. Whatever sorrow she might have felt over the death of her baby brother was well hidden behind careful makeup and a professional manner. I watched her fix a separate smile on each of the diners at a table for four. It vanished as her eye caught a problem at another table. With a tiny gesture she sent a waitress scurrying to solve it. I opened the door and went in.

With Lincoln Center dark, Sunday was the slowest day at Christine's. The place was nearly empty. Toby was off, but the Sunday/Monday bartender, Walter, greeted me by name and made a show of wiping down the gleaming bar. I would probably have been his first action of the day had I gone to the bar, but I disappointed him. I walked directly to Christine. She was still talking to the table for four, her back to me. She turned and started to fix her welcome-to-Christine's smile. When she saw me, her face went dead.

I said, "May I have a table? It'll just be me." She stared at me, then led me wordlessly to one near the back of the room. As I sat I said quickly, "Christine, I really am sorry about your brother. You must know I had nothing to do with his death. Can we talk about this?"

She handed me a menu and said, "Your waitress will be glad to tell you the specials." Her tone was neutral and her glance, as she left the table, didn't seem hostile. I had hope.

I ordered a martini and drank it slowly. Restaurant owners are more likely to stop by and talk when you're having your drink than when you have to respond through a mouthful of food. But she never came near me. There were only four or five other parties in the room, and it was hard for her to appear busy, so mostly she disappeared into the kitchen.

Eventually I gave up waiting and ordered the steamed halibut. I could hear my mother's voice saying, "Never order fish in a restaurant on a Sunday. Where would they get it?" But I had discovered I was less hungry than I thought, and everything else on the menu seemed too much. The fish was good, redolent of ginger, but I didn't eat much of it. I pushed it around on the plate for a while and then called for the check.

I think Christine had expected me to have coffee, because as soon as the waitress went off with my new credit card, she made a beeline for the table. "Yes," she said, "I think I would like to talk. Not here."

"Can you cut out?"

"Not for another half hour."

"You know I live in the neighborhood." It was half a question, and she nodded. I gave her my address and as soon as Gloria came back with my credit card, I left.

Half an hour later Christine Stavros was sitting on my couch but not settled into it, her back ramrod straight, and I was offering her a Mexican brandy, the nearest thing I had to cognac—about as near, I apologized, as Mexico is to France. She turned it down. She wanted to talk. I got the feeling she hadn't come to hear what I had to say but to unburden herself.

"Mr. Saldinger . . ." she began.

I said, "Everybody calls me Mike."

She nodded but didn't do it. "I may owe you an apology. I know I do. In L.A., when we . . . met—I guess you could call it a 'meeting'—my brothers . . ." She trailed off and then she said, "Do you mind? I will have that brandy."

While I poured her a stiff one neither of us said anything. She was organizing what she wanted to say and I wasn't going to intrude on that.

She took the brandy and said, "What we were doing, my brothers and I, when we turned on you that way with all that anger—and again I apologize for it, it was unfair—we were trying to show Niko, show him through you, that we cared. Actually the whole fuss was to cover our deep feelings of guilt."

"Guilt about what?" I was all ears.

"About not doing for Niko any more. About, finally, digging in our heels."

"I still don't understand."

She took a long swallow of the brandy. Then, "You thought Niko was a dreadful person." She waited. "I know you did, didn't you?"

I don't like to answer questions when I'm not sure of their purpose. I kept my mouth clamped shut and made an ambiguous gesture.

"Well, he was," she said. "Dreadful."

That freed me up to add my assessment. "Of course I didn't know him, but I'd guess he wasn't easy to get to like."

"Yes," she quickly countered, "but you have to understand where he was coming from, what made him that way."

"That's true," I said. True of everybody. Down what winding, rock-strewn path were we headed?

She said, "Niko was spoiled rotten as a child and the boys and I were largely to blame. Can you imagine what it must have been like to have three older brothers and a sister and a doting mother? Who did everything for you? I mean everything? Because you were the baby, the helpless, adorable, incredibly bright baby of the family?"

She waited for my response. I had no intention of checking the flow of the narrative. I said, "I've seen it. It happens in families."

She said, "The worst of it, after all the attention we showered on him, all the love and concern, Niko grew up disdaining—*despising*—everything we stood for. Phil, Alex, and Connie worked so hard, sometimes sixteen hours a day, until they had pooled enough money to buy that rundown diner. And then again sixteen hours a day to build the place into something. All the while putting away enough so they could send me to the C.I.A. to study—"

"The C.I.A. . . .?"

"The Culinary Institute of America in Hyde Park. Afterward they backed me in Christine's. Niko despised all that. I had gone to Hunter for two years, but Niko was the first in the family to graduate from college, and he went to one out of town. Not a great one, but a private college, and the boys paid for all of it. They didn't even ask him to pitch in with a part-time job while he was at school. He was to devote himself to learning. But nothing the boys did really registered with Niko. He never stopped accusing them of having an immigrant mentality. He said they didn't have enough self-esteem to climb out of the dishwater. He said he was going to be the first member of the family to make it without using his hands. Niko was going to make it with his fingers. On a typewriter. Movies, novels, television—he was going to write them all, become famous, lift the four of us out of the dishwater."

"And . . . ?"

"After college the boys continued to support him. Nearly totally. While he wrote. Or said he wrote."

"He probably did." I knew he did. I had seen the stuff, pounds of it.

"I suppose he did," she said quietly. "I'm being hard on him. Every once in a while he'd sell something to some tacky magazine. But for three years he took the boys' hard-earned money with barely a thank-you. And once Christine's was going well, he would come in there at night and latch on to the actors or directors from Lincoln Center, the dancers, the people who worked at the network news studios nearby—anybody remotely connected with show business. His soul brothers.

"I finally put my foot down. The boys had done enough; it was my turn to take some responsibility for Niko and I wasn't going to be a patsy. I offered him a job and a proposition. He could write during the day and use his charm to run the front of the restaurant at night. He wanted to mix? Let him mix for a living. And eventually I would make him a partner. It was a very good deal. He turned me down. 'Patronizing,' he called it—when he had lived on patronage all his life. But I had convinced my brothers to take him off the payroll. We had him backed into a corner. He had to find some way to earn his keep.

"And he came up with one, a totally yuppie concept, his idea entirely—that precious health food store he decided to call Nature's Buddy. Most of the capital for it came from me, and most of the work organizing it was done by his friend Leon, who then pretty much ran the place while Niko mostly 'wrote.' Niko was embarrassed to be a shopkeeper. He hung out even more at my bar, drank more, bothered my customers more, boasted more loudly about his writing, and let his store run into the ground. He was heavily in debt to his wholesalers and someone would have to bail him out.''

''Who?''

''I told him, not me. The banks turned him down and his creditors threatened. He was ready to borrow from a loan shark. There's one comes in to the restaurant. Luis Vico. You know him?''

''Someone pointed him out. Short, very little neck, hardly any eyes?''

''And absolutely no heart. I was terrified and Niko saw it. And took advantage of it. He swore if I bailed him out he would devote himself to his business and turn it around. I didn't want him mixed up with Vico, so a month ago I lent him fifteen thousand dollars. I told him that was it. I had convinced my brothers that from here on out it was sink or swim for Niko. He was nearly thirty years old. For his own sake as well as ours he was going to have to make it on his own.''

She had drained her brandy and now she put the glass on the coffee table. ''In my heart I knew he would never make it. He drank, he gambled, he had no head for business. And his friends were like him. What he had was a hot temper and a mouth full of boasts. Did he have enemies? I wouldn't be surprised if he had many.'' She looked straight in my eyes. ''No, you didn't kill him.'' She tried to lighten it. ''You don't eat enough red meat to be a murderer.''

''Apology accepted,'' I said. I had her blessing,

good. Was this it? But she was not getting up. And now she was holding out her glass.

"One is usually my limit, but could I trouble you for a touch more of that . . . uh, brandy?" She may have read a look of concern on my face; if she did, she read it wrong. She said, "Yes, it is a little harsh but once your tongue is vulcanized you can't tell it from Armagnac."

I poured her another, stiffer than the first, and this time I took a splash for myself. My look of concern had sprung from a suspicion that "One is usually my limit" meant she had something further to say that might call for courage from the bottle. I braced myself for it as I gave her back her glass. She picked up the thread of her agenda.

"My apology was for having accused you of murder," she said. "Not plagiarism. You did steal Niko's television idea."

I said, "I damn well did not. Where did you get that idea?"

"I was there when it happened."

"Impossible."

She said, "You're not qualified to say that."

"What's that supposed to mean?"

She swirled her brandy and took a sip. "Do you remember how you were when you first started coming to Christine's over a year ago? When you first moved to the city?"

"How I was? In what connection?"

"Your emotional state. My help got to know you, and so did a few of the regulars. They felt sorry for you, this poor sap whose wife had dumped him without warning somewhere out there in the upper-middle-class suburbs. You flapped around like a fish on the dock, a writer who couldn't write, or didn't write, or wouldn't write. You were at my bar in a fog three or four nights a week—dazed and rambling, pouring out to anyone you could corner what that woman had done to you. You were still trying to convince yourself it had really happened."

I said, "If you're making a point, why don't you get to it?"

"This went on for two months—three? it seemed never ending—before you got a grip on yourself and the drinking tapered off. And somewhere during that period, sometime near the end of it, one night you were at the bar bending Niko's ear—"

"No way. Yes, I drank a lot when I was first separated. And I don't doubt that I may have occasionally made an ass of myself. But not with Niko."

"The regulars had learned to avoid you. You were a one-note bore. Niko was the only one in the house who would listen that night. Not out of charity. You were a writer, and you were in show business. Some of the magic might rub off. So he stood still for it while you poured out your troubles."

"I would have had to be mighty drunk."

"Believe me. I happened to be at the bar going over reservations for the next night. You interrupted your sad song to signal Toby for another drink. The break was just long enough for Niko to take the floor. And I heard him. Not all of it. But he told you a story that had a New York cop in it and a ranch in the West and a murder the cop has to solve to pay for the ranch. That's what *Corrigan's Way* is about, isn't it?"

"Yes. And it's been described that way in newspaper and magazine previews of next season's shows. You're more likely to remember that, or a recap of that from Niko, than a rambling conversation between two drunks at your bar all those months ago, at a time when you were trying to concentrate on

something else. I don't remember your brother telling me any story like that. I don't remember ever—
ever—talking scripts or stories or anything else having to do with television with Nick Stavros. Period.''

"That doesn't surprise me. I don't think you're a calculating thief. As I said, you were pretty far gone that night. And I can't recall your letting Niko corner you again. Soon after that you started coming into the place late enough so you didn't have to wait at the bar for a table, and you began drinking less. You turned out to be kind of amusing sober and there were plenty of other people willing to talk to you.''

"But you do happen to remember my socializing with Niko that one time. Long enough to lift his idea, huh?''

"I remember him telling it to you, yes.''

"Pretty convenient, your paying attention, wasn't it?''

"Toby remembers the incident too. I asked him yesterday.''

"Your employee. I don't doubt he remembers what you remember.'' This dialogue was souring rapidly. "Is all this going to figure in a legal action?''

"It may very well. Wouldn't there be poetic justice in my brothers and me getting back some fraction of what we laid out for Niko?''

I thought, some fraction! The numerator could be many times the denominator. What I said was, "You seem to know an awful lot about me—when I drank and when I stopped, what I talked about and who talked to me. You know that about all your customers?''

"No.'' She drained her glass. "But it happened I was interested in you. At first it was the sheer pity I might have felt for a stray cat. And then, when you sobered up, it was . . . well, it was interest. And I think you had some in me.''

Now what kind of game were we in? I said, "It took me until very recently to get interested again in any woman.''

"I don't think I could have been that mistaken . . .''

"Okay, I was curious sometimes. It happens when you eat alone and forget to bring something to read. Those outfits you wear that are always perfectly coordinated and look like they're straight from the dry cleaner?'' She had held the floor too long, shaken me too much; I wanted to shake back. "I sometimes wondered if your underwear was as neat and perfect, or if you were wearing a blue bra that had been in the washing machine too many times and pink panties that were crawling up your ass.''

She took hardly a beat. "Which way would have fed your fantasy?''

I wasn't going to fall into that trap. I said, "If you were interested in me, you covered it very well. Never a hint.''

"That's because of my rule. Never date the customers.''

"Inviolable, huh?''

"If I expect them ever to come into the restaurant again. It was different with—what was his name?—Seth Blau.''

I could feel the blood go to my head and fill my ears. "You went out with Seth Blau?''

"He didn't tell you?'' She seemed surprised. "The night you brought him into Christine's for dinner a few months back. Don't you remember introducing him? I knew he was only east for a day or two to meet with you about your project and that he'd be flying straight back to Los Angeles. So there'd be no harm in going out with him.''

"When did he even get to ask you?" I couldn't believe this. ·

"When he walked to the back to pick up his coat. I guess you kept yours at the table. He was very adept.''

"Was he?''

She caught the innuendo and laughed. "At asking. We went out that same night. He never told you?''

I shook my head slowly.

"I suppose because it wasn't much fun for either of us. Oh, he was very California, made all the right moves, but I had to work hard to keep from laughing. Maybe he was too young, maybe too much in the shadow of the big brother he kept talking about. We made an early evening of it.''

"Is that supposed to get you Brownie points?''

"You wanted to know, so I told you.'' She put her glass down and looked steadily at me. As steadily as she could; she was half in the bag. She said, "I'm considering a new rule. Something to the effect that after two very large Mexican brandies it's perfectly all right to date a regular customer.'' She uncoiled from the couch and walked slowly toward me.

I said warily, "Dating. How would that affect the legal action?'' My skin was starting to tingle.

She said, "Not in the least. Why should it?''

She had to take only two more steps and then our arms were around each other at the same time, our bodies pressing tight. She felt marvelous. I said, "I haven't done much of this in a long time.''

She said, "Lucky me.''

                                  * * *

I would have preferred it the other way, but it turned out that her underwear matched perfectly and fit flawlessly. No matter. The sex, rapacious and adversarial, was terrific. Afterward, while Christine smoked a cigarette, I almost said, "Was it as angry for you as it was for me?" Instead, I moved toward her and we did it again.

Later, halfway between sweet sleep and waking, I felt the warm breath of her mouth at my ear. I expected a few at least half-tender words. What she said was, "You know, I have the proof of what Niko claimed. Before he left for California he gave me an envelope to hold for him."

I chose to believe she was bluffing. I wasn't up to another B. and E.

CHAPTER TWENTY-ONE

She didn't stay the night. She said when you ran a restaurant your reputation had to be as clean as your kitchen. It was nearly three when I walked her out to find a taxi. I was careful of my flanks until I reminded myself that my nemesis had left town.

We huddled on a cold street corner for ten minutes waiting for a stray cab. From time to time Christine ran a hand lightly up my crotch, as though I needed to be reminded of the last few hours. I didn't. But despite her aura I had managed to turn my thoughts elsewhere. Her mention of an envelope Niko had left her was weighing on me heavily. I resisted asking her about it directly. Instead, leaning shamelessly on our altered relationship, I asked if she would reconsider launching a messy legal action.

"Not a chance," she said. "I told you, the money will mostly go to Phil, Alex, and Connie as partial payment for all they did for me. For Niko I'm thinking of the recognition—his name up there on a television screen. It's the best memorial I could offer him.''

"Is it," I said flatly.

"You don't understand, do you?" she said. "Niko was terrible with money, an open faucet. But it wasn't money he wanted from you people, it was validation as a writer. That would have brought him the respect he was looking for.''

A taxi was pulling up. "I, however,'' she concluded hastily, "have no problem with gouging you guys for every cent I can get.'' She kissed me quickly and climbed in the cab, her good legs flashing.

It was nearly four before I fell asleep. On the one hand, the sex—I wasn't willing to call it lovemaking —had eased my tensions. On the other, nearly everything else that happened with Christine had heightened them. How much had I subconsciously, subliminally—however I might have done it—borrowed of Stavros's concept? Or had Christine made up that idea because it could result in something tangible for Stavros's heirs?

I would have liked to believe this last. With the fevered clarity that sometimes comes in the middle of the night, I found myself again denying the probability that a germ of an idea in the air at Christine's those many months ago had lodged in an alcove of my brain. But the possibility was stirring some guilt in me. I had to remind myself that most story ideas are sparked by a germ in the air somewhere. Then I went back to refusing to believe it had happened in this case. My development of the idea too closely resembled Stavros's. It was beyond mere inspiration from him, beyond coincidence. Either I was being hoodwinked in some way I didn't yet understand, or Stavros had told me even more than Christine claimed to remember. And I refused to believe the latter. Just about one hundred percent.

An insistent signal from the front-door buzzer roused me from a dreamless sleep. My clock radio said 10:57 A.M. I couldn't remember the last time I had slept this late. My conscience must have somehow resolved my concerns. I went to the bedroom window and looked out at a tall, thin black man holding the handlebars of a racing bike. A messenger. I wasn't expecting a messenger. After some cautious back-and-forthing on the intercom, I established that he was carrying a delivery from Hal Patch's ad agency. I threw on a robe and went down and collected it.

As promised, Hal had come through for me. The envelope contained two 8-by-10 glossies. One was a composite picture from a commercial agency of an actress named Jenny Haycroft—Jenny with a shopping bag, Jenny swinging a tennis racquet, Jenny drinking a glass of juice, Jenny in a nightgown yawning. She was my Jenny-from-the-beach, all right, every bit as delicious as I remembered her. On the picture's back was a listing of her commercial credits. Decent credits. In four years she had made nearly two dozen local spots and two national, including the cereal spot I had caught her in. As a commercial actress Jenny was getting by.

The other glossy was from a theatrical agent, a head shot with a few sculptured shadows and highlights calculated to bring out the subject's character. And they did. My Jenny was more than just another pretty face. But the back of the head shot showed her theatrical credits, and these were very thin. Four parts in dramatic TV episodes in four years, only one of them important enough for the character to have

been given a name. She was a day player, my Jenny,
and a marginal one at that. The commercial work
was keeping her alive while she pursued her serious
acting career. I remembered Al Vecchi's analysis of
her shopping list: it held plenty of low-end products
to stretch the budget.

The back of the head shot also tipped me to how
hungry Jenny Haycroft was for theatrical work. Ig-
noring the risk of attracting heavy breathers, she
had inked in her own phone number beneath her
agent's. I bypassed the agent and called Jenny.

It wasn't much after eight in the morning in L.A.,
but I got a machine. "Hi! Yes, it's me, and this is
Sunday night. Listen up everybody, I'm leaving for a
shoot in Baja at seven A.M. They say it's a hundred
and ten, so weep for me! Back Tuesday night. Love
you, whoever you are!"

Tuesday night I would be in L.A. It would be my
pleasure to personally strangle Miss Gosh-do-you-
really-work-in-TV with my bare hands.

By four in the afternoon I had been through the
script one last time and placed it reluctantly in the
hands of Federal Express. With my pampered brain-
child now loose in a cruel world, I called to check on
my biological children in their temporary home in
Irvington. Benjy picked up. All was well. He and
Jane were loving the adventure, and he gave no hint
that he missed his old dad. I didn't even get a wail of
protest when I told him I was going back to L.A. in
the morning.

Since the kids were happy where they were, I
thought it best to play it safe and let them stay put
until I had a better sense of where Mack and I were
headed. I had Benjy call his mother to the phone
and she agreed; better safe than sorry. Nothing re-

motely suspicious had gone on, but the kids were
enjoying the change and so was she, so they'd stay
where they were until they had some further word
from me. Very reasonable. Who could say? One day
all the acrimony might be drained and I would look
on Helene as a friend. But not soon.

I called American and booked the flight that
would land me in L.A. at noon, about two hours
after the revised script would be delivered to the
Blaus at their office in the Valley. By the time I
checked in at a hotel, the script would have been
copied and distributed, and there could already be
new sets of notes waiting for me in envelopes
marked "Hold for Arrival."

With that unpleasant prospect before me, I called
Winnie at Waxroth's office, asked her to reserve me
a room at the Hollywood Claverly—my affection for
the Desert Palm had long since faded—but please
not to tell anyone yet where I was staying. Let them
hold their goddam notes until they had a chance to
reflect on them. Then I called Vecchi at the Hollyview.

His room phone was picked up by a woman who
said in an accent I couldn't place except that it
wasn't Hispanic, "Meester Vesky in botroom."

When he eventually came on I identified myself,
but Vecchi didn't speak until I heard a door close.
He said, "That was the new maid. I can't pronounce
her name and I'm not exactly sure which country in
Asia she's from. Whichever, she's from the mountain part. She's been making eyes at me, so yesterday
while she was doing the room I asked her what time
she got off work. She said, 'Why wait till get off
work?' and she quoted me what she said was a very
special price. Not special enough. I have nothing
against sex with working girls, but I'm used to being

comped. We agreed to remain just friends. What's up?''

I said, "Change of plans. Kornbluth wants me to come back out tomorrow. Can you stay there?''

"I'll fake something. Your shadow still hanging in there?''

"Mack the Knife. I'm pretty sure he's gone back to L.A. He's more secure on his home turf and he must know I'll have to show sooner or later for preproduction notes and that I'll be running around exposed. Can I count on you to keep an eye on me for a few days?''

"Better. We'll nail the bastard. I've been thinking about him. About who's winding his clock. Haven't you? For Chrissake, it's getting embarrassing. This is our business, you and me. We solve crimes.''

"Wrong, Al. You solve crimes. I invent solutions, then I write crimes to fit them. No help here.''

"Solutions I've got plenty,'' he said. "I've knocked myself out spinning solutions to this one.''

"I'll listen to one.''

"To show where my head is taking me? How about this? It's you. You're big enough to have done the dirty, you're in good enough shape, and you have a reason. It's already stuck in Dunleavy's tooth. You killed Stavros.''

"Dunleavy has a limited imagination. I expect better from you.''

"So follow me while I make the case. You did it to get rid of competition that could be a major headache for you professionally and moneywise. That's a given. Now here's the cute new part only a TV write would dream up. After you do Stavros, you know there's a chance you'll be the number one suspect. So you trump up a story: Stavros's killer is after you too. To prove it, you claim he almost knocked you off at the Desert Palm. But who's ever seen this Mack the Knife except you? For that matter, who's ever seen your alibi girl at the beach except you? You made them both up, a killer covering his ass. Not bad, huh?"

"Not bad. Maybe you should be in my end of the business. But not good enough. Somebody did see Mack the Knife. Remember Cissy, the English girl with the lethal gin bottle?"

"An actress. Who's conveniently left the country. Maybe you wrote her the best part she ever had."

"Cissy's a dancer, and dancers can't act. Anyway she can be found. And questioned."

"Okay, no problem. Version two. You were attacked for real at the Desert Palm. You and Cissy. But the attacker was only a free-lance burglar—a lucky accident you made good use of when you got back to New York. You turned it into a kind of TV story. You know the one, you've probably written it —innocent man stalked by relentless killer who has already struck once. It stirs up a shitload of sympathy. Except nobody followed you to New York, because this time there is no killer. Except you, a second time, when you had to do that doorman on West End Avenue when you went after the piece of registered mail."

I said nothing.

"Saldinger? You there?"

"Of course I'm here. Where do you think I am?"

"Do I hear you getting hot under the collar?"

"Damn right."

"How come?"

"I'm jealous, you bastard. You tied this crime into such a neat package I'm the only one who knows for sure it didn't happen that way."

"Good. I wanted you to see how I'm going crazy

with this thing. I can shape it a million different ways. You want to hear another?"

"Save it. I'll see you tomorrow. I'm staying at the Hollywood Claverly."

We hung up. Son of a bitch, that *was* good.

I was looking forward to sacking out early; I still had some sleep to catch up on. But first I cleared the decks for the trip with a few calls.

Somehow the first one was to Sarah Cole. Anyway, to her answering machine. I didn't recognize her recorded voice, although I had heard it on my machine. It was liquid, with very little density, as though any vagrant breeze could blow it away. And it was sad. She apologized in her message for not being at home and she swore absolutely to return all calls promptly.

I said, "It's Saldinger, and you don't have to return this one. I'll be in L.A. tomorrow for the sole purpose of keeping my promise to have dinner with you. Well, it's almost my sole purpose. I'll be at the Hollywood Claverly, but please keep that our little secret. Our first. Leave word there of your availability and I'll adjust to your schedule, which I hope is crowded with delights."

I hung up, surprised to find myself thinking, But I don't hope that at all.

I called Dunleavy's number and got Detective Ossian. I told him I was letting them know, as requested, that I was on my way west again. Ossian said, "I figured. *Daily Variety* says your project is All Systems Go for immediate production. At least three unions were on golden time all weekend. I guess the network's trying to catch Trig Bascomb with his pants down, huh?"

I said, "You'd know more about that than me. All we get here from L.A. is sports scores."

He said, "You're missing a lot. Oh, don't forget to let Lieutenant Folsey there know you're leaving town."

"Will do." And I got off. I had no intention of calling Lieutenant Folsey until I was safely on the other coast. I saw no reason to trouble trouble.

Some kind of telepathy may have been at work. That or Ossian. Less than an hour later Folsey called. "Do you know where my precinct house is?" he asked.

I said, "I've walked by."

"Good. Could I bother you to drop around for a few minutes at either nine-thirty tonight or at six tomorrow night? Whichever is convenient?"

"Would you mind telling me why?"

"It's an identification thing."

"What's that?"

"It's a routine we have to put up with here." He was getting impatient with me. "Dotting the *i*'s and crossing the goddam *t*'s."

I said, "Yes . . . ?" And then, "And you need . . . ?" He would have to be a lot more forthcoming.

He took a moment. He didn't like having to give away this much but there was no way around it. He said, "A couple that was in the building on West End that night and went to Bermuda for the weekend? They're back."

"Yes . . . ?" My pulse quickened, but I played it as slow and dumb as I dared.

"These people were in the elevator around one A.M. with someone who got off at a high floor. They were—"

I said, "Excuse me, Lieutenant. The police have been taking a lot of my time this past week. Here and in L.A. I want to cooperate but I don't want to waste any more of my time. Or yours. You say someone got off 'at a high floor.' If you knew it was Stavros's floor you'd have said so. Am I wrong?"

"You're right, Mr. Saldinger, that's very good. We don't know what floor it was. Just a high one. I can see where you have the kind of mind it takes to write those crime shows. I'll have to catch one of yours. But this happened after one o'clock in the morning. We rang every bell on the high floors. Mostly family people. There was none of them came home nearly that late that night. Whoever got off at that high floor probably had no business on that floor."

"So what is it exactly you want from me?"

"I don't usually have this kind of conversation on the telephone." He weighed his options and decided there was no use pussyfooting. "I'd like to put you in a lineup with some police officers, make sure this couple back from Bermuda doesn't recognize you. It won't take twenty minutes of your time."

I said, "You may have heard that I was just in a lineup in L.A. And a witness there made me. Luckily I was able to prove I was somewhere else at the time. I don't know how much luck I have left. So you'll understand if I'm not anxious to be stared at by strangers."

"These particular witnesses eyeballed someone in an elevator. A small elevator with good light. There's not much chance of mistaken identity. I wouldn't worry on that score."

"If you say so. But I still don't know why you're coming to me on this."

"Come on. Your connection with the person

owned the apartment. Logic tells me I have to. Wouldn't you?"

"I'd want to think about that."

"I already have. So which will it be? This couple is available at nine-thirty tonight or at six tomorrow night."

Without a moment's hesitation I said, "Six tomorrow works better for me."

I would figure out a story on my way to the Coast.

PART THREE
N.Y. TO L.A.

CHAPTER TWENTY-TWO

The Hollywood Claverly Hotel—Claverly as in Clay and Beverly Winters, the husband-and-wife team who built it with unerring bad taste in the twenties—was a healthy cut above the Desert Palm. That still registered a good four cuts below, say, the Bel Age. Having sunk to rock bottom in the seventies, the Claverly had been bought by a consortium that gave it in the eighties the kind of cosmetic makeover that was more flash than substance, but good enough to make it an acceptable address for budget-minded business travelers.

These, so far as I could guess from the crowd in the lobby when I checked in, were mostly minor executives in the Colombian division of the mood-elevating game. They huddled in twos and threes in the corners, heads bent low and not quite facing each other, voices subdued but charged. They may have chosen the Claverly for the same reason I had: it was a high rise, and the competition would have some trouble getting at them. It was true that Stavros had been offed in a high-rise hotel, but I was not going to open my door to Mack the Knife.

My room proved to be a bit larger than a walk-in closet, but it was doggedly cheerful. And I liked looking down on worn-out but haunted Hollywood Boulevard, with the stars in its sidewalks reminding passersby how fleeting is fame. I waited until I unpacked to open a message the desk had been holding for me, an envelope addressed in a scrawl I recognized from his script notes as Vecchi's. No other messages, no call from Sarah.

Vecchi's note said, "I had a couple of good schemes for getting hold of this but I didn't have to use them. I lifted it from behind the reception desk in the office while the girl was in the can." It was unsigned. Attached was the current membership list of the Pacifica Tennis Club. I read through it and recognized a few names—character actors, a director, a couple of writers. They could mean something or, more likely, nothing. It seemed hopeless.

But then I read through it a second time, more slowly, and stopped in two new places. There was a Vince Cooper. Vince. What was Trig Bascomb's Vince's last name? I couldn't remember having heard one. Did his kind of Vince have a last name or was it vestigial and dropped soon after birth? Trig's Vince looked as if he could be a tennis player, and there was no court at the Bascombs'. So? The other name that stopped me was Wesley Bothwell. I couldn't be absolutely sure, but that sounded like Sarah Cole's Wes. I was almost positive. And what if it was? This exercise wasn't really going anywhere.

The phone rang. It was Sarah. She said, "Good, I caught you live. Welcome back. Welcome home. It really is your home, Saldinger, you've just been fighting it all these years." Even on the phone the sadness beneath the gaiety was as evident as a cloud crossing the moon.

I told her that when I heard her voice it did seem like home, but only then. And I asked her when she was free to have dinner.

She said, "You name it, the sooner the better. You have a first-rate vanishing act."

"I'd say tonight, but I literally just dropped my bag and I don't know yet when I may have to do my dancing bear act for the brothers Blau. Tomorrow?"

"Fine. If it turns out you are free tonight, call. As it happens, my calendar is clear. I keep it that way for easy reading."

"I'll call. Sarah, your ex, Wes. What's his last name?"

"What's the difference? He's dead."

"No, I mean it."

"Why?"

"Because . . . I know he plays sort of post–Ivy League types. Some producer was asking me if I knew someone for a part in— It's Bothwell, isn't it?"

"Steer the work somewhere else. Wes will never be Emmy material."

"Forget the job. It's just that at the time I blocked on the name. I hate when that happens. It is Bothwell, isn't it?"

"I'm not sure I want to have dinner with you if we're going to sit around swapping stories about Wes Bothwell."

"We won't, I promise. I'll call."

We hung up. So it was Bothwell.

I caught the Blaus together in a casting session. They both got on the phone. Behind them somewhere I could hear my own lines being spoken badly from an earlier draft of the script. Or was it the lines that were bad?

Seth said, "Hey, pal, how was your flight?"

Werner said, "Get on your horse and come out here. I have some notes from our female lead and I want to put you together with Jerry."

"Jerry?"

"Bayliss. Our director."

From what I knew, Jerry Bayliss couldn't direct the mouse to the cheese. The best anyone could say for him was that his pictures were in focus. And when you saw them you decided that was his first mistake. I said, "You got him, huh?"

Werner caught my tone. "With two days to principal photography, who did you expect, Scorsese?"

"Doesn't Bascomb have director approval?"

"He has veto. But he's not talking to us, so how can he exercise his veto? Get out here, Mike. There's no time for chit-chat."

"Wait a minute. What about my new draft?"

"Copied and distributed. You want a critique? After the picture's made. Where are you calling from?"

Did I have to tell him? "The Claverly."

"God. Be here in twenty minutes." They got off.

I was half out the door when I remembered to come back and put in a call to Lieutenant Folsey, NYPD. He was in.

I said, "I'm sorry, Lieutenant, I got an emergency call from my production company too late last night to let you know I couldn't make our date today."

"Where are you? Are you in California?"

"They needed me fast and I had to grab the first flight out this morning. If you still want me to come in—"

"Damn right I want you to come in."

"You sound as if I'm trying to dodge you. You

want to call my producer? This picture begins shooting on Thursday."

"When are you coming back to New York?"

"The minute I'm released. Two or three days."

"Make sure it's no longer. You understand?"

"You're making this sound a lot heavier than you did yesterday. Is there something new?"

"Since you asked. I had another talk with that couple I told you about. From the elevator? Trying to get some kind of fix on the man they saw. It wasn't easy."

I liked the sound of that. I said, "Didn't you say it was late at night? Could they have been drinking?"

He said, "Well . . . I won't get into that. But something did come back to the wife. And then the husband remembered." He stopped.

Forcing me to ask, "And what was that?"

"She thinks the man may have had a bruise. On his cheek, his forehead. Somewhere on his face."

I said, "I can see where you'd be concerned. Listen, they're calling me in to a meeting, but I'll shoot back to New York the first chance I get, my guess is two days at the most, help clear the air. Sorry, I'll have to get off."

I did. And looked in the mirror. The damn bruise had been fading but it still had a good week to go. Wild horses couldn't drag me back to New York before then.

At the studio gate in Burbank the guard gave me directions to the Blaus' production headquarters, a building heretofore unknown to me and not easy to find. They somehow always were. Then he assigned me a parking space about a quarter of a mile from it, no big deal in New York but an affront in L.A., especially in the Valley during a midafternoon temperature rise that felt as if someone had opened the oven door. When I finally found Building 27C and stepped into the air-conditioned lobby, I was doubly refreshed. I found myself face-to-face with Al Vecchi. I greeted him like a twin separated at birth and asked him what he was doing here.

He said, "Waiting for you. I knew you'd be heading this way. The trades are full of what's happening on this production." He came close to blushing. "Yeah, I'm reading the trades. And if *I* know where you'll be, your friend Mack the Knife knows, so I thought, just in case . . . I wasn't doing anything anyway . . . Did you get the list I left at the hotel?"

"The tennis club membership. I don't know what to do with it but I've got it. Thanks."

"Hey, I needed the exercise." He must have read my face. He said, "No, I didn't walk to the club. I meant the mental exercise. No more walking. The network insisted on laying a rental on me. A midsize. Would you believe it?"

"Who's romancing you?"

"You're right, word got around on what I'm doing —for Kornbluth, not you—and now someone else is after me to toughen up their shows." I now noticed he was wearing a new sport jacket in a soft sand color. It almost fit.

"Couldn't be better for you, Al. Being loved is good; being loved by the competition is heaven. You're not still handling your own negotiations . . . ?"

"Why not?"

"Please, let me get Wolf Waxroth on it. No job's too small for Wolf if he sees a chance to thrust the knife in deep and give it some wrist action."

"Let me think about it. They're waiting for you upstairs." We started up. He mumbled, "I've already been approached by a couple of agents. I took a meeting with one.'' I'd been gone less than a week and a new Vecchi was emerging. In another few weeks he'd be saying, "You know, I could live here. The vegetables are fresher and they've got a really first-rate symphony orchestra.''

Upstairs we made our way along a corridor past six or eight actors sitting, standing, or pacing with script pages in their hands, all of them absorbed in getting a fix on the character they were preparing to read for. I didn't recognize any of these people, but two of them flashed generous smiles my way. They may have remembered me from previous such sessions as someone from the creative side, or, more likely, they may simply have decided I wasn't an actor so why take a chance of possibly offending an executive with a vote in casting? Actors on their way up smile a lot. I had long since vowed sooner to indenture my children to Zaire ivory poachers than encourage them in a career in acting.

Vecchi elected to post himself in the corridor just outside the door of the room they were using for casting. I waited to slip in until an actor who had just finished reading opened the door to come out. The Blaus, barely visible through a cloud of blue smoke, were comparing notes with Jerry Bayliss and the casting director. The group had obviously been at it for many hours. The cigarette butts, plastic cups and sandwich plates, soda cans, and crumpled notepaper were stacked in geological layers. A secretary passed me on her way out, probably to fetch the next actor. The selection process had the feel of a longshoreman's shape-up and it operated on the same principle. Never mind the right actor for the right role. Even with production schedules less frantic than this one, there was rarely time for that kind of luxury. The strongest people available that day and willing to work got the jobs.

I didn't see why the Blaus had been in such a hurry to summon me. Nobody here even acknowledged I was in the room, and this session still had hours to go. The script had twenty-nine speaking parts. Three or four so-called starring roles would have been cast without auditions. I guessed they would be trying to cast about half the rest today. I sat in a corner and squirmed through one more reading. I often squirmed when I hadn't yet got the dialogue right or it was being read by someone wrong for the part. Rather than submit to more of this, I came up behind Seth and tapped him on the shoulder.

That brought the proceedings to a very brief halt for cursory greetings all around and introductions where necessary. Jerry Bayliss and I each told one flattering lie about each other's work, and then Werner, who seemed to be functioning at warp speed, shoved a page at me with what he said were the complaints and queries from the actress who had been signed yesterday to play opposite Bascomb. The widow. She would get second billing, below the title.

"Work on these for Ellie," he said. "See if you can make her happy without pulling out any threads. In a few minutes we're taking a break here so I can sign contracts. That'll give Jerry a chance to walk you through the New York sets and talk down the action. We didn't have time to rig the stunts your way, but Jerry has some ideas."

I wanted to say how surprised I was, because I understood Jerry hadn't had an idea since he tied the heroine to the railroad track. But I held my tongue, retreated to my corner, and tried to read

Ellie Wister's note. Another actor was struggling with my dialogue and I had to stop to reedit that in my head.

When I was finally able to concentrate on Ellie, I found that most of what she had to say made sense and addressing it would create no problems. Relieved, I put the note away. This was no place to work and I had something on my agenda more urgent—a talk with Seth Blau. No reason not to steal him for a few minutes. Seth was a fifth wheel in this room anyway; his vote might even be counted as a negative. I walked up behind him, tugged his sleeve, and mimed that I needed him. He followed me dutifully out of the room and back into the corridor, now rapidly filling with more actors. Most of them would have to wait, sweating bullets, until after Werner signed his contracts.

"What's up?" Seth asked. He hadn't the least idea.

"Not here," I said, and led him down the hall. I found an empty office, ushered him in, closed the door. Before he could open his mouth I said, "Why didn't you tell me you went out with Nick Stavros's sister?"

His eyes widened. But just for an instant. He said, "Easy, pal. It was no big deal. You'd have been one of the first to know if we'd gotten engaged or something."

"I hear you didn't get engaged or anything. Did you get to meet Niko?"

"Stavros? Hell, no, I'd have told you if I did."

"He was in the bar the night you and I had dinner at Christine's."

"How would I know? I still don't know what he looked like. Maybe Christine doesn't introduce her men to the family on the first date. I just saw her that once. I never mentioned it around here because it wasn't especially memorable. It wasn't especially anything." He looked at me speculatively. "Did I miss something?"

I said, "I want you to lie awake nights wondering about that. Did you bring up *Corrigan* with Christine?"

"No. And Mike, I don't like being grilled as though I'd committed a crime."

"Join the club. Sorry if I stepped on your toes. Would you rather I took this up with Werner?"

His tone softened. "Let's clear it up here and now. What exactly is your problem?"

"You came east with Werner's notes. And yours. For the sole purpose of going over the story with me. Your head was full of *Corrigan,* that's what we talked about for two days. And you're telling me you went out with Christine and the subject never came up?"

"It was my last night in town. I was trying to romance the lady. Murmuring television stories in her ear wasn't going to do the trick."

"You and I went to her restaurant from my apartment. You had your copy of my presentation with you."

"In my coat pocket. In a manila envelope. And yes, I suppose if Christine and I had ended up at her place, or my hotel, and I took off my coat, followed hopefully by my jacket and pants, she might have found a chance to sneak a peek at the outline. But what we did was go someplace in the neighborhood where they played jazz, and we had a drink. One each. The air went out of the balloon fast. I don't do great with women in the East. Maybe it's the water."

I wanted to say that eastern ice cubes didn't have

"Blau Brothers" stamped on them. Instead I said, "You didn't take her home?"

"I dropped her in a taxi. I didn't even take her phone number. It's not the kind of story you tell when you're sitting around bullshitting with the guys. Listen, I understand where you're coming from but you and I are shooting blanks and I gotta go. They'll be looking for me."

I said, "Right. Okay, thanks. I appreciate your telling me the way it happened."

He nodded and walked out. That was a big fat nothing.

So was my walk-through on the New York sets with Jerry Bayliss, Vecchi trailing. A number of interiors were under construction, and the studio's standing New York street was being frantically touched up, redressed, and rigged for some stunts. This was all to figure in the opening sequence of the picture—Corrigan's last gritty New York case, the one that decided him to put in for early retirement and a bucolic new life in the Pacific Northwest.

I passed Vecchi off to Bayliss as the network's technical adviser on police matters before I realized, right, that's what he was. I had been telling lies almost by reflex this past week. Bayliss did most of the talking on the tour. A leather-fleshed man in his fifties wearing, yes, a safari jacket, he used his arms a lot to describe the simple stunts he had devised to replace mine. He explained them, and he reexplained them, and then, to make sure I had gotten it, he explained them again. He was very pleased with what he had come up with.

I quickly understood that Bayliss's changes had nothing to do with "not enough time" to rig the set the way I had written the sequence; he just wanted to do the action his way. It wasn't worth my energy to argue with the director. Not this director, determined to kick up his heels for a movie star in a pilot after years of pulling the plow in episodic television. I agreed to come back the next day, when the set would be close to finished, and make the notes I would need to adjust the pages to Bayliss's action.

Vecchi and I left Bayliss to huddle with the production designer, and we walked back in silence toward the front of the lot until we were out of earshot. Then Vecchi said, "They make you earn every cent, don't they?"

"Beats laying linoleum," I said. "But just."

CHAPTER TWENTY-THREE

I holed up in my cheery room at the Claverly the rest of the day, alternately staring out at the sun glinting off the chinoiserie on the facade of Mann's Chinese Theater and pushing out script revisions on the computer the Blaus had rented for me. I started with Ellie Wister's notes because they were intelligent, had Werner's endorsement, and would go fast. I had brought the script west on a floppy and that kept the typing to a minimum. After Ellie I braced myself for Jerry Bayliss's three tightly handwritten pages.

To address the most broadly philosophical of Bayliss's notes would have required a new script. "Too late!" as Warner Oland, playing Charlie Chan, said when his number one son, Keye Luke, came running up with a clue after Charlie had solved the murder. "Save for next case." As for Bayliss's page notes, he was mostly showing off that he had read every word of the script. Werner had slapped a Post-it on the first page that read, "Do what you can with this, but don't agonize. The top priority now is window cuts. Myrna says we need five minutes."

I took Werner's first sentence as a license to do as little as I could with Bayliss's notes short of outright insulting him. But I disagreed with the need for cuts. I have a better feel than a script supervisor's stopwatch about how long my scripts run. This one seemed right—maybe six or seven minutes above air-time, the minimum cushion the editor would need. I would take out a minute or so and be prepared to argue.

By the time the Chinese theater lit up for the evening, word of where I was staying had leaked around town, and I had to stop a few times to take phone calls and once to receive more notes—from Kornbluth this time, by way of the Blaus. I went down to the lobby to pick these up. I had left word with the desk to send nothing, and especially no one, to my room.

Kornbluth had scrawled across the envelope with a marking pen, "Mike, call me!"

I called him and he took the call.

"Hi," I said. "You having a problem with the draft?"

"The draft? No, that's okay. I sent the Blaus a few notes." His mind was miles from the draft. He turned from the mouthpiece, probably to his secretary. "Thanks, Eileen. Would you close the door, please?"

He was back on with me a moment later, anxious, but with his voice much lower. "I had a call," he said. "From the sister."

"Christine Stavros called you?"

"The sister!" he snapped. He was letting me know not to use names. "She says she has it in her possession."

"Has what?"

"You know, the original."

"What does she want?"

"Mike, does she? Does she have it?"

"I don't know," I said. "She may be bluffing."

"She *may* be?"

"What do you want me to do, prove it? You want me to break into her apart—"

"Mike!"

"No, I don't know absolutely that she's bluffing. I don't know where the truth is anymore. What is she asking for?"

"A reasonable, she says, cash settlement."

"Can't your people find her a few bucks, quietly, and end this thing?"

"Plus she wants recognition—screen credit—for the brother as co-creator."

"That's a Writers Guild call."

"Only if you contest it."

"Damn right I contest it. That's out."

"The whole package is out. Do you understand? No deals. New York would drop the ceiling on me. We've got to hang on, push ahead, make the picture as fast as we can."

"And when she goes public with a lawyer?"

"By then we're at least deep in production and we can't lose Bascomb anymore. And we hope she's bluffing. What about that?"

I said, "She's bluffing. The more I think about it the surer I am." But my first answer had been closer to my true feeling. Christine had been straight with me; somehow I didn't think she would lie this extravagantly. I don't know what she had in her possession but she thought she had the goods.

* * *

.

The interrupting phone calls came about once an hour. The first was from Wolf Waxroth, warm as toast. How did my flight go? was I comfortable at the hotel? blah, blah. He couldn't have been more attentive. He knew I knew he had tried to screw me with Bascomb and he would have to make nice for a while, maybe even take my calls. I asked how Phoebe was.

"Phoebe?"

"The migraines."

"What can I say? Thanks for asking. How is the script coming? Is Jerry Bayliss, that lox, giving you trouble?"

"I made the changes," I said. "Will Bascomb show up to play them?"

"He has a makeup call first thing Thursday morning. He'll be there, I guarantee." He paused for effect. "Mike, he loves the new scenes."

"How do you know?"

"I established a relationship with Bascomb, remember? I was in contact just this afternoon. Not directly. With his trainer, whatever, at the house. Vince what's-his-name. He says Trig is very pleased. He pointed you in a direction and you built on his foundation. Trig likes that."

"Vince said all that? The man must have verbal diarrhea."

"Mike, you're set with Bascomb. The man is reassured."

I said, "He made a mighty fast turnaround. You're telling me he's now prepared to honor his contract with the Blaus just because he feels okay about a scene where a widow teaches him to handle a canoe?"

"My reading is no, the script changes are not all of it. Basically he needs an excuse to report to work.

What I hear is, he put out feelers for a film deal and nobody felt back. What's he going to do, sit home and play gin with his wife? By the way, I hear, a lovely woman.''

An hour later I had a call from Rudd Cole. Sarah had told him where I was staying. "Nice choice," he said without much preamble. "A lot of big stars stay at the Claverly. The last, I believe, was Carole Lombard, in 1936."

"They're coming back," I said, "but only to the lobby. They can get what they need there to make them happy."

"Everything but a three-picture deal at Fox." He didn't even pause. "What exactly happened in that apartment house on West End Avenue last week? Curiouser and curiouser, as Alice remarked years before she went into that sitcom about the diner."

"You're right, it was curious," I said, "but the full story had better wait until we're warming ourselves over a drink in front of your ceramic logs. There may be a docudrama in the making here."

"Forget docudrama. One more permutation in this tale and you're into mini-series. Torn from tomorrow's headlines by greedy fingers. Do you have time for one more smashing solution to the murder of the Greek?"

"Save it for when I can enjoy it."

"I figured. You must be hacking away at changes. I only called to pass along Jasmine's *'Mi casa es su casa,'* which sounds nifty in Japanese. Okay?"

"Thanks, Rudd," I said. And then, slyly, "Oh, and thanks for that call the other day to Helene. She was touched that you took the time to think of her."

"Oh, that. Well, yes . . . uh-huh. What are friends for?"

"Exactly. Good night, Rudd."

I had had him tongue-tied for a moment. But I didn't have the faintest idea why.

Right after a dinner break in the lobby restaurant, where I dined on the regional delicacy you can't get in New York, the New York strip steak, Seth Blau called. I had gone back to wrestling with Bayliss's notes, a couple of which there was no way to duck. It was nearly ten, and behind Seth I could hear a cocktail piano.

"How's it going?" he asked. He sounded slightly oiled.

"Moving along," I said. "I should be finished in a couple of hours."

"Good. We ran the current draft through a script service. It's got scene numbers and it's being boarded. So this set of revisions will be going into colors." Why was he telling me things of absolutely no interest to me? He said, "You'll bring the revised pages to the studio in the morning?"

I said, "No, you'll have to send somebody for them. I have something to do in the morning."

"You're not coming out?" He sounded dismayed.

"The work will be on a floppy. You'll have to print it and read it and compare notes with Werner and Bayliss before you're ready for me. I should be there by then."

"Good. Because we have to talk."

"Don't worry. You'll all get your crack at me."

"No, I mean you and me. Away from the others."

"Oh?" What was that about? "You don't want to talk now?"

"No."

"Whatever you say." Whatever it was, he knew how to whet my appetite for it.

As soon as I hung up, I remembered to call Sergeant Dunleavy. I left word with the detective who answered that I was back in Los Angeles and the sergeant could reach me through the office of the Blau Brothers in Burbank.

I finished the notes at about a quarter to two. I turned off the machine and tried to go to sleep. It took me about an hour.

CHAPTER TWENTY-FOUR

On my list of things I didn't miss about Los Angeles during that long drought in my employment that kept me mostly in the East, rush-hour traffic stood near the top. The bad taste came back this morning; the streets moved no easier than I remembered. Jenny Haycroft, I had learned from the third phone book I searched, lived in Culver City. To make it to the studio from her neighborhood I would have to double back at a crawl more or less to my start point and then creep and stall a few miles beyond it. Every painful inch I made in the direction I was going I would have to eat coming back.

I had left the hotel at seven-thirty A.M. to make sure I nabbed the elusive Ms. Haycroft before she left her apartment, room, house, whatever, for the day. At eight-thirty, still short of my goal, I wondered if I was about to blow it. There was small comfort in knowing I was not alone in my frustration. Somewhere behind me in the line of cars, Vecchi's rented

Ford occasionally stuck out its blunt black nose as he doggedly followed me.

Jenny's address turned out to be a long, two-story wooden box in an anything-goes zoning district. Two rows of apartment doors all opened directly to the outdoors, motel style. Jenny's was on the second floor. Those apartments, each featuring a huge picture window, were reached along a deck. Jenny's drapes, like all her neighbors', were drawn. Permanently, I supposed. Otherwise, as at a motel, a passerby on the runway would be able to count the teeth of anyone inside.

I tapped her door knocker twice with no results. But I hadn't expected any. She had returned late last night from Mexico and she could be either fast asleep or in serious trouble in the bathroom. I knocked again, louder and longer. This time from somewhere behind the thin door I heard shuffling, rustling, and finally footsteps. And then from directly behind the door, her voice.

"Who *is* it?"

"Global," I said. "I've got your check." Global was her modeling agency.

"Check? What check?" she asked, and flung the door open irritably.

She passed the morning test. No makeup, hair a mess, just rolled out of bed and wrapped in a ragged cotton robe, she looked ounce for ounce as good as she had in that cereal commercial. To my taste, better.

"Oh, God," she said. She knew who I was.

"Yes, Jenny, it's your friend from New York," I said. "The one who's in television. Actually right in it. Okay if I come in?"

"No." She clutched the robe tighter around her, a strange display of modesty from a woman who had been roller-skating in Venice naked except for that sprayed-on coating of Spandex. She bit her lip and reconsidered. "There's a café on the south corner, far side. Give me ten minutes."

"No you don't," I said. "You have a bad track record keeping dates with me."

She said, "You know where I live. Where am I going to run?" I knew she would show up.

I said, "Five minutes. Don't dress to impress me. It's not a commercial callback."

I left my car and walked to the place. Vecchi followed in his car and parked almost directly across the street. He must have seen Jenny when she opened her apartment door. As I walked past him he rolled his eyes heavenward and mimed a kiss-kiss.

She showed in not much over five minutes. I was sitting at a table but I hadn't even been brought my coffee. She couldn't have improved on herself if she had taken another hour. Her attire gave me an entirely new appreciation for jeans. I ordered her a coffee, and she asked if I minded moving to the back table. I didn't, and we did.

She was nervous and she was trying to overcome it. When we were settled she said, "I told you I had a feeling we'd run into each other again."

"Jenny, this is running into each other only in the sense that the Patriot runs into the Scud. And that's about the way you ran into me that day at the beach. I was targeted, wasn't I? For how long?"

"About fifteen seconds."

"Tell me."

She said, "You don't remember me, do you?"

"From before the beach? No. And you're not easily forgotten."

"It was over three years ago. A TV movie called *Promises I Never Made.*"

"A family drama. I wrote it. You weren't in it . . . ?"

"I read for you. You and three or four other people. I wasn't sure who was who, but you were at the casting session."

"You have a remarkable memory."

"I don't get that many theatrical auditions. It was for a small part, and I didn't get it. You were the only one at the table who looked at me as if I had a chance."

"Not to discourage you, Jenny, but could I have been looking at you simply because you're good to look at?"

"I hope not."

"So that day at the beach . . ." I prompted.

"It happened almost instantly. I was skating, I recognized you, you were dressed like you had just come from the East, and I figured you could be here for a new picture."

"All that in fifteen seconds?"

"It can happen in ten when you need it. I need it. So I put my improv classes to the test. If you had come to town for a picture, and there was a part in it for me—any part—I wanted a shot at it."

I said, "If that's what you were after why didn't you introduce yourself as an actress?" But I thought I already knew that answer.

"Because that way I'd have lasted three minutes with you. One more eager young actress on the make. You'd have been bored out of your gourd. The way I did it, I kept you interested."

I said, "And then, when I would get to know you for the refreshing person you were, you would reveal yourself as an actress?"

"I'm very well trained, Mr. Saldinger. I'm a Carnegie-Mellon graduate and I studied at the H-B Studio in New York."

"*In* New York? Right in it?"

To her credit, she blushed.

I said, "Hats off to your improv classes. You fooled me, I freely admit it. So why did you stand me up at Musso and Frank? And please don't tell me about your sick grandma in the Valley."

The hard part was coming. She said, "I had every intention of keeping that date."

"So . . . ?"

"I had the TV news on as I was getting ready to leave the apartment. And there was this item about the man who was pushed through the hotel window on the Sunset Strip. Awful. And they flashed your picture, with your name. And gave the impression that the dead man had somehow been causing you trouble."

"So that made you think the police might want to question me about the crime."

"The TV said that man was killed shortly after noon. Around the time you were with me. If the police did question you, I was afraid you might tell them that."

"What's wrong with that? You were my alibi."

She didn't answer right away. "What's wrong with it, Mr. Saldinger, is that I told my husband I was having dinner with a girlfriend."

"You have a husband?" I said stupidly. "Back there in that apartment?"

She nodded. "Taking a shower. I told him I was going shopping."

I took a moment to regroup. "I'm sorry, Jenny, there's no way around it. You're going to have to vouch for me with the police. They're hounding me not only for this murder, but for another one in the East. Cops will soon be taking numbers for me, like in a bakery.''

"What about my husband? I'd rather not have to tell him I lied to him.''

"He'll never know. I'll work it out with Sergeant Dunleavy of the L.A. police.''

"But suppose it does get out . . . ?''

"Then tell him what happened. It was perfectly innocent. You and I ran into each other and remembered that other meeting years ago. We saw each other at the beach and then never again until I looked you up because I needed the alibi. That's the truth, isn't it?''

"Do I really have to do this . . . ?''

"I'm afraid so.''

She sighed. "Okay. But I was right, wasn't I? You *were* here for a picture, and you're here for it again. *Corrigan's Way.*''

"A pilot.''

"My husband's an actor too. Blond, outdoorsy, twenty-eight. Is there anything in it that's right for either of us?''

"I'll talk to the casting director. Meanwhile I'll give you Sergeant Dunleavy's number and I'll alert him to expect a call from you.'' I took a beat. "Jenny . . .''

"Yes?''

"Suppose there had been no murder that day and you had shown up for our dinner date. How far were you prepared to go to make an impression?''

"The truth?'' She hesitated. "I'm sorry, Mr. Saldinger. Not very.''

CHAPTER TWENTY-FIVE

When Vecchi and I finally got to the studio, a production meeting I should have sat in on had just broken. Casting was again fully under way and elsewhere on the lot contracted feature players were filing in and out of wardrobe. I ran into the production designer, who looked busier than the legendary one-armed paperhanger; he told me his paperhangers and scenic artists were even busier. This picture was heavier with golden time than the Los Angeles basin with smog.

Wolf Waxroth had been right, as he usually was in such matters: word had come from Trig Bascomb's camp that the star would be available for work at the start of production tomorrow. He would provide his own wardrobe—subject, of course, to the director's veto. I could just picture Bayliss vetoing Trig's chamois jacket with velvet trim and Trig finally blurting out, "I don't do scenes where I debate wardrobe with the director."

It turned out there would not be enough time to

light the New York interiors for shooting tomorrow. The location manager had come up with a practical location, reasonably close, at which to do the body-in-the-lake sequence; they had decided to go with that first. The unit manager was juggling and rejuggling his board to make the schedule work both logistically and budgetwise. I was impressed with the determined speed with which the picture was proceeding. And watching Jerry Bayliss work, I began to understand why Werner had been willing to settle for him. Now that the film was on go he wasn't going to spend a lot of time sitting around pondering "the style of the piece." He would knock out the pages.

I spent the rest of the day absorbing notes through Werner or Bayliss to reconcile the script with the realities of casting, physical layout, the production schedule, and last-minute second thoughts. Thank God there was no flood of notes to wrestle with from Program Practices. Network cutbacks for economy had axed the house censors first; every production furnished its own conscience. God save America, I thought, from Werner Blau's conscience.

I fought Werner and Bayliss to a draw on further script cuts. They agreed to limit them to one minute and to let me find the minute. As always, the most expendable lines turned out to be my prize jokes.

My pulse was beginning to quicken; tomorrow the camera would roll. Several strings of cheap thread spun over many months would come together to weave what would eventually be just another cheap garment. Nonetheless there remained a tiny element of magic in the process and it never failed to produce a cheap thrill of expectation. Once in a while, once every four or five years, the expectation was realized.

All through the day Seth kept darting urgent, meaningful glances my way. They said, When can we talk? But we were never alone. In any case I was under continual pressure to turn out pages for still another color of paper. I couldn't afford to take time out for Seth Blau.

I took only two short breaks. One was to call Sarah Cole for her address in West Hollywood. I told her I would come by for her probably by eight, definitely by nine, but not to be discouraged if I was later, and could I please give her the responsibility of making a reservation somewhere? My custom on coming to L.A. had always been to head dutifully for the restaurant I had been told on my last visit was "a must." Invariably I could now bowl in the place. Sarah was plugged in; she would spare me that embarrassment.

The second call was to Dunleavy. It was my pleasure to inform him he would be hearing from a Ms. Jenny Haycroft, my beach alibi.

"I heard from her," he said, less than overwhelmed. "An actress. She's coming in later today, after she reads for a prune commercial. Oh, and Lieutenant Folsey, in New York, wants you to call."

I had no intention of calling Folsey. Nor, now that Jenny was in my head, would I suggest to our casting director that he consider day-player work for her or her outdoorsy husband. Not because Jenny had bruised my ego. But if it should come to Dunleavy's attention that I had thrown a job her way, he would suspect a quid pro quo that might invalidate her as my alibi. Maybe later, when the heat was off me and the series was into episodes, I would look for something for her.

* * *

I came out from under the revisions at about six o'clock. My last remaining task for the day would be to walk through the New York sets, interiors and exterior—the stage with the interiors adjoined the New York street—and make notes for adjusting the action in the sequence to the configuration of the sets. I had seen the current shooting schedule; the New York sets wouldn't start shooting until Tuesday. Once I saw the sets, I could use these few days to try and improve on Jerry Bayliss's routine take on the action.

The few days would also help me with Lieutenant Folsey, NYPD. If he pressed the Blaus to release me to return to New York, they could honestly claim my presence in L.A. was essential to the production. And if by Tuesday the fading bruise on my forehead had not entirely disappeared, I would find some other way to make myself essential here. The pair of ditzes in that elevator had been too drunk, and too much time had gone by, for them to identify a man about whom they could remember not one physical fact other than he might be sporting a bruise somewhere on his person.

This would be the time to give Seth Blau the few minutes he had been pleading for. The Blaus were still in session with the casting director and Bayliss, reading minor female roles. I came into the corridor outside the casting room and found Vecchi sitting there, totally relaxed, shamelessly enjoying the parade of women passing into the room. They were mostly mature character actresses, but from Vecchi's face you would have thought he was ogling starlets. I gave him high marks for his total lack of ageism. Seth spotted me as soon as I cracked the door. He had obviously been waiting. He slipped out and followed me wordlessly to the office where we had had our little conference yesterday. Vecchi barely glanced at us as we walked by.

There were no preambles. Something was weighing heavily on Seth and he was anxious to unburden himself. He said, "After we talked yesterday, I started thinking."

That would be a novelty; Werner did almost all of Seth's thinking. But I kept my mouth shut and arranged my face to show sympathetic attention to what he had to say.

He said, "You asked me if I told Christine Stavros anything about *Corrigan*. And I told you, no, nothing. That was the truth. And then you wanted to know if your story outline could have gotten into her hands—"

"And you said only if you took off your coat and maybe your pants. Are you going to tell me that happened?"

"I wish. I told you I had the script in my overcoat pocket. On the coat rack at the back of the restaurant."

"In a manila clasp envelope."

"That's what I got to thinking about after I left you yesterday. That envelope."

"Go on."

"I put on my coat when you and I left your apartment. I rolled the envelope and stuffed it in my pocket as far as it would go. But which pocket?"

"Which pocket?" I echoed stupidly.

"I'm right-handed. My *left* pocket. Always. Last night I tried to shove a rolled manuscript-sized envelope in my right pocket. It was awkward, unnatural. I suddenly understand why the sword always hangs on the left."

By God, he *had* been thinking. "Are you telling me," I said, "that when you took your coat off the rack when we left the restaurant the envelope was in your right pocket?''

"I hadn't thought about it since—why should I?— but it came back to me last night. Because of the way you bitched yesterday. When we left the restaurant there was a moment when that envelope somehow felt as if it was in the wrong pocket. But just a moment. And to tell you the truth, I can't say for sure it happened."

I said, "It would have taken, what, eight or ten minutes to read that outline? Christine didn't do it. We were in the restaurant early and it was packed. She was all over the room taking care of customers. I doubt she ever left the floor."

"The brother?"

"Niko was at the bar. I didn't introduce you but I did tell the bartender you were my producer in from the Coast for a story meeting. Niko could have heard that. He must have heard that. And seen the envelope sticking out of your coat pocket."

"Son of a bitch," Seth said, and then, embarrassed, "Listen, I'd appreciate if you didn't mention this to Werner."

"It wasn't your fault. Nobody protects television series proposals like they were the family jewels."

He said, "You don't know Werner. It's my fault when we're shooting exteriors and it rains."

That may have been why he had shoved this memory to the farthest recess of his mind—fear of Werner. A minute later, reassured by my promise not to expose him to his brother, he excused himself to return to the casting room.

I sat in the gathering dark pondering what Seth had told me. Jenny Haycroft might at this moment be lifting a murder cloud from my head, but I had

never taken that seriously. Even my worst enemy
would be hard put to believe I could push a man
through a window. But at least one or two of my
lesser friends might entertain the possibility of my
committing plagiarism. And now that cloud appeared to be breaking up. Second only to the possibility of hearing again from Mack the Knife, it had
been the heaviest cloud hanging over me.

What had I known of Niko's idea for a television
series? And when, as the old saw has it, did I know it?
I tried to review the evidence, circumstantial as it
was, speculative as it had to be, of the evolution of
Corrigan. My conjectures, I believed, were fair and
reasonable.

Very possibly, I now found myself willing to admit,
some fragment of a story Nicholas Stavros had
pressed on me when I was in an alcoholic fog at his
sister's bar may indeed have lodged in a recess of my
brain. And months later it may or may not have surfaced in an altered form that gradually evolved into
Corrigan. By that time Stavros had doubtless gotten
wind of a *Corrigan* project in the works—it had
popped up in TV columns—and wondered whether
I had stolen his story. Why? Because he had told me
a story, it must have been about a cop, and therefore
in his mind I might very well have stolen it. So he
had "borrowed" Seth Blau's copy of the *Corrigan*
outline at the restaurant long enough to read it.
And he had found, or thought he found—would I
ever know which?—some element of his invention
in the material. He might then have begun to believe it was *all* his, that this was the very story he had
told me. So he had gone home and written it down,
very close, but not too close, to the way I had written
it. By which time he was so convinced that this was
the way it had always been that even his sister had

come to remember it that way, as well as Toby the bartender. No wonder Niko had worked himself into a rage against me.

At this late date I honestly couldn't say what *Corrigan* owed to Niko's input. Did I have a debt to his estate? I went through it all again. It was possible that what he told me that night related not at all to the *Corrigan* idea, or it related so remotely that he deserved no share of the credit for it. It was also possible that Niko's story had something of *Corrigan* in it, but that I had still come to the idea independently, without reference to my subconscious. It wasn't, after all, that exotic a concept. The same idea comes to several writers often enough—and paranoia is sufficiently widespread—that professionals often make amateurs sign a release before they will read their material. I knew I could never have been drunk enough to *invite* Stavros to tell me his television story. Only certifiable insanity could have induced me to do that.

What was clear to me now was that Nick Stavros had never had in his possession a registered-mail envelope with an original manuscript predating my written *Corrigan* proposal. That threat was a scam he had dreamed up in his righteous anger at me after reading my outline. So what, I wondered, was in the envelope he gave his sister to hold before he left on his fateful trip to California?

CHAPTER TWENTY-SIX

When Orson Welles went west to make *Citizen Kane,*
they showed him through the sound stages at RKO
and he said something like, "This is the biggest set
of electric trains any boy ever had." He had it more
or less right; the working part of a studio has always
looked to me like a giant playpen. By day, that is,
when there are people around to play in it. Studios
are meant to be filled with people—before, behind,
and beside the cameras and sound gear and end-
lessly fiddling with the lights; and where there are
no cameras, building sets or tearing them down, or
trucking them in or out, or repainting the floor. At
night, when the studio streets are empty and the
vehicles don't move and the open elephant doors
make black holes, the stillness rings in the ears and
the cavernous stages have all the appeal of a mauso-
leum.

The huge stage that held the New York interiors
for *Corrigan* was marked off with cautionary "Active
Set" tapes, but at the moment I was the only activity.

The scenic artists and lighting people who would be working into the night were, I guessed, on a dinner break. Notebook in hand, I picked my way around the areas of wet paint and the places where furniture and props were already in place. Making an occasional note as I walked, I had to be careful not to trip over stage braces or thickets of cable.

Vecchi had said, "Right behind you," when I told him where I was going but I could tell he was reluctant to tear himself away from the people-watching that had hypnotized him outside the casting office. I had gotten used to his dogging me and I suddenly missed his bulking presence.

I moved on the stage from Corrigan's gritty squad room to his tiny office to a lush Wall Street broker's office to a cheap saloon to the hallway of an old brownstone and then to its gloomy basement. Most of these sets were standard and predictable and I moved quickly, sometimes around the sets, sometimes through a door on one set to get to the next. I marveled, as I always did, at the power of artifice. I knew I was on a sound stage, but I was also in that squad room taking in its yellowing WANTED posters and half-expecting its occupants to drift in to answer the battered phones. And I smelled the success of that Wall Street broker in his soft leather furniture, his hunting prints, and his gleaming fruitwood desk. Through his high-rise window I could almost glimpse the Trinity Church spire.

The brownstone basement was the most convincing—unpleasantly dank-seeming under the single standing work light. Even the stairs, rising supposedly to street level but ending twelve feet in the air, barely dissuaded me from the uneasy feeling that rats were scrabbling in the corners. These basement stairs were going to figure in action also involving a number of props, and I stopped to make a note on the placement of the stairs and the props—two suitcases, a bicycle, some cases of wine.

It was while making my note that I heard a sound I wasn't entirely comfortable with. I would have preferred rats; this was the sound of a man moving too lightly and cautiously to be either crew or a security guard. For all I knew, the movement had been going on all the time I was on the stage but my own footsteps had covered it. I put the notebook in my pocket and gave my attention to listening. Very slowly, some distance off, I heard a door open on a set. My gut tightened. I didn't like being pinned here in the basement. And then I reminded myself this wasn't a basement and there were plenty of ways to leave it.

Thus encouraged, I took advantage of being in the one set that could afford me an overview of the stage. The stairs were practical, and very solid. They had to be; three people would be fighting on them. I tiptoed up for a look around, stopping only one step short of the one that led into the void. The maze of walls below and the occasional work lights gave me a limited view of the stage. It was like looking down on a pinball machine with most of its lights out. But I stayed with it.

After a bit I was rewarded with the shadow of a head and shoulders moving across a wall of the squad room. Even as distended as it was, I thought I recognized that shadow. Or had apprehension stirred my imagination?

The shadow disappeared in a direction I calculated would make its creator visible, if only partly, as he crossed the length of the squad room. And an instant later, and only for an instant, I saw just the top of a head moving in my direction, the dirty blond hair combed straight back. A glimpse was all I needed to recognize Mack the Knife. My blood surged and I bounded down the stairs. Too carelessly; one step boomed. But by that time I was racing around and through the tangle of props, flats, lights, dollies, and cables, headed for the elephant doors coming at me dead ahead, and the open air. My feet had wings.

A moment later I was looking down the New York street, a hundred yards of turn-of-the-century brownstones to my right, the theater, shops, and an office building to my left, all false fronts erected decades ago. Mack had to have heard me running; he had abandoned stealth and was running now himself. I could hear him, still on the stage, banging against obstacles as he made for the doors. I hadn't come out the doors I went in. Disoriented, I couldn't remember whether the front of the lot was behind me or ahead. I began to run the length of the New York brownstones. Almost at once I knew I had made the wrong decision. I was headed toward the back lot—the foreign streets, the western street, the small town square, acres of fake buildings. They would be absolutely dead at this hour, without lights or security; a shot from Mack's small-caliber pistol would not be heard. Under no circumstances must I allow myself to be trapped back there. So what were my choices?

Mack had not yet come out of the stage but I could hear his footsteps approaching the elephant doors. I was confident I could keep ahead of him. This past year of five- and six-minute miles in Central Park made me secure in that department. So long as he didn't dead-end me somewhere. Or get close enough to take a shot. In the gathering dark I was a poor target and I ran bent forward to make myself even less of one.

The unbroken phalanx of brownstones, with their wide, stepped entrances, pretended to offer refuge. There were doors at the tops of the stairs, and windows; and basement doors and windows. But these were not practical openings. They were either fake, or they were nailed shut. I might as well have been running along the Great Wall of China. A fake New York, unlighted and unpoliced at night, was no more sheltering than the real New York.

Wrong. There was, I remembered, at least one practical door here. Jerry Bayliss had shown it to me yesterday on our tour. It was at the top of one exterior stairway, the main entrance to one of the brownstones. Corrigan was to follow the heavy through that door. The interior would be shot on the stage, much of it in the basement I had just left. But Bayliss and I had climbed those exterior stairs and talked in that doorway about the action that would play there. If I could find it, a sort of plan was forming. But which door was it? I hadn't paid much attention to Bayliss, and these damn brownstones, for all the differences in detail, looked pretty much alike. Rivers of sweat were streaming down my neck.

All of this flashed through my head in the six or seven seconds it took me to reach halfway down the New York block. It was at about this point that Bayliss had stopped in the course of his tour, and I thought I recognized the brownstone with the practical door. It had to be the one with double posts framing the door. Or was it? I dashed up the steps. Nothing. Even before I reached the doorway—beautifully crafted, architecturally authentic—I could see that the door was a fake and that this way was a dead end.

I turned and took the stairs back down two at a time. In my peripheral vision I saw Mack, out of the stage now. He had looked the other way before turning toward me; he knew the way to the front of the lot. Even in the dark, the way he held his right arm I was almost certain he was holding that damn pistol. If I lost my concentration now, I would panic.

I decided the door I wanted was the one to the adjoining building, the one with a griffin under an arch over the door. It had to be. I turned and streaked up the stairs. Mack was sprinting toward me and there was no question now: that was definitely a pistol in his hand. I pushed the door. Nothing. But this was a door, a real one. It was swollen shut. I pushed again. It opened.

Of course there was nothing behind these brownstone facades but the long braces that held them up. But here, where the camera would show someone walking through the door, a portable tower of hollow tubing platformed over with wide planks had been wheeled up so the actors would have something to step onto. As of yesterday the crew had not yet butted the platform against the inside of the door. Now I saw they still hadn't done it: there was a gap of a couple of feet between the platform and the doorjamb.

I jumped across to the platform and dropped flat on the loose planking. With my feet I pushed back against the swollen door until it was firmly closed. I continued to push and the tower rolled away from the door another couple of inches. My mind raced like film that has slipped its sprockets.

I had to wait only a couple of seconds. Mack's body thudded against the far side of the door. The shock wave came through the soles of my feet and pushed the tower out another inch or so. But the door didn't open.

I pulled back and scrambled to my feet as he charged the door a second time. This time it flung wide and Mack hurtled through. Too late to check himself, his foot hit air; true to character, dumb as a post, Tom tricked again by Jerry, he dropped straight down. As he fell, the hand without the gun managed to grab the edge of the platform. For a moment while he hung from it, I met his eyes, not so much angry or surprised as simply uncomprehending. I stomped on his fingers. "You fuck," he gasped, and dropped like a turnip sack eight or ten feet to the ground. Twisting an ankle, I think, because he let out a sharp cry.

I jumped back across the gap and through the open door. He took one wild shot, not even close, but close enough, that sent a splinter flying from the door. I was on one side, he on the other, of the Great Wall of China. I bounded down the stairs. When I got to the bottom I shouted, "Security!"

My voice gave him a clue and he fired again quickly, three shots that ripped through the thin fabric of the fake stones of the brownstone. These were closer; I heard them singing in the air over my head. Silently now, I zigzagged the hell out of there.

All the way back to the front of the lot, I never saw a security man; the way it always is when you need a cop. Not until I reached the first of the office structures did I see a sign of life. Anyway, by then Mack could have been anywhere; it was a two-hundred-acre lot with, to my knowledge, at least four gates.

I figured to lay the problem in Vecchi's hands. I would know what to do next if I was writing the situation; in the round it was more in his line. I went back to casting to look for him. But they had broken, he wasn't anywhere in sight, and the two secretaries mopping up the paperwork didn't know where he was. They thought he had gone looking for me.

Some bodyguard. I thought, you get what you pay for.

CHAPTER TWENTY-SEVEN

All the way to West Hollywood I stewed over Vecchi's having vanished the one time I really needed him, and I drove past the address on King's Road Sarah had given me. It was time to knock off. Vecchi's services as a volunteer had gone beyond what I had any right to expect. And I still needed him; Mack had demonstrated that well enough. I pulled in to a gas station with a phone booth and left messages for Vecchi at both the Hollyview and the Claverly. I said not to worry about having missed me, and that I would be at Sarah Cole's. I left her number. It was just after nine o'clock.

I could see Sarah's apartment house whole from where I parked a block away. Uniformed doorman, curved driveway, terraces heavy with specimen plants, custom drapes on oversized windows: solidly middle class. I couldn't remember whether this was the place she had shared with Wes. It seemed more Wes than Sarah. Wes's folks had money. But so did Sarah's. I walked the curved driveway to the fountained lobby. The concierge announced me and I went up.

She was dressed the way her mother might have dressed, in silk pants and a blouse in jewel colors. More an at-home than a going-out outfit. Her shiny hair was pulled back from that perfect oval face by a scarf. She looked a shade less drawn than last time, more serene. We hugged and I looked around the living room. Good furniture in muted colors.

"Good room," I said, and then I noticed the little dining table set for two. "Is that for us?" I said. "I thought we were going out . . ."

"You're standing in the foyer of this week's hot new dinner spot," she said. "Sarah's formerly Sarah and Wes's." That answered that question.

"But I didn't want you to go to any . . . I told you to make a reservation . . ."

"For what time? 'Would you please hold a table for precisely thirty minutes after Mr. Saldinger should happen to leave the studio, if they let him go?' Don't look so nervous. You must know that the daughters of good cooks are also good cooks."

"I don't doubt it. Are you as . . . adventurous as your mother?"

She smiled. "I try not to compete. No abalone ceviche. We're going more home style. Shrimp and rice. Already cooked, so there's no turning back. You look really beat. They giving you a hard time at the studio?"

"Even worse than usual." I was tempted to tell her but I suspected she had troubles of her own. "You can't begin to imagine."

She said, "Then you'll want a drink. What will it be? Oops, inattentive question. Beefeater martini, straight up, twist."

She made the martini, not that badly, poured a

sherry for herself, and we settled on the couch and made small talk, memory talk, the best kind, for ten or fifteen minutes. Eventually I worked my way around to, "So how's the work going on those sitcom scripts?"

She said, "What sitcom scripts?" She read my confusion and added, "They're history."

I said, "But I thought . . ."

"It never should have happened. I don't like sitcoms, I don't watch sitcoms, so how could I write a sitcom?" A tremor had come into her voice.

"Then why did you . . . ?"

"Ever get started? Dad's idea." Her dark, sad, intelligent eyes looked deep into mine. "He thought it would save my life. The work, the discipline, and finally the sense of accomplishment. Didn't I have a sense of humor, hadn't I published a few short stories? Of course I could do it. Dad is so quick, so agile, he can write anything. As his offspring, so could I. Well, surprise, I couldn't."

I said, "He thought it would save your life from what?"

She took a beat. "From death, Myron. He thought I was going to kill myself. He may have been right."

A deep sadness settled on my heart. "When was that?"

"When Wes left. And forever after." Her voice was almost all breath, no substance. "You can't know how many times I told myself, 'How weary, stale, flat and unprofitable are the uses of this world.' No actor will ever play Hamlet long enough to catch me."

I didn't know what to say. I said, "I'm sorry. Sarah, I'm so sorry. I knew you were unhappy. I could see at your parents' that you weren't over Wes . . ."

"Oh, I think I am. Wes started me on the downhill

slide but I left him far behind. Everything else piled on and the dark started to close in. Dad knew what was happening.''

"Not your mother?"

"Mother has never known any of it. I didn't want her to and Dad agreed. He was ferociously protective. And when I hit bottom he thought he had my salvation. Writing would bring me back into the world.''

"He got you those sitcom assignments . . ."

"By selling his soul to Wolf Waxroth. Much as he hated television Dad agreed he would come back to it if Wolf could get me work. Wolf showed some producers my stories, got me the meetings, swore on his mother's head that I could do the work, and then whispered behind my back that if I couldn't, Rutherford Cole would backstop me. Why do you think he could so confidently offer Dad to Trig Bascomb to replace you like a tough steak sent back to the kitchen? Yes, I heard about that. Wolf delivered. Dad owed him.''

"So you did the work . . ."

"Dad meant so well, but those writing assignments were the worst thing he could have done for me. I couldn't do them.''

"He didn't help you?"

"I wouldn't let him. That would have been hideous, it would have defeated the whole purpose. I sat here at my machine day after day, week after week. The nights were worst of all. Would you believe it stretched into months, nearly three? Staring at a blank screen, then making a hundred false starts and floundering and faltering and producing scenes that went nowhere or didn't fit or weren't funny. While the walls of my life closed in and I realized how totally worthless I was.''

"Nobody, least of all you, should measure herself by how she writes television."

"Don't I know? That's how confused I was. I got so turned around I eventually thought I had written something that might be worth showing. I had finished both scripts and they didn't seem that bad. I had absolutely no perspective, but what did I know? Maybe I needed some distancing, maybe they were actually good. Even if they weren't exactly right, they were first efforts and wiser heads would see the gold flash through. I turned them in. Both scripts. And held my breath." She was reliving the moment and the pain showed.

I said, "Sarah, you really don't have to—"

She said, "No, let me finish. Two producers, two shows. Both scripts came back the next day. Killed without comment, both of them. I thought I didn't care. Those silly little sitcoms? I despised them. And to be judged by people who ground out twenty-two sausages a year? Never. So what did I do? I went into a tailspin. Plummeted straight down through my previous bottom. Dad could tell at once on the phone—"

"Was that only a week or so ago, when I was visiting—?"

"Yes, you were with him when I called. He sent you out of the room. He was so frightened for me. Scared stiff. He talked and talked. But no, I didn't want to see him, and no, I wouldn't go for counseling. I knew he despised that anyway, they'd made him do it in prison. Eventually he calmed me down. And I said if they got you to come to dinner I'd come too."

"Why?"

"Saldinger." There was a trace of tease in the sadness. "You've always been special to me, you must

know that. From the very first. Didn't I tell you I felt
a mysterious bond between us?''

"Sarah . . .''

"No, let me. First it was a schoolgirl crush that
began on a picnic to Ojai when I was ten. You
wouldn't remember. That grew into a teenage
crush. Even your marriage failed to dampen it. Or
my leaving my teens. Or Benjy's birth. Down deep I
always felt one day you would turn around and see
me—see me really—for the first time. Yes, like in an
old movie. And that would be that.''

"You hid it very well.''

"I internalized it. It was silly, of course. A fantasy.
On the reality level I knew it would never happen. I
wasn't stupid, and I would never have done anything
to get in the way of you and Helene. I functioned
very well. At school, and then at work and with my
stories. There were boys in my life and later men,
some very nice ones. But I never dug in deep with
anyone. At some level there was always that dopey
expectation . . .''

"And Wes?''

"Don't you remember when I locked in with
Wes?''

I shook my head.

"When you moved back east. L.A. to N.Y. That's
when I finally gave up hope, abandoned the fantasy,
and faced life. I gave myself totally to Wes, no
strings, no regrets.'' She fiddled with her empty
glass. "Flash forward. Is that how you say it?''

"I guess. I've never used it.''

"Flash forward a few years. Wes dumps me, and
then I learn that you were dumped months before.
Two free souls, grown up, the years that separate us
no longer of any real consequence. Fantasy could
become reality, almost pedestrian. We could meet at

a church supper and no one would give it a second thought. Or a synagogue mixer. Well, almost. I write you a note about your divorce, but there is no reply.''

"I told you at your parents' that I wasn't up to—''

"No matter, it wasn't meant to be. Not then. But your being there that day in my father's office when I called from the bottom of a well—. That was positively eerie.''

"Sarah, you're extremely vulnerable right now.''

"Am I ever! That night with you at Mom and Dad's? I was in the worst depression, in the icy grip of anxiety. Still am, mostly. But that night I felt it lift just the least little bit. Two percent? Two percent was like standing on a mountain. In the driveway after dinner I came this close to asking you to come home and make love to me.''

She read my uneasy look and said, "Don't worry, I'm not going to propose it tonight. You'd feel you were taking advantage of my damn vulnerability. What we're going to do instead is maybe have one more drink—''

"Uh-uh, no more for me.'' A second martini and I was afraid I might forget her vulnerability.

"Okay. Then we'll eat our shrimp and rice and we'll talk. General talk. Of cabbages and kings. But I simply had to say what I said.''

"Have you told your father how you feel about me?''

She said, "And my mother. You bet. You know what? They think I'm on to something they're very much in favor of. Their only caveat is that maybe you and Helene will find your way back together. Because of the children.''

I smiled, suddenly remembering. "Rudd checked that out in his flatfooted way. He called Helene the

other day to make sure she was deliriously happy
without me. She thought he was kind of loopy."

"He is, a little. But not about me."

I said, "Sarah, you are an extraordinary woman in
just about every way I can think of. You don't need
that confirmed by anybody. Certainly not by anybody in television."

She listened, and nodded slowly. Then she got up.
"Shrimp and rice?"

We stuck to shrimp and rice and cabbages and
kings; we knew that was safest. The time spun by.
Not long after coffee—it was close to midnight—I
beat a firm retreat. I didn't even risk a good-night
kiss. I promised to stay in close touch. Sarah stood in
her doorway until I got in the elevator. She looked
tired and strained and beautiful.

I left the building so deep in thought I wasn't
aware of someone coming up quickly behind me until my shoulder was firmly grabbed. I felt a giant lick
of fear as I was spun around. It was Vecchi.

He said, "I figured you were still up there. I was
just about to ring up. Come on, we'll take my car."

"Where to? And where have you been?"

"I'll tell you in the car."

CHAPTER TWENTY-EIGHT

On the way—he still hadn't said where, but we were driving across Laurel Canyon toward Studio City—Vecchi filled me in on his disappearance at the studio. He claimed he hadn't intentionally deserted me. A couple of minutes after I went off to study the New York sets, he had torn himself away from the casting office—with some reluctance, he admitted—and set out to find me. But instead of going to the sound stage, where I had headed first to make notes, he had gone directly to the New York street. When he didn't find me there, he had kept walking straight on back past New York, in confusion and wide-eyed fascination, until he was deep in the warren of back-lot standing sets.

"I don't know how, but I got so far back," he said, "I could have sworn I was in the town square in Agrigento," he said. "I was expecting to run into my great-aunt Rafaella filling a water pitcher at the fountain. And then I heard what could have been a shot. Three more made it definite. I ran forward to where I thought it came from, the back side of the New York street, the nothing side. Maybe fifty yards along the wall I saw this guy through the braces that hold up those fake buildings. He was half running, half limping. He didn't look that kosher. And then I spotted the pistol."

I said, "That was Mack the Knife. I was on the other side of that New York wall, beating it the hell out of there. What did you do?"

"Kept way back out of pistol range. What do you think, I tackled him? I was lucky it was dark enough so he didn't spot me and I stuck to his tail. I followed him through the lot a few blocks to a gate—not the main one, this one was handling mostly truck traffic. By now he was down to walking with a slight limp and he had the pistol in an ankle rig. I could see that if you don't have a vehicle, and you act like you belong, you can walk on and off the lot. And that's what he did—walked out through the gate to an old Ford Fairlane parked two blocks away and drove off."

I said, "And that's it?"

"Except I took his license number." He pulled a slip of paper from the pocket of his mock turtleneck shirt. "I've developed some contacts in the LAPD while you were east. You can stop calling him Mack the Knife. His name is Victor Petrik, forty-one years old. I don't guess the name rings a bell."

"No."

"Me neither. Or my contacts; he's clean, no record in California. So I figure we'll have to introduce ourselves, do a little exploratory surgery." He handed me the slip of paper. "Here's his address in Sherman Oaks."

"You're going to call on a man with a gun at one o'clock in the morning?"

"Not without an equalizer," Vecchi said. He reached in his glove box and came out with a massive gun; even I could tell it was a .45.

"Where did you get that?"

"I told you, I've developed contacts. Don't worry, it's legal, I just got the waiting period waived." He tucked it under his belt. "It's bigger than we need, but the main thing is to make a good impression."

It was one of those half-number addresses that turned out to be a very small one-story frame house up a narrow driveway behind a more substantial house finished in stucco. The small house had been re-sided many years before with a weatherproof synthetic made to look like brick. It was now cracked and peeling; so much for trompe l'oeil. A battered Fairlane was parked in the driveway. We had to squeeze past it to get to the house.

If there had been a dog we'd have heard him by then, so we did a three-sixty around the house. There were no curtains and the shades were all up. Victor Petrik had nothing to hide, at least from the neighbors. We could see in pretty well even with no lights on: kitchen, living room, two small bedrooms, bath. Salvation Army rejects for furniture except for a fancy exercise rig that filled the middle of the tiny living room. Sun-faded wallpaper. One bedroom was empty and looked as if it hadn't been used for years. In the other, peacefully asleep in a standard double bed but alone, was Mack the Knife, a.k.a. Victor Petrik.

There was no use hollering for the police. At the moment I couldn't think of one piece of physical evidence to tie him to either crime. That's why Vecchi had proposed "exploratory surgery." One more B. and E. My last, I vowed. Absolutely.

The windows were double-hung. We tried a few but they were locked, so we zeroed in on one in the living room, the farthest from Petrik's bed, and Vecchi cut a small hole in it with a glass cutter. He had selected a pane he calculated would drop back noiselessly onto the cracked leather couch when he tapped it, and it did. He unlocked the window and we climbed in. And tiptoed toward the master bedroom. No cat, no child, no wife on hand. Nobody here but us chickens. The house reeked of the cheap cigars I remembered from my previous encounters with Mr. Petrik.

The floor groaned some, but we made it through the bedroom door and all the way to Petrik's bedside without disturbing him. His breathing was even, he was sleeping the sleep of the just. With his eyes shut he didn't look quite so stupid. Vecchi came up next to his head and stuck the .45 in his ear. I grabbed his ankles through the covers. His eyes sprang open.

Vecchi said, "That's a forty-five in your ear. Move an eyebrow on your own and it will take a week to scrape your brain off the wall. When I tell you to do something, do it. If I ask a question, answer it. Where's your gun?"

Petrik said, "Night table drawer."

With his free hand Vecchi felt around in the drawer, came out with the gun, and handed it to me. I let go of the ankles to take it. I checked to make sure it was loaded, slipped the safety, and pointed it at Petrik. Basically for effect. I had never fired a handgun, and I wasn't absolutely sure I had the safety off.

Vecchi stepped back a couple of feet and said, "All right, nice and easy. Hands behind your head, then sit up and swing your feet slowly over the side of the bed. Do it now. I've got a very nervous finger."

Petrik complied exactly. Vecchi backed up and sat facing him on the windowsill, too far away for Petrik to reach him but close enough that the .45, pointed between his eyes, must have looked like a cannon. Without having to be told, Petrik kept his hands clasped behind his head. He knew enough to respect the man he was dealing with.

Vecchi said, "I don't know you and you don't know me. But you know my friend here; you've been trying to kill him for a week. So here's the deal. I don't give a fuck whether I blow your head off and we drive back to the hotel—I'm behind on my sack time—or you answer my questions and we leave you for the police. Does it make a difference to you?"

He said, "I'll answer the questions." He wasn't that dumb.

Vecchi said, "Who are you?"

"Victor Petrik."

"Why were you trying to kill Mr. Saldinger here?"

"It was a job."

"Victor, you're answering slow and you're not answering full. Don't make me have to pull the information out of you because this is a heavy piece and if it gets heavy I'm going to blow you away. What do you mean, a job?"

"I was hired to kill him. For pay."

"Hired by whom?"

"I don't know."

"Victor, were you listening to what I just said?"

"No, I mean it. I don't know who it was hired me. I answered an ad. In an outdoors magazine. For an ex-military man to do security work, good pay." He had learned not to wait to be prompted. "I was in 'Nam for ten months."

"You answered to a box number?"

"With my phone number. I wrote I'd do whatever the man wanted. He called. He wanted to know if I was ready to do anything at all. I said that's what I wrote. I could tell he was getting to something but I didn't know what. He got to it real slow, couple of weeks. He called here four or five times, two or three times where I work. He wanted to make sure I really meant it. If it was a him."

"You couldn't tell if he was a man?"

"Not for sure. Not the way he whispered. He never gave a name or nothing. He was careful to make sure I didn't have a clue who he was. I guess he was afraid of blackmail. Or maybe if I was caught, that I'd talk."

"Like now."

"Yes, sir."

"So you agreed to commit murder for someone you didn't know, just because he or she asked you on the phone to do it?"

"No, sir. It was for the money."

"You got paid in advance?"

"Partial. He sent me five thousand dollars, cash."

"How?"

"By mail. Packed in a candy box."

"How much more did he promise?"

"Ten thousand."

"Victor, stop jerking me around. I'm getting annoyed with you and I'm real tired of holding this heavy gun. I don't know why I'm wasting my time here. Are you telling me someone you never met told you if you killed a couple of people he would send you ten thousand dollars? And you agreed to do the job? Even you can't be that dumb."

"I'm not dumb! Half the money was in the candy box."

"So he sent you *ten* thousand dollars."

"No. Five, and half the ten."

Vecchi glanced at me. Was he not getting something or was Petrik incapable of explaining it?

I said, "Victor, you mean he took the ten-thousand-dollar balance, cut the bills in half, and sent you half of each bill?"

"They was all hundreds." He couldn't see why it had taken us so long to understand something so simple. "When I did the job, he'd send the other half." It seemed perfectly reasonable to him and, when I reflected on it, to me too.

Vecchi resumed his grilling. "Okay, Victor, tell me about the first killing. Nicholas Stavros."

"The guy who hired me—I'm almost sure it was a guy—he calls and tells me the man he wants to get rid of is finally here in town. I don't have a good description of the target, but I do a little snooping and find out he's got an appointment at this TV network around ten, ten-thirty, the next morning. I figure if I go down there and hang around the lobby and check the names when people sign in at the desk, that's a sure way to make him. I used to work in security. Not there, but the studios, the networks, they're all the same. What I've got to go on is I'm waiting for a Byron Saldinger, who wrote a script called *Corrigan's Way*.

"No Byron Saldinger signs in but there's a kind of fidgety guy in the lobby who talks to the guard but doesn't sign in. After a while someone, some executive—I think the guard calls him Mr. Cornbloom—he comes from the elevators, looks around, and this fidgety guy jumps up and says, like, 'You looking for the man who wrote *Corrigan's Way*? That's me.'

"They go in the back and I wait for the fidgety guy to come out. He leaves the building and I follow him to breakfast and a long walk on Sunset, and then back to his hotel on the Strip. I was lucky to go up in the same elevator with him and I'm right behind him when he opens the door to his room. I wasn't figuring to do the job right then but it was so easy I go with it. I'm in before he can close the door and I heave him through the window. Could I have a glass of water?"

Vecchi and I were in a stunned silence. I broke it. "Finally. Niko finally got someone to give him the recognition he wanted for *Corrigan*."

Vecchi turned to Petrik. "No water till you're finished. When did you find out you'd killed the wrong man?"

"I was listening for the story on the radio. When I heard it, with the wrong name—Stavros?—I couldn't believe it. I looked in his wallet. Yep, Stavros. You know how the fuck I felt? I could kiss the other half of those bills good-bye if I didn't do the job. That's when I went to work and found out from his agent Mr. Saldinger was staying at the Desert Palm. You know what happened there."

Vecchi said, "So you never finished the job and you never got to collect."

"Yeah."

"So where are those half bills?"

"The chest behind him." He had never looked at me. I couldn't blame him, based on our relationship to this point. "Bottom drawer."

I went and got the bills. They were still in the candy box. A hundred half bills, all crisp hundreds. "What happened to the good five thousand?" I asked.

"It's with my brother in Cheyenne," he said. "We had our eye on the down payment for a half interest in a cattle ranch. Five years we've been looking to get in on that spread."

I said, "Victor, you said you used to work in security. What do you do now?"

"Maintenance."

"What kind of maintenance?"

"Tennis courts." He caught Vecchi's impatient look. "I'm on the crew at the Pacifica Tennis Club."

"Where's your phone?" I asked.

"In the parlor."

I said, "I'm going to make a long distance call. I think you owe me one."

He shrugged but he still didn't look at me.

I went in the other room and got Christine Stavros's number from New York information. She picked up on about the eighth ring. She sounded underwater. "Who *is* this?" she gargled.

I told her.

She said, "Do you know it's a quarter to five in the morning?"

I said, "You won't be nearly so mad when I tell you I can get you back two thirds of that fifteen thou you gave Niko."

She said, "How?" She was suddenly awake.

I said, "Do you have the envelope he gave you when he went to California? I mean, there. At home?"

"What if I do?"

"Don't be paranoid. I'm calling from L.A. Get it."

She was off the phone for only a minute. When she got back on she said, "So?"

"Does it have any stamps or marks from the post office?"

"Those would be inside. Niko put the package in this envelope for me."

"Open it."

"Niko said not to."

"Niko's dead. You want your ten grand?"

I heard the sound of tearing paper. I said, "What's inside? A mailing envelope?"

Disappointed, a little sheepish: "A cereal box. Scotch-taped closed."

"Open it."

Silence, then more tearing sounds. Then silence. Then, "Jesus."

I said, "It may take a while but I'll see that you get the other half of those bills."

I went back in the bedroom and said to Vecchi, "Nothing good ever happened to Niko. Couldn't you guess he'd be killed by friendly fire?"

I would never again feel guilty about what, or if, or how much I may have borrowed from him. Not once I knew the son of a bitch had paid to have me murdered.

EPILOGUE

Jerry Bayliss knocked out the pages and kept the *Corrigan* shoot right on schedule. The action scenes went without a hitch and Trig Bascomb could not have been more professional or more cooperative. The canoe sequence with the widow, played by Ellie Wister, was almost a gem. Other pieces came together okay. People connected with the picture told each other and anyone outside who asked, "We're right on schedule." And you can bet your ass, when "We're right on schedule" is the watchword, the picture will never blow anyone away.

The only slight hitch in this trouble-free production came in post. Werner's very good tight cut of the picture, after he dumped the director's cut, was nearly thirty seconds short—I told them, I told them —and they ended up having to pad with scenic shots of the fruit farm that doubtless sent viewers to the fridge for another beer.

But the network was delighted with the numbers. And the critics were kind to Bascomb. He was widely applauded for his deft comedy, not only in the canoe handling scene but for Corrigan's wry dealings with the locals in fruit country. More, his "vulnerability" was noted approvingly in several reviews.

I liked seeing my name up there, uncluttered by disclaimers. "Written by Byron Saldinger." By itself. Full screen. The guaranteed twenty-two–show season was going to get me out of my financial hole and then some. If the series took hold and I lived sensibly, I would never have to worry about money again.

It never happened. When the series episodes began to air, the numbers went straight to the basement. Audiences had tuned in the pilot to get a free look at the movie star they had once paid to see in theaters. They didn't much like him on television. The pace of television production didn't allow the Blaus to protect him from himself the way the movie makers had. Bascomb had aged and it showed, and he looked out of place on the small screen. His timing was not the old Trig Bascomb timing. After four increasingly disastrous weeks on the air, the network bought off his contract. It cost them a bundle but they felt it was worth it. Trig seemed relieved. He turned his hand to full-time ranching and he told interviewers he had never been happier. Vince Yarrow—that, it turned out, was Vince's full name—managed the hands on the ranch.

The show's cancellation was a tough break for Jenny Haycroft. She played Corrigan's niece from back east in one episode, two days' work. She wasn't half bad. There was talk of making the niece a recurring character, but this turned out to be one of the episodes that never aired.

Corrigan's Way was replaced by an action-adventure series with mystical overtones, *Wu*, starring a Korean weight lifter named Kim who had never be-

fore been on television; the viewers ate him up. Kim
was discovered by Sheila Bannister, Oscar Kornbluth's mousy Director of Development, who shortly
thereafter succeeded Kornbluth as Vice President
for Development. Matt Clay moved up to the direc-
torship and was replaced as Manager by a nineteen-
year-old college dropout named Tad Pomerantz who
observers in the advertising community predicted
would turn television on its ear within five years.

Oscar Kornbluth got a development deal with a
production company. Not a bad deal, but he had
been eased out of the network fifteen months too
soon for a really good one. His failure at the network saved his marriage. Kornbluth couldn't really
afford a divorce anymore, and he and his wife sat
down and worked out their problems. His engine of
ambition was grinding to a halt. He spent more time
with his little girl, and Mrs. Kornbluth was soon
pregnant again.

Sergeant Dunleavy, LAPD, and Lieutenant Folsey,
NYPD, shared credit for solving the two linked
murders in L.A. and N.Y. Folsey "found" the Post-it
slip on Nick Stavros's desk with the phone number
of the Pacifica Tennis Club, and after Dunleavy
questioned the staff at the club, Nicholas Stavros's
back phone bills were found to contain calls to the
residence of one of them, Victor Petrik. It didn't
take long for Petrik to break down and confess. Not
surprising. He had already confessed once, although
he never brought that up. Maybe he thought the two
guys who had come through his window in the middle of the night were a bad dream. Petrik's guilty
pleas saved two states the cost of trials; consequently
he will be back on the street, if he keeps his nose
clean, in eighteen years. Dunleavy got a merit pro-
motion to lieutenant and an even better barber.

The half bills in the candy box that had been held as evidence against Petrik were eventually returned to Christine Stavros, who Scotch-taped them to the halves in her possession and divided them among her three brothers. When the Stavros brothers finally and clearly understood that Niko had ordered my murder, they sent about four square feet of moussaka to my apartment with what was intended, I supposed, as a note of apology. It read, "Compliments of Clytemnestra Restaurant." I never saw their place, but I continued to eat at Christine's when I was in New York. I like the food. I decided I liked Christine. But by unspoken agreement that is as far as it ever again went.

Wolf Waxroth negotiated a substantial deal for Al Vecchi as technical adviser at another network. One of the provisions of the contract was that Vecchi agreed to meet, consult, advise, and answer the questions of all writers the network referred to him, but he would not be required to read any of their scripts. To my relief, Vecchi quickly got over his "this isn't such a bad town" phase. He took to calling L.A. "Yonkers on the Pacific" and went back to his inimitable New York wardrobe.

During the months I worked as one of three executive producers on the ill-fated *Corrigan,* I rented an apartment in Westwood and brought Benjy and Jane out to stay with me for the summer. Their mother was grateful, as she had to spend much of those two months in the library. The Professor was out west looking for a better job. Or maybe just any job; I wasn't sure and I didn't care. One Sunday afternoon when I was taking the kids to a movie in Hollywood, I drove them past the Desert Palm. They got very excited over the Casbah architecture and asked,

please, please, could we move in there? What do
kids know?

Since *Corrigan* remained alive in production all
through that summer, Sarah Cole turned out to be
an enormous help with the kids. I sometimes called
on her to keep them entertained after day camp
when I had to put in extra hours at the studio, and
then we would have a pickup supper. We did manage, all of us, one truly memorable Sunday picnic at
Ojai.

Vecchi helped some too. The last time was on a
Saturday when I was called to the studio on no notice and he volunteered to take my place with the
kids on a promised trip to Disneyland. He came
back looking like a lost turkey and said, "I'd rather
put in a double shift on the Brooklyn waterfront."

Sarah and I took Benjy and Jane to the airport on
Labor Day for the flight back east for the opening of
school. There were fierce hugs between the kids and
Sarah, with tears on both sides, solemn promises to
write, and an exchange of gifts. Sarah got a Minnie
Mouse T-shirt.

The show went belly up in October. I came out of
it with enough to pay down my considerable debts
and take care of Helene and the kids for the next
year. I had no immediate work prospects but Wolf
said not to worry. What he actually said was, not to
worry *yet*. So instead of worrying, I blew the little
that was left on a holiday on Kauai—after careful
consideration, and a solemn regard for the responsi-
bilities involved—with Sarah. She had been steadily
on the mend since April and was at work on short
stories again and a nonfiction assignment from a
national monthly.

Sarah and I left for the airport from the Coles'
house in Benedict Canyon after a good lunch in

Rudd's office. He and Jasmine saw us to the front door and stood there watching us drive off, their arms around each other, until we were down the driveway and out of sight. And, for all I knew, longer.